MW00794930

NAIVE IN PARADISE

Chapter One

It was a deceptively beautiful day—barely a cloud in the sky and the humidity off the charts. The trek from the house to the Hummer engulfed my body and refused to let go. After barreling down the two-lane highway, my irritability lessened when my best friend, Fabiana Merceau, finally eased her foot off the gas and slowed somewhat from driving like a maniac.

I turned in my seat and stared out the back window, then threw my hand out, slapping Fab on the shoulder. "Turn around."

"You could ask a little nicer." A pout in Fab's tone.

Just as I was about to make a threat that I wouldn't follow through on, she jerked the wheel and hung a U-turn, barely touching the brake, and somehow managed to keep us from swerving into a ditch along Mangrove Road, which wasn't its name but would be a fitting one. I was loath to be out here in what felt like the middle of nowhere, as I believed nothing good happened in this wilderness area. Fab would disagree. The hot French woman had been unable to resist another hottie in a sportscar, who'd rolled up alongside her soon after we left the compound, varooming the engine—race time. The man behind the wheel of the Ferrari had gunned his engine, the Hummer accepted the challenge, and the race was on as they sped along neck and neck… for a few miles anyway. Before turning, Fab had hung her hand out the window and waved to the other driver, who'd slowed when she did. He'd reciprocated, then blew up the road and disappeared in a blink. I wanted to clap but kept my relief in check.

I jabbed my finger at the windshield. "I saw a female, and it looked like she tumbled into the ravine. There's not a lot of water down there, but enough that she could drown." I rolled down the window and hung my head out. "There she is." I waved at the woman hauling herself out of the grassy muck. "You need help?" I yelled.

Fear filled the woman's face, a definite "deer in the headlights" look as she stumbled backwards out of sight.

Fab jammed on the brakes and came to a stop just past where we'd last seen the woman.

I threw open the door and jumped out, Fab right behind me.

The woman peeked out from between the tangled limbs hanging from several tall trees, making eye contact. The blood draining from her face, she squeezed her eyes shut and curled into herself.

I trudged down the side of the ravine, slogged

through the ankle-deep muck, thankful to have on a skirt, and barely managed to stay upright. "We're here to help." I extended my hand. "We'll give you a ride wherever you need to go."

"Go. Just go. Before he finds me," she croaked.

"It's a long walk back to civilization," Fab told her, peering down from the roadside, where she'd remained.

"Whoever you're running from, we'll help you get away, take you wherever you want to go," I told her in a reassuring tone as I stumbled the few steps to her side, fighting to keep from falling. After an up-close inspection, I guessed the woman to be twentyish, and it was evident that someone had used her as a punching bag. "How about we take you to the hospital? Get you checked out." I shuddered at the bruises, new and old, on her face and the ones on her arms and legs that could be seen where the baggy men's t-shirt she wore ended.

"He'll find me for sure," she whispered.

"I can promise you that whoever he is, he won't find you." I held out my hand. After some hesitation, she slipped her hand in mine, and I helped her up the slight incline. With every step, she winced in pain. It didn't help that she was barefoot; if she'd had shoes before she fell into the ravine, they were nowhere in sight.

"He found me last time," she whimpered as we reached the roadside. "Said if I ran again, he'd kill me."

"All the more reason to get you out of here." I coaxed her toward the SUV.

"You promise not to take me to the hospital? Or call the police?"

"Promise." I opened the car door.

"Take me away from here." She batted a tear from her cheek. "Anywhere is fine. Then let me out, and I'll figure out where to go next."

Fab had spread a beach towel over the back seat. It took the two of us to help her inside, every move eliciting a groan of pain. Once seated, she slumped over, rested her head against the window and closed her eyes, taking deep breaths.

"I'm Madison. That's Fab." I pointed.

She hesitated for so long; I didn't think she was going to give her name. "Susan?" she said tentatively. I knew it was a lie.

"Do you have family or friends in the area?" I asked.

Fear flooded her face, and after several seconds, she mumbled, "No one."

I grabbed another towel from the back and handed it to her. "Feel free to stretch out on the seat. If you fall asleep, I'll wake you when we get back to Tarpon Cove." The girl was exhausted. Her eyes fluttered closed, and she didn't open them again as she stretched out.

Fab had looked her over from head to toe more than once before closing the door and sliding behind the wheel. She glanced over at me and whispered, "She needs a doctor."

"I promised no hospital."

Fab scanned the highway in both directions—not a car or person in sight. "What are we going to do with her?"

"She's terrified of someone." I flipped the visor down to look in the mirror, and she hadn't moved. "She's been pretty battered and isn't in any shape to have gotten very far. That means whoever she's running from might not be far behind."

"Let's get the heck out of here." Fab pulled onto the road heading back to Tarpon Cove, the first town at the top of the Florida Keys, and didn't speed off in her usual fashion.

I leaned back against the seat and pulled out my phone. I'd proven in the past that I could come up with a plan in a second, and now was the time to capitalize on that skill. I scrolled through my contacts for ideas. Macklin Lane would be my first call—she was the property manager extraordinaire who managed my beach-front property and the loons that lived there with finesse. Another plus, she never skipped a beat at any request I made. I glanced into the mirror and was certain that Susan was asleep. I felt assured that, even though I was hitting the speaker button, we wouldn't be overheard. From experience, I knew that if you want to be part of a conversation happening in the front, you have to scoot up and hang your head over the seat. This way, Fab wouldn't grumble about being left out the whole time I was talking. Neither of us were fond of repeating conversations—something was always left out in the retelling.

"It's your favorite boss," I said when Mac answered.

"Figured as soon as I put my feet on the desk you'd be showing up or calling, and here you are. Makes me a mind reader." She laughed at her humor.

"I've got a favor to ask. To be honest, I didn't know who else to call. That said, feel free to say no."

"Must be a doozy."

I already knew we were booked up at The Cottages, a ten-unit property I inherited. "Would you rent your spare bedroom for a day or two?" Before she could respond, I told her how Fab and I found the girl and that I didn't know anything about her except that she reeked of fear.

"If she's as beat up as you say, what if she dies?" Mac asked. "You're the do-gooder with little thought to the consequences; as for myself, I'd prefer not to end up in jail."

"That's why my next call is going to be to a doctor that makes house calls."

Mac snorted. "I guess you've forgotten that the one we had on speed dial moved away. The rest are too busy, with folks so stacked up in their waiting rooms, they only have to yell 'next.'"

"I can find someone," I said, more to reassure

myself than her. "I'm thinking that after a day or two of rest, she'll get back on her feet and be able to tell us how to help her. If it turns out she really doesn't have anyplace to go, I can hook her up with a women's shelter with professionals that will know how to help her."

"Do I have your promise that I can call at any time and you'll come pick her up? No arguing."

Fab snickered.

"At the first sign of anything you don't like, you get hot on the phone."

"You can count on it," Mac said emphatically.

"There's one more thing—since we don't know what or who she's running from, we want to keep her presence a secret," I said.

"Got it. See you in a few."

We both hung up.

"Do-gooder sums you up," Fab said with a snort. "Mac had a good point about Jane Doe dying. We'll all end up in jail for a long time. And not as cellmates either."

"Her name is Susan," I reminded her in an uppity tone.

"When pigs start flying."

I laughed, which pleased Fab, and scrolled through my phone again. No doctors, but the next best thing. "Hey baldie," I said when Casio Famosa—retired decorated Miami detective—answered. I wasn't sure if he shaved or waxed, as I hadn't asked.

"You must want something, since you're being

so nice," Casio grumped.

"I need a doctor that makes house calls and pronto. If you want details, you'll need to swear on a body part to keep quiet."

"Pinky swear, like my daughter insists on."

Casio's wife had succumbed to cancer several years ago, and he took his role as his four kids' remaining parent seriously. He always worried about making the right decisions, but they adored him, so he was doing something right.

"I'm happy your kids are training you right." I told him about the girl we found and the condition she was in. "Maybe... since you're a retired cop, you could give us your two cents. Gratis, of course."

"You know what they say about good deeds? I can smell trouble from where I'm sitting, and I'm not even close by." Casio grunted. "My best advice is to take her to the hospital. Since that probably blew through your ears, knowing you, where are you taking her?" I told him. "Let me make some calls, and I'll get back to you." He hung up.

"Here's my free advice," Fab said, looking in the rearview mirror. "It's incredibly nice that you didn't leave Susan on the side of the road. Not that I would've, but then, I didn't see her."

"The advice?" I rolled my hand.

"Her problems appear to be huge, and I'm suggesting that you not get any more involved than you already are. Find the women's shelter you mentioned and make it their problem; they'll know what to do. If not, they can get the answers."

Fab was right. It was good advice that I should listen to. After the doctor checked her out, I'd research women's shelters and give one a call.

Fab turned off the main highway into a residential neighborhood, made two more turns, and backed into the driveway of Mac's yellow house across the street from two properties I owned—The Cottages, which backed up to the beach, and the apartment building next door.

Chapter Two

It didn't surprise me to see Gertrude Banner—aka Rude, the manager of my apartment building—sitting on Mac's front porch. Besides their being friends, it had proven to be the best seat on the block. The older woman could sniff out a situation that was none of her business faster than anyone I knew, and would make it her mission to hotfoot it around the neighborhood and ferret out additional information whether she was asked or not.

As I got out and reached for the back door, I heard the slapping of feet coming down the steps. I turned and looked down to see what was making all the noise. Both women had on horrendously ugly oversized flip-flops and socks. Who paired the two together? These two. Mac had on open-toed purple socks that matched her toenail polish, and Rude had donned a pair of men's socks, the toes covered in dirt.

I opened the door and gently nudged Susan awake. Her eyes flew open, and she squealed in fear.

"You're safe. No one's going to hurt you," I reassured in a quiet tone. "Since you don't have anywhere to go and dropping you off on the side of the road isn't an option, I brought you to a friend's house for a couple of days." I helped her to sit up.

"I don't want to impose," she said, less fearful than when she first opened her eyes.

"I promise you'll be safe here. It's just until you figure out what you want to do next." She slipped her hand in mine, and I helped her out of the car.

Fab made the introductions.

Rude waved wildly.

Susan squealed, stepping into my side, and squeezing her eyes closed.

Rude ignored her reaction and closed the distance, putting her arm around the girl and leading her toward the stairs. "Don't you worry about anything. A few days' rest, some good food, and you'll be able to think clearer," the older woman said in a tone that didn't brook any argument.

Mac slid up on the other side of Susan, and the two women helped her up the steps and into the house, Fab and I right behind. Before we could get the door closed, a beat-up Mercedes blew into the driveway, and an older man got out, grey hair sticking on end. He was wearing wrinkled shorts, a tropical shirt, and flip-flops, a doctor's bag in his hand.

"Which one of you is Madison?" he grouched as he eyed Fab and I.

I checked him out from head to toe and stepped forward. "That would be me."

"Dr. Blunt. You don't look like you're in dire shape." He squinted and gave us both the same assessing stare. "Making up ailments so I'll step on it?"

"You the friend of Casio's?" I asked. He nodded. "He didn't send the text he promised, so it's taking me a minute to catch up. You still licensed and in good standing?" I returned his snooty stare and ramped it up.

Fab chuckled, knowing I'd learned that look from her.

"I'm somewhat retired but still make house calls for my daughter's general practice, calling on patients that can't get out," he said in a raspy voice. "Where's the patient? I got the backstory from Casio, so no need to hear it again."

"Try not to scare her." Fab matched his stare, then flicked her finger toward the stairs. She pushed the door open, and the three of us went in the house.

"This is Dr. Blunt," I introduced. "He's here to make sure that you don't need more care than we can give you."

Susan, who'd been sitting on the couch next to Rude, sidled across the cushions in an attempt to go… where, I wasn't sure. Rude tugged on her arm, so she didn't get far. "He'll find out," Susan whined.

"You're safe here," I reassured her. "No one's

going to find out anything. As for Dr. Blunt, he's restricted by patient confidentiality."

"Madison is right," Dr. Blunt said, crossing to where Susan sat and standing in front of her. "One of you needs to stay. I'll call the rest of you when I'm finished with my examination."

Rude hooked her arm around Susan and motioned for her to stand. "We'll use the guest bedroom." She moved her hand under Susan's elbow and led her down the hallway. "Don't you worry; I'll be right by your side."

Once the bedroom door closed, Fab said, "Ask the doc about women's shelters; if he doesn't know, he can tell you where to find the answer. If not, Tarpon Cove Hospital should know."

"Surely there must be someone she can call. Friend? Family?" Mac asked.

"After some hesitation, she told us that there was no one," Fab said. "Highly doubt that Susan is her name."

"Susan—or whatever her name is, doesn't matter—is holding up really well, considering someone kicked the stuffing out of her and it appears to have happened several times," Mac said. "Probably a husband or boyfriend. She's lucky to be alive. I suggest that Rude and I play good friend/better friend, and I'm the latter. Rude can be the one to squeeze every last detail of her life out of her, which she's good at, and I'll be the sympathetic one. If that works, then we'll know how to help her."

"You do know that she's going to have to want help?" Fab said. "You might gently remind her that her cooperation would go a long way in helping her situation. When her batterer finds her gone, he'll start looking, and according to her, he's not likely to give up. Being one step ahead would be in her best interest."

"I'm thinking he's not going to be able to track her down anytime soon, since the two-lane highway where we found her is fairly remote and doesn't have any cameras that I've ever seen," I said. "I kept my eyes peeled on the way back to the Cove, and we weren't followed. The chances of anyone showing up here are slim unless she has a tracker planted on her."

"It's possible that whatever property she escaped from is outfitted with cameras, since we both know a lot of criminal activity goes on back in those weeds." Fab waved me off before I could raise an objection. "I know what you're thinking—that I'm about to suggest we go back and check out the area—and I am not."

Relieved, I said, "You should be the one to discuss the tracker issue with her, since you're the most knowledgeable on the subject."

The doctor spent an hour with her, which surprised us all. That was more time than I'd spent with any doctor during an office visit. He came out of the bedroom and crossed to the kitchen to wash his hands. "As you know, I can't share anything she said, but I will tell you that she answered all my questions succinctly and didn't elaborate. It's my opinion that if she goes back to where you found her, she'll end up dead. Her body has taken a tremendous pounding and won't be able to take much more. I gave her my card and told her to call anytime and that I could refer her to a woman doc, as she needs a complete examination."

Fab asked him about a shelter that specialized in abused women.

"Good idea." The doctor nodded, rattling off a name and number. "They'll be able to answer all your questions and get the girl help. Under her fear, she sounds educated. Maybe you can convince her to take control of her life and help herself, so any other assistance she gets won't be a waste of time."

"Thank you, Doctor," I said.

"Just Blunt." He reached in his bag and handed me a business card. "You need another house call, you've got my number. Leave a donation at my PayPal address. Don't break the bank."

"I'll take care of this right away," I said. "I own Jake's out on the highway; you ever stop in, drinks are on the house."

"How do you know Casio?" Fab asked.

"That's need-to-know." Blunt smirked and traded glares with Fab, both enjoying themselves. He waved and banged out the door.

Minutes later, Rude came out of the bedroom

and shut the door softly. "Kathryn is sleeping. Didn't get her last name, but I will. Once she figures out none of us are going to turn on her, she'll be more forthcoming. Her boyfriend did this to her. I didn't get his name. Yet. When I do, I think serving him up as an appetizer for the local alligators would be fitting."

"The doctor didn't elaborate on any health issues," Fab said. "I take it Kathryn's going to be okay with some rest."

"It will take more than rest," Rude said with a huff. "Loverboy used her as a punching bag, cracked a couple of bones that need to be x-rayed. Blunt thinks more thorough medical attention is in order, since she was unclear about the last time she'd seen a doctor." She spit out an angry sigh. "She's riddled with old and fresh bruising. There were some other lacerations that I couldn't identify that had the doc cursing under his breath. Poor thing tried to reassure us both that 'they don't hurt that much.' She didn't move a muscle during her examination, but pain continually flickered across her face. Blunt did his best to talk to her about her options but stopped when she started to cry. I told her I'd listen to the good doc and repeat everything he said when she was feeling up to listening."

"You ready to disclose your next plan?" Fab asked.

"I don't have one," I said with a sigh. "When do we have a cottage opening?"

"The last thing Kathryn needs is to be by herself," Rude said adamantly.

I agreed. "Since you've bonded with Kathryn, based on the fact you got her real name out of her, reassure her however many times she needs to hear it that she's safe and we're going to keep her that way."

"The boyfriend needs to be stopped," Fab said. "At some point, he's going to miss his punching bag, and when he can't find her, he'll go looking for another one. Who knows what he's done to other women in the past?"

"If she's willing to share her story, I'll send Casio over," I said. "Women, for whatever reason, find him charming."

"That's because he's hot." Mac made a sizzling sound.

Chapter Three

The morning sun shone through the glass pocket doors, signaling that it was time to get up. I rolled over and cuddled up to Creole. Waking up in this double-king-size bed the size of a football field would be coming to an end soon, although I'd put in a request for one when we moved into our new house. We'd been staying in Fab and Didier's guest bedroom while Creole and I negotiated a deal with them on the house next door, which they used to own. The renovations would be done soon.

Creole and I were the first to live on the street originally; then Fab and Didier had bought at the opposite end. As a wedding gift, Fab's father, Caspian, bought up the rest of the block and installed security fencing and a gate at the front entrance, and we named the entire area "The Compound." Then Marcus had come to town. Even Creole hadn't known he had a twin brother, let alone such an unpleasant one. We'd lost our beach house because of his illegal dealings and opted not to fight anything in court, as the buyer was Caspian—another gift for Fab. Creole and I had decided we didn't want the beach house back—too many bad memories—and Fab and Didier convinced us to buy one of the other two houses on the block they owned. I'd thought that Caspian would flip over the sale, but he was agreeable, since it was Creole and me. I'd heard rumblings about Fab renting the other house, but thus far, she'd been mum about it. I'd wanted right of neighbor-refusal in the sales contract, but Fab had laughed.

"Who's going to get up and make the coffee?" Creole nuzzled my neck.

"I say we flip."

Creole unleashed a growly laugh. "You mean that imaginary coin of yours, where you always win?"

"That would be the one. I say we stumble out to the kitchen in all our bedhead glory just to irk the perfectly groomed Fab." How she managed to look perfect first thing in the morning remained a mystery.

A loud banging on the door interrupted my good idea. Jazz and Snow, who'd been asleep at the foot of the bed, lifted their heads and let out faint meows.

"Knock it off," Creole roared.

I stuck my head under the sheet and laughed. "Tell her she's scaring the cats."

"Coffee's ready," Fab yelled back.

"Bedhead it is." Creole rolled off the bed and took me with him. He tossed me one of his dress shirts, which had been draped over the chair, then reached out and messed up my hair, which didn't need any more help sticking on end. I squeezed around him and brushed it out, then pulled on a pair of sweatpants.

"You need to put on a shirt?" I raised my brows.

He shook his head. "Going to show off my pecs."

I tossed him a t-shirt. "I don't want anyone but me staring."

"In case Romeo forgot to tell you, we're having a meeting in ten minutes," Fab yelled from the hallway.

"What's she talking about, Romeo?"

"I forgot." His lips were curved upward, eyes full of humor when they met mine. "Instead of a family dinner, we decided on breakfast. Get the day started with a good brawl."

My family was notorious for airing grievances over dinner, although it had been a while. "Meeting? That calls for sprucing up, even if just a little, or listening to jokes for probably ever." I tugged on his hand. "No time for fun and games in the shower."

We were showered and dressed in record time. He curved his arm around my shoulders as we walked down the hall to the mammoth kitchen, where he picked me up and set me on a stool at the island.

"My humblest apologies for my wife's appalling behavior." Didier faux glared at Fab.

Our husbands—both over six feet, lean, with hard muscles and rumpled black hair, their blue eyes twinkling with amusement; the picture of hotness any time of day—each went by only one name. People often referred to them by Fab's and my last names, and they went with it without a blink.

Didier handed Creole and me mugs of our favorite brew, set one in front of Fab, who sat opposite us, and took a seat next to her. He never complained about whipping up the different blends, unlike Fab, who thought we should all drink the same thing.

"Morning coffee is going to be a thing of the past with you and Creole moving," Fab said with a full-on pout. "I don't want you to be in a hurry, even though renovations will be done soon. In fact, I want written notice."

I covered my face and chuckled. There was no convincing the woman that nothing would change just because we moved down the block. "It's a two-minute walk. You can kick the door in there, just like you did this morning, and I'll return the gesture."

"You two look like you just rolled out of bed." Fab smirked.

"When the princess screeches from the hallway… here we are." I laughed at her.

The doorbell rang.

I noticed none of them looked surprised. Last to know was annoying. I glanced out the kitchen window and couldn't miss the black Escalade that had just pulled up. "I'm assuming that's food, since family's about to descend, and you can't have a food fight without it."

Didier groaned. "You need to behave."

"There's only a slight chance of that."

Fab slid off her stool and crossed to the door. She opened it and stood back, and the invitees all trooped in at once.

"You're oh so lucky that I'm not sitting here with my hair stickin' on end." I glared at Creole, trying to keep the smile off my face.

I stood and gave Mother and her husband, Spoon—his first name was Jimmy, but no one ever used it—a group hug, then relieved my brother of one of the pink bakery boxes that were a family favorite and set it on the counter. Wait until Brad's six-year-old daughter, Mila, found out that she'd missed out on family fun just because school was a higher priority.

Caspian enveloped Fab in a hug. Their resemblance was obviously noticeable, with their dark hair and blue eyes. They greeted each other in French and began laughing.

Just as she was about to close the door, Fab peeked out and stepped back one more time. Chief Harder, Creole's ex-boss from his undercover days, swaggered into the house like the honcho he was used to being. Now that he was retired, he'd ditched his usual suit for a pair of tan shorts, a short-sleeve shirt, and deck shoes.

He'd opted to keep his Chief moniker and was called that by almost everyone in town. It surprised me to see him at a family meeting.

"I set the table out on the patio." Fab motioned through the glass doors leading to the pool area and beach beyond.

"All by yourself?" I asked.

Fab stuck her nose in the air and ignored me. She looped her arm in Mother's, and they walked outside. Even though Didier did all the cooking, Fab, being the consummate hostess, knew everyone's favorites.

The women in the family turned the kitchen over to the men, who worked well as a team, since they'd done it often enough. The food was arranged on a couple of large serving trays, and Didier and Creole each grabbed one. Brad carried out a tray of pitchers of orange juice and flavored water. A large coffee urn already sat on a side table.

There was little talk as we consumed the soufflés and breakfast pastries. I wanted to ask when this meeting was organized and how I'd known nothing about it, but there was no way to ask and not sound surly.

As the dishes were being cleared away by Spoon and Brad, I asked the Chief, "What brings you to a family meeting?"

"I like to stay on top of things, even if it's none of my business." He smiled cheekily.

"I believe that, but I'm also betting that you

have something up your sleeve."

"When the Chief called to speak to my wife, I invited him," Didier said with a hint of amusement. "That way, everyone can hear firsthand what kind of job he's got for the two of you."

It surprised me that the Chief kept calling, since Fab showed a definite lack of enthusiasm for his jobs. She didn't know how to tell him no without causing hard feelings. "You shouldn't leave your phone lying around." I shook my finger at Fab, who shot a glare at her husband at hearing what he'd done.

"Creole calls it phone poaching and brought me up to speed on how it's done," Didier said.

"Call this meeting to order." Creole slapped his hand on the table. "While we're on the subject of phones, I want Madison and Fab to know that I had tracking apps installed on all our phones, so our whereabouts can be tracked at any time." He pulled my phone out of his pocket and handed it to me.

"Are you expecting trouble?" Caspian asked, concern for his daughter in his tone.

"Just being vigilant," Creole reassured him.

After the ordeal with Marcus, Fab had upgraded the security around the compound and her house and installed a system at our new house.

"That doesn't mean you stop calling when something hits the fan," Didier admonished us.

"That reminds me…" I picked up my phone and checked the screen. "We need to check on Kathryn later. No urgent texts or calls, so that's good."

We'd told the guys about the previous day's adventure, and they'd agreed that the man needed to be found and locked up. Preferably not by either of us. I now told everyone at the table about yesterday's drama.

"Casio told me about the woman you rescued yesterday," the Chief said. "I thought it was nice of you two to stop and offer her help when most would've kept on driving."

"It was all Madison," Fab told everyone.

"If you can get her full name, I'll pass it off to one of my old detectives and have them run a check—maybe a missing persons report was filed," the Chief said. "If you ever need a police contact here locally or in Miami, just give me a call."

"We discussed having Casio talk to Kathryn," Fab said. "On one of my other cases, he was able to charm information out of the female victim and even talked the so-called husband into hitting the road without making any financial claims when I would've shot him." She grinned at the groans that went around the table.

"I'm thinking the best person to get Kathryn to open up is Mother." I smiled at her. "Her parenting skills have been tested, raising me and my brother. Someone less sneaky would be easy for her."

"I'd love to help." Mother flashed me a huge smile.

"As long as you assure me that it won't turn into anything dangerous," Spoon grouched.

"I'm thinking that Kathryn has to have family," Fab said. "If they're estranged, maybe they can make up now. She's not going to be able to put her life back together without some help. As for the abuser, I can't wait to give his name to the cops."

"I'll stick around after everyone leaves, and we can talk more," Mother said.

"Anything new on the Boardwalk project?" Caspian asked.

The Boardwalk was a family joint venture focusing on a collection of rides, attractions, shops, restaurants, and a hundred-slip marina. Creole, Didier, and Brad dealt with the day-to-day management and oversaw construction. The rest of us were silent investors and only consulted when a vote was needed on a new project.

"We've got our eye on acquiring more land for a future project," Brad updated us. "I'll be emailing a report to everyone this afternoon."

"Anyone opposed to the property report that I sent over a couple of days ago?" Didier asked. No one objected. "Now that it's been verified that there won't be any building restrictions, we'll be submitting an offer."

"Since we've expanded our office space, and the phone seems to ring off the hook, we've decided to hire an office manager," Creole announced.

Why was he looking at me? What was Creole up to? I looked over my shoulder, wondering if someone had shown up that I hadn't seen and he was talking to them. Nope. Coast clear. "If you think I'm the woman to run your office, the answer is N. O." I pointed to Fab. "Hire her. The phones will stop ringing. Problem solved."

Didier laughed and got elbowed.

"One of the reasons for this meeting… You can take it from here," Creole said to Brad.

Brad glared at him. "After a short discussion, we decided that we needed someone to keep us and the office organized, and since none of us has any time to spare, your name came up as the obvious choice to do the interviewing."

What a crock!

"All in favor." Brad's hand shot into the air, along with everyone else's. "Great. It's unanimous." He banged his spoon on the table for effect.

"Except for me." Spoon held up his hand. "If you want, I'll beat the rest of the voters up… except the women."

"That's why you're my favorite." I winked at Spoon. I swear his cheeks pinkened. "I'll be sending over a contract that will outline my stipulations, and the three of you will sign." I wagged my finger around.

"Now for the other reason I'm here," the Chief said. "You have a lease agreement for me to sign?"

"I didn't know how serious you were, since you just threw it out yesterday," Creole said. "I made notes on what we talked about. I'll pass them off to Madison, and the two of you can negotiate the lease."

"And here I thought it was a done deal." The Chief glared at Creole, then turned to me. "I'm interested in the second floor. I've got the cash and references."

"What's wrong with the cubicle you're renting down in Marathon?" Fab asked in a bossy tone.

Didier nudged her.

"That cubicle was a two-story office building." The Chief matched her tone. "I'm surprised your husbands didn't tell you. That's the main reason I'm here."

"What could it be?" I tapped my cheek.

"Two nights ago, there was a break-in. Everything was destroyed with a sledgehammer. We know, since it was left behind. If that wasn't bad enough, then the offices were doused with gas and set on fire. The flames were doused pretty quickly because the sprinklers came on, but everything flooded. Total loss."

"One of those pretty-boy partners of yours?" Fab asked. "You remember, the ones you booted out the door?"

The impetus to the Chief's retirement was that he'd been offered a partnership in a private investigation firm in Marathon. Once he discovered its gross mismanagement, he bought out the other partners. It was clear there was more to that story, but who had the nerve to ask?

"Perps in jail?" I asked.

"No all around," the Chief said.

"So…" I looked around at all the eyes on me. "You want to bring all this unfinished drama into our neighborhood? Creole's always been adamant that I not lease to criminals or trouble—maybe not the latter explicitly, but I got the unspoken gist." I smiled at him, enjoying teasing him.

"You're turning me down?" the Chief said in disbelief. "I thought we were friends."

"Can you assure me that our building isn't going to burn to the ground?"

"Since it's cement, we'll at least be left with a shell," Creole said.

I gave him the not-helpful stare. "Since you began negotiations with Creole, I'm going to let him handle the rest of the deal."

Creole leaned over and whispered, "I don't want to."

I tried not to laugh.

"Local cops don't have anything on who started the fire," the Chief said. "That's why I want to hire Fab to snoop around, ask a few questions. Maybe someone saw something and will talk to her. And until someone's been arrested for setting the fire, I'll meet clients away from the property."

"You want someone to cozy up to a stranger and get their life story, you've got the wrong girl." Fab poked her finger in my direction.

"Back to the lease," I said. "Here are the rules: Pay on time, and the second time the cops get called because of your antics, you're out. There will be no court hearing. You and your boxes will be set out in the parking lot. I'd prefer sidewalk, but we don't have one. If you think I can't follow through, think again." I shot him a ferocious stare.

"Where do I sign?"

"One more thing: any issues, you call immediately. I don't want a small leak to turn into water gushing through the walls. We're not slumlords." I looked at Creole. "You get to handle the paperwork, dear." He shook his head.

The Chief reached down and picked up his briefcase, opened it, and handed a file to Fab. "Here's the police report and a set of keys so you can have a look around inside if you so desire. Pictures of its current state are on the top."

"As long as we're agreed that I get to choose my backup," Fab said as she flicked open the file. "We'll get on this case of yours today, at the latest tomorrow."

"Anything else that needs our attention?"

Brad asked and, not waiting for an answer, said, "Great. Let's do this again sometime."

Chapter Four

"A tray of coffees would be a good icebreaker," Mother said, as I opened the car door and she climbed in.

I leaned in and kissed her cheek. "I'm happy that you're coming with us to Mac's. If anyone can get Kathryn to open up, it's you."

"If I'm going to need a firearm, I'll have to stop by the house or borrow one of yours." Mother shot me a cheeky grin.

I slid into the back seat. "No shots will be fired today. Hopefully."

Fab revved the engine and shot out of the driveway, then slowed going down the street, coming to a stop in front of the one-story white Key West-style house that would soon be home to me and Creole. Two construction trucks were parked in front of the house, the green privacy fence rolled back.

The three of us leaned forward.

"Aren't you worried, letting Creole make all the decisions in the renovations?" Mother eyed the house.

Creole had wanted to surprise me, which made me squirm. We'd compromised. "I got to approve materials, and thus far, I haven't had a single objection. I don't have any doubt that it's going to look amazing; he renovated the beach house himself and did a great job. I did negotiate carte blanche for the patio and beach. He laughed, thinking I meant a couple of chairs and done." I didn't tell them that I'd had a professional layout drawn up and, in the spirit of fair play, showed him what I had in mind. I got a resounding approval and handed it off to the contractor.

"Did you hire the decorator you told me about?" Mother asked with a sneaky smile.

"Not certain she's going to work out." I made a sad face. "I emailed her late last night and haven't heard a word. Besides, she's being dramatic, wanting to make every decision."

"You're a pain," Fab snapped. "I got your file, and if I have any questions, I know where to find you. Your mother volunteered to help, and the two of us have cooked up a little surprise for you."

Surprise again. Everyone in the family knew I didn't like them. "One would think you two believe I can't decorate my own house."

"It's not that," Mother reassured me.

"Just remember: beachy, comfortable, and minimalist."

"Creole took me aside and told me, 'Keep the receipts.'" Fab mimicked him.

Mother and I laughed. I would have loved to

see her reaction when he issued his edict.

"This is going to be fun," Mother insisted. "I'm looking forward to shopping. I know you don't like matchy-matchy dishes, so that's a good reason to hit up the flea market." Fab groaned, which Mother ignored. "I'm happy to be included in this project." She patted Fab's shoulder.

"We'll plan a girl trip and drag grouchy along whether she likes it or not. Besides, she's a good negotiator." I scooted up and hung my head over the seat.

Fab drove out of the compound and hit the main highway.

"You need to give me an idea of what kind of information you want from Kathryn," Mother said. "The young woman has been through a lot. I'm not comfortable strong-arming her, but I'm certainly willing to help in any way I can."

"We need information on how to help her," I said. "There must be someone we can reunite her with. At least, I'm hoping."

"Neither of us are going to be a party to putting her out on the curb like she first suggested," Fab said.

I once again went over everything that had happened from the moment we found Kathryn. And how little we were able to find out about what went down. It surprised me that she'd allowed us to help her, but I figured her fear of her abuser made us the better choice. We wanted to help Kathryn but needed her help to do it.

Mother's face was awash in emotions—shock, anger, and sadness.

"What Kathryn needs is a heart-to-heart chat with a mother figure who won't brook any nonsense and won't steer her into the weeds," Fab said.

"I'm not sure what you have planned, but I don't think making her the center of attention in the living room with everyone staring would be a calming situation," Mother said.

"I'm going to introduce the two of you," I said. "Then leave so you can have a private talk."

"If we had contact information for her family, we could approach them and see if there's an interest in reuniting." Fab turned off the main highway, made a couple more turns, and then into Mac's driveway. "The other issue is the abuser's name. I refuse to call him a boyfriend. He has to be stopped. It's impossible to believe that he won't do it again."

Mac was sitting on the front porch, her feet up on the railing. She waved.

I got out and opened the passenger door, extending my hand to Mother.

Fab came around the front of the SUV. "Including you was a great idea. I take all the credit." She and Mother laughed.

"One of your many good qualities is that you're a rock in a crisis." I enveloped her in a hug. "I think your no-nonsense mothering skills are just what this situation needs. And you're pocketing a couple of those favors you covet. Not that you need them."

Favors were a form of currency in the family that had spread to our friends. They came with one condition—no whining when cashed in.

"We should all go out to lunch, get our drunk on, and stick Madison with the check," Fab said.

Mother laughed. "I'm in."

We walked up the steps, said our hellos, and sat down.

"Kathryn's asleep. That's about all she does. And when she wakes up, she eats like a bird and picks at her food." Mac pulled her phone out. "If I don't text Rude and tell her you're here, I'll never hear the end of her incessant whining. She's spent the most time with Kathryn and gotten her to open up a little. Rude should be the one to tell you." She typed out a text.

I turned and looked across the street at my two properties. Both appeared to be drama-free, which didn't happen often. "While we're waiting, what's going on at The Cottages?"

Mac had long said that she didn't mind living across the street from where she worked and claimed that it made it convenient to spy on goings-on. That had proven to be true in the past.

"Miss January has a bone to pick with me." Mac grinned. "I'm thinking you can straighten it out. I'll be right behind you to see how you accomplish it. Learn from the master and all."

Miss January was one of two original tenants that I'd inherited from my Aunt Elizabeth along with the property. Doctors had written her off for dead, which hadn't slowed her down as she kicked along, subsisting on vodka and cigarettes.

"How about a hint?" I asked.

"Nope."

Rude came running out of the bushes in front of my apartment building. She'd been manager for a while—she didn't put up with nonsense and was immune to sad stories. She tripped twice, in danger of falling on her face before she made it across the street, skidded to a stop on the sidewalk, bent over, and gasped for breath.

"You need me to call 911?" Fab yelled.

Rude straightened and yelled, "Naw."

Both Fab and I eyed her sandwich flip-flops, the soles made to look like two slices of bread with meat, lettuce, and tomato in between. No sign of mayo or mustard.

"I'm surprised you let Rude one-up you on shoes." I stared at Mac's bare feet, happy that I hadn't added the word weird.

Mother looked down, probably hiding an eyeroll, not wanting to break her own rule that they weren't allowed. Which didn't stop anyone. Nor did the threat of premature wrinkles.

Mac scrunched up her nose, shaking her head. "I saw them first. Tried them on, and they're not comfortable."

Rude raced up the steps. "Did you tell them?"

"We don't have all day." Fab tapped her watch. "We've been waiting on you for a rundown on the information you were able to get. This better be good," she said with mock impatience.

Fab's fan club of two grinned back at her.

"Kathryn's a semi-local girl, has family in Miami. Well-to-do folks," Rude said.

As I suspected, although it was hard to tell because she was so soft-spoken, I'd guessed her to be well-educated.

"There's a slight problem. Her family thinks she's dead. And Kathryn claims to have been such a disgrace to the family that they wouldn't want to see her even if they knew she was sucking air."

"They think she's dead?" Fab repeated.

Rude nodded. "I didn't get all the details, but I'm working on it."

"I can't believe that they wouldn't want to see her again. What could she have done that they would cut all ties?" Mother asked.

"Start at the beginning," I said.

"Kathryn has a tendency to ramble sometimes and at other times goes silent. I had to be patient, wait her out, knowing she'd start talking again. I didn't question her directly, as I didn't want to freak her out."

"And?" Fab said, radiating impatience.

Mother reached out and patted Fab's hand. I tried not to laugh.

"The boyfriend, Colton, wasn't really her boyfriend, just someone she dated a few times, unbeknownst to her parents."

Mother nudged me.

"Whatever happened in the past, I have immunity," I told her.

"Kathryn thinks this Colton character drugged her, because she doesn't remember how she ended up in the Keys, tied up and his prisoner."

"How did she supposedly die?" I asked.

"He boasted that he rigged a car explosion with two bodies inside and showed her a news report that verified it."

"Since her death warranted a news story, it would follow that either her family is of some importance, or the explosion was pretty spectacular," I said.

"Did Colton brag about how he managed to get two bodies incorrectly identified?" Fab asked. "That would take some connections, and he'd owe someone big time."

Rude shrugged. "I wondered but didn't ask."

"Dickhead went to her funeral," Rude related, "not wanting to pass up the opportunity to take pictures of those grieving Kathryn's demise. Swell guy that he is, he shared them with her. As if that wasn't enough, he went back once the headstone was put in, took pictures, and gloated as he showed them off."

"Dickhead's a fitting moniker, more so than his real name," I said.

"Kathryn told us that the dude lives in a small, rundown house close to where you found her," Mac said.

"She doesn't have a clue what he does for a living, only that he leaves the house every day for a few hours," Rude said.

"How long was she kept captive out there?" Fab asked.

"We figured six months, maybe a little longer."

"No way he could ever let her go. I can't imagine being tied to a chair for the rest of my life…" Fab grimaced.

"Rest of her life is right. She believed that it wouldn't be long before she died from one of his beatings."

"It was a hard story to listen to," Mac said.

"Why does she think her family wouldn't want to know she's alive?" Mother asked.

"She called herself a wild child. Her father told her on more than one occasion that she was a pain in the ass," Rude relayed.

Aren't all kids at one time or another?

"Having had two kids, I'm certain I had that sentiment more than once." Mother smiled at me. "But there's no way I would've wanted either of my children dead."

"I'm happy that Brad and I turned out to be decent adults, and you were along for the ride." I bumped my head on her shoulder.

"No parent wants to suffer the loss of a child," Mother said.

"I had no clue what we were getting into when we picked her up," I said. "The story gets worse the more we hear."

"Kathryn will need identification to get her life back on track," Fab said, going into investigator mode. "You can't do anything without it. Since she's been declared dead, it will be next to impossible to be declared alive. I've read a couple of stories of that happening, which went into detail about the difficulties, but never saw a follow-up story, so I don't know if they got it worked out."

"We're getting ahead of ourselves," Mother said. "The best thing to do is ask Kathryn what she wants and then offer our help to that end."

"You want me to wake her?" Mac asked.

"I'm going to introduce Kathryn to Mother, and it will either go well or it won't. I'm betting on the former." I motioned to Mother, and we went into the house. I knocked on the bedroom door and heard a quiet, "Come in." I opened it and gave Kathryn a reassuring smile. "I'd like to introduce you to my mother. Madeline Spoon, this is Kathryn."

Kathryn responded with a weak smile.

"I brought my mother to talk to you, thinking she was a better person to confide in than any of the rest of us."

Kathryn's cheeks bloomed with color, and she appeared flustered.

"Five minutes." I held up my hand. "You're free to talk about whatever you want, or not, if that's what you want."

Kathryn nodded.

I left the room, closing the door softly, and went back to the living room.

Fab, who was standing at the front door, opened it and stepped back. "Fingers crossed we're able to help her."

Chapter Five

"While Mother is talking to Kathryn and hopefully convincing her that she needs to trust someone, as hard as it seems for her right now, I'm going to wander across the street and mediate between Miss January and Mac."

"This ought to be good." Fab followed me across the street to the ten brightly painted cottages I owned. They'd been built around a u-shaped driveway, and the property backed up to the beach.

Mac had joined us, but Rude stayed behind, in case Mother or Kathryn needed anything. I wouldn't have put it past her to press her ear to the door.

I scanned the property while walking up the driveway and caught sight of Miss January. Slumped in her chair, housedress bunched around her thighs, she was fascinated with the blue sky, staring intently as she sang off-key, the tune unidentifiable, squealing out the high notes despite the cigarette dangling from her lips. Not wanting to startle her, I called out, and when she looked my way, I waved and hopped up the steps to her porch. "You doing okay?" I wasn't going to bring up whatever was irking her with Mac. Fingers crossed that she'd forgotten.

Miss January stopped singing and sucked on her cigarette, forgetting it wasn't lit, then blew air out of the side of her mouth. She leaned back and peered around me. It took her a minute to focus, and then she glared at Mac. "She stole Kitty. Again." She jabbed her finger in Mac's direction. "I want her back. Could you go get her for me? She climbed up on the top of the shelf unit in the office."

No, no, and no. I was tired of having the feline restuffed. I turned and glared at Mac to wipe the smile off her face. "Poor Mac," I said with feigned sadness.

"What happened?" Miss January squealed.

"I know that you miss your cat." That is, when you have a lucid moment and remember her. "But Mac bonded with Kitty. You know how lonely she is. She doesn't have a boyfriend and you do, hot sexy man that he is." He wasn't, but…

"I got lucky when I met Captain." Miss January gave me a toothy grin.

If he knew about her track record, he'd wonder about his own luck. Her exes tended to end up dead or in jail.

"If you could share custody, then both of you would be happy." At some point, she'd forget, and this would become a non-issue.

A milk truck zoomed into the driveway and

squealed to a halt. A twenty-something jumped down. "Hey, Janny." He handed her a tablet. "You know the drill." He produced a pen from behind his ear, and she scribbled her name. He set a shopping bag at her feet. The upside to Miss January's daily vodka delivery was that she didn't get lost going to the liquor store.

She reached down the front of her dress, pulled out cash, and handed it to the guy.

"You're the best." He saluted and made a running jump back into his truck, then pulled up to Joseph's door and got out with a case of beer. He banged on the door, reminiscent of a cop knock, and after a minute, the door opened and cash exchanged hands. The beer delivered, he got back in his truck and backed out to the street.

Miss January's door opened, and Captain stuck his head out. He winked at Miss January, which elicited a giggle from the woman. He stepped out and picked up the grocery bag, peered inside, and shoved it in the cottage. Then he helped her to her feet and steered her inside.

"Nice to see you, too," I said to the man's back, which filled the doorway.

Captain turned. "Yeah, hi." He kicked the door closed.

Fab laughed. "How long has he lived here? And in that whole time, I've not heard the man say six words."

"Once or twice, he's strung a sentence together. Maybe," Mac said.

I cleared the steps in one jump and managed to land on my feet. "You're fired," I told Mac. "Seriously, the cat! You hoaxed me. Guess what? Be on the lookout for payback."

"Hold on," Fab said. "You need to rethink firing Mac, because I'm telling you now, I'm not sitting in that office. I won't even come visit when you're forced to do it."

"It wouldn't take long before you shot someone, and problem solved. Word would spread, and no one would want to stay here." Mac grinned.

"Where's the lookalike that you had made?" I asked. "The one that was supposed to sooth Miss January in her catless moments."

"For that, you need to point the finger of blame at Rude." Mac waved hers around. "Furrball took a shine to the pretender and ran off with her. He's kept her hidden. Probably buried somewhere." Furrball was a twenty-five-pound Maine Coon who fit right in, completely unable to stay out of trouble.

"No worries," Mac assured me. "When I find it, I'll give it a good scrub."

Fab snorted and made a face.

"While you two entertain each other, I'll go check on Joseph." I cut across the driveway, leaving the two of them laughing. His door stood open, and I stuck my head inside. He was reclined in his easy chair in boxers and a t-shirt. "You staying out of trouble?"

Joseph lifted his head and nodded. "Me and my girlfriend are sharing a beer." He held the can up to her lips. "Maybe not."

"Hey, Svetlana." I waved to his sexy blonde blowup girlfriend. She'd been bequeathed to the old goat a few years back, and it'd turned his life around; he stopped getting into trouble, which put an end to picking him up from jail.

Just then, another tenant, Crum—shirtless, his white hair sticking on end—rode in from the beach on a water bike with ginormous tires. The retired college professor had pitched buying a couple of unusual bikes for the guests to use, and thus far, they'd been a hit.

"If you need anything, I'll be around for a few more minutes," I said to Joseph and walked over to Crum.

"Before you say no—" Crum held up his hand. "—this bike can be ridden in the water and on the sand. Not too much on the concrete or it could ruin the tires."

I was happy to see that he had on board shorts and had, for today anyway, ditched the too-small speedos I'd seen him in before. I'd banned him from wearing his favorite—tighty-whities—in public.

"I gave Crum the okay on this one," Mac said as she and Fab walked up. "I think it's going to be popular. How did the test ride go?"

"Works good. No problems at all in the water," Crum said.

"This one, I really like," I said. "We should have at least two, as most of our guests will want to go riding in pairs."

Fab circled the bike, checking it out while Mac answered her questions.

I turned away and lowered my voice. "I want two for my new house. I'll surprise Creole with our first beach toy."

"If my supplier's got them, do you want me to make the deal?"

I nodded.

Rude whistled from across the street and waved for us to come back.

"That must mean that Madeline's finished talking to Kathryn." Fab linked her arm in mine and pulled me away. "You're better at these emotional scenes than I am. I'll sit close by and smile encouragingly."

"Let's hope Mother convinced her that the only way to help herself is to talk to someone."

Mac had lingered to talk to Crum. When finished, she ran, catching up to us and following us up the steps and into the house.

Mother and Rude flanked Kathryn on the couch. Fab and I sat in chairs across from them while Mac dragged over another one.

"You've been amazing to me, and I want to thank you for everything you've done," Kathryn said in a soft tone.

"I'm happy that we saw you on the side of the road and were able to stop," I said. "We'd like to offer more assistance in wherever you want to go from here."

"Madeline was quite convincing; she reassured me that I could trust all of you." Kathryn smiled at Mother, who shifted closer, giving her a hug.

"Rather than have Kathryn repeat her story, I suggested that she tell all of us at the same time," Mother said.

"The last night of my normal life... I didn't appreciate it enough at the time," Kathryn said. "A couple of my girlfriends talked me into coming to a college party down here. It was at a condo in the middle of town. Once I got there, I realized that everyone was older, and I didn't recognize a single person. I wanted to leave, but my friends wanted to finish their drinks. That's when Colton Roberts came up, the one face I recognized from campus. He steered me out on the balcony so we could talk. The next thing I knew, I woke up in a strange place, tied to a bed." A tear rolled down her cheek.

Mac got up, handed her a box of tissues, and passed out bottled water all around.

"I hadn't been awake very long when Colton kicked the door open, in a rage that it had taken him so long to get me. I don't know out how long he'd had it planned, but from the way he talked, it had been a while and the wait had frustrated him." Kathryn took a long drink of her water. "I threatened him," she scoffed. "Warned him that my dad wouldn't give up until he found me, and then he'd kill him. He bent down, nose to nose, and laughed." She leaned into Mother.

"Take your time," I said.

"Days went by… maybe… I couldn't keep track of time. Colton held me in a dingy shack, in a room with black paint on the windows, which were boarded over. I never knew what day it was. I made the mistake of asking once, and he blacked my eyes, screaming at me that it didn't matter." She closed her eyes and rolled her neck from side to side.

Mac stood and collected the empty bottles, exchanging them for full ones. It proved to be the short break that Kathryn needed.

"I hung onto hope that my dad would find me—he's a man who never gives up—and then Colton showed me my obituary online. I was in denial, but there it was, and the site looked legitimate. He also showed me news coverage he'd recorded." The color drained from Kathryn's face as she said, "I knew then that he'd never let me go." She gulped in big breaths. "I want to go home. But I was the adventurous one, doing things I shouldn't; my sisters were perfect. I want to apologize. But after they've grieved my death, how do I just show up?" Tears rolling down her face, she jumped up and ran to the bathroom.

"If Kathryn wants to talk again, I'll be out on the porch." Ignoring everyone's surprised expressions, I stood and walked out the door, gulping in the fresh air. The door opened immediately.

"That was a hard story to listen to." Fab came up and stood by my side, and we both stared off down the block.

"It was a terrible story when I thought we were talking abusive boyfriend. But kidnapping… He was never going to let her go. He couldn't." It had me flashing back to what had happened with Creole's brother, still immensely painful, even after everything Creole had done to scrub the unpleasant memories.

"I'm happy that you saw her attempting to climb out of the bushes." Fab wrapped her arm around me.

We stood in silence.

"We need to get her over her reticence about seeing her family. She needs them; they're the best ones to help her through this awful ordeal," I said.

"Agreed."

The door opened, and Mother beckoned us inside.

Kathryn was sitting on the couch, and although her eyes were red from crying, she looked much calmer. She took a deep breath and confided, "My father is Henry Beckett, and I'd really like to go home."

Fab's eyebrows went up. "The corporate mogul?"

Kathryn nodded as another tear slid down her cheek. "I can't just call… Without my phone, I don't have the numbers. I could call my dad's office and say… What? I'm his deceased daughter? Even if I could get put through to his assistant, she'd hang up. Going home… I can't get past the security guards."

"How about we break the news to him?" I said, flinching inside, thinking this idea had all kinds of ways of going wrong.

"You'd never get past his bodyguards. There's two of them, and they're formidable." Kathryn smiled weakly.

"You let us worry about the logistics," Fab said.

"I love my family. I'm so afraid. I couldn't bear it if my dad rejected me, told me to go away."

"I'm telling you, that's not going to happen." Mother hugged her.

"You haven't mentioned one good reason why your father wouldn't want a second chance to wrap his arms around you," Fab said. "You know how many times he and your mother have probably wished for just one more chance to tell you that they love you?"

"Tell them about Colton," Mother said.

"Do not confront Colton. At least, not by yourselves," Kathryn warned. "I escaped once before and got out to the highway, but he found me and beat me until I passed out. After that, he threatened to kill me if I broke any more of his rules. I think he enjoyed tormenting me." Her hands shook while she spoke. "If he feels threatened, there's no telling what he'll do."

"Did Colton have any help that you know about?" Fab asked.

"On several occasions, I heard a woman's voice coming from the other room, but only at night. I don't know what their relationship was, if she was there willingly or if he had her tied up like he did me. During the day, he left me tied to a chair in the bedroom. He put me in front of a laptop that showed every move I made, and often threatened that he'd know if I moved. Then he locked the door. The whole time, I never saw anyone else."

"Can you give us any clue where Colton held you?" I asked.

"Both times, I crawled through bushes and shallow dirty water to the highway. I had no clue where I was or which way to go. The second time I attempted to escape, I doubt I'd have gotten much farther down the road if you hadn't stopped. I'd already made up my mind that if Colton caught me again, I'd goad him into killing me rather than go back."

"Do you know what kind of car he drove?" Fab asked.

Kathryn shook her head. "The whole time he held me, I was only out of the house twice. Both times I escaped, he was away. There was a rundown car parked beside the house; I assumed it didn't run. He didn't have a garage." She stared back and forth between me and Fab. "If Colton catches either of you snooping around or, worse, finds out that you were the ones to help me, he'll kill you."

"We should report this Colton character to the cops," Mother said.

"No," Kathryn said emphatically. "I'm not ready for that. You said I could trust you, and I'm asking you not to."

"I've got a couple of cop friends that would be eager to see Colton off the streets," I told her. "If he's holding another woman, then they need to know now so she can be rescued. I'll keep you out of it as long as I can."

"I'd really like to lie down again," Kathryn said. "I want to thank all of you for everything you've done. I don't know what you were doing out there that day, but I appreciate your taking a chance on helping me. If you hadn't..." She shuddered.

"We were only there by a fluke; I'd taken a wrong turn," Fab said. "Neither Madison nor I like that area—too remote for us."

Mother's radar went off. She knew Fab was lying—Fab never took a wrong turn ever. Mother stared her down until she looked away.

I'd let Fab tell Mother she was drag racing.

Mother extended her hand to Kathryn, who stood, and the two went into the bedroom.

"Kathryn needs to report this to the cops now, so they can document her injuries," Rude said.

"Her father is a powerful man with lots of connections," Fab said. "I'm certain he'll call in the cops. No way is he going to let Colton get away with everything he's done."

I pulled my phone out of my pocket and called Xander, our go-to information guy, as I went out to the porch, craving sunshine on my face. Hot on my heels, Fab came up and stood next to me.

"This is a rush," I said when he answered. "I've got two names for you: Henry Beckett, corporate bigwig, and Colton Roberts. Especially interested if the latter has a criminal record."

"I'll get right on it and get back to you."

We hung up.

"I met Beckett a few years back, at one of those South Beach parties you like to turn your nose up at," Fab said. "He showed up with his wife, and they both charmed the room and talked to everyone. He didn't have a wandering eye—attentive to his wife, who he kept by his side. I remember wishing I had a man like him."

"Now you do." I smiled at her. Fab and Didier garnered attention wherever they went but only had eyes for each other. "I want Kathryn to have the happy reunion she's hoping for. If Colton hadn't beaten the confidence out of her, she wouldn't be so worried over the outcome."

"I have no doubt that you're going to make this happen. When you do, give Beckett, Colton's name and location, and I'm willing to bet he'll disappear without a trace and no one will ask any questions. I imagine his death won't be fast."

I grimaced at the thought. If Colton knew Kathryn's background, he'd leave town if he were smart. "There's an upside to one of us getting around." I pointed at her with a smile. "You can call Beckett, set up an appointment."

"Mr. Beckett, sir, remember me? Not going to work because he's not going to remember, and even if he did... Your idea needs to be reworked."

I made a face.

"How about we just happen to bump into him?"

"Are you forgetting he has muscle? They're going to make sure we don't get within arm's length." I air-boxed, which garnered a smirk from Fab.

Mother came out the door. "Kathryn curled up in a ball and went to sleep. She's a lot stronger than she thinks, and with a little rest, she's going to be eager to get back to her life."

I enveloped her in a hug. "You rock."

Chapter Six

Before leaving, I stuck my head back in the door and thanked Mac profusely, promising to keep her updated on anything we found out.

Fab pulled out of the driveway and stopped at the corner. "Where to next?"

Mother's phone rang, and she took it out of her pocket, glancing at the screen. "Hi, honey," she answered. She turned to me. "Do you need me for anything else?"

"We're headed down to Marathon to check out the damage to the Chief's business." I tapped Fab's shoulder for confirmation, and she nodded.

Mother wrinkled her nose and turned her attention back to her phone. She spoke for a few minutes and ended the call with a kissy noise.

"I'm assuming that was your husband," I said, loving that I could tease her. "Unless you're fooling around."

"No chance of that," she said with a smile. "The other fellow would end up dead, and Spoonee wouldn't be happy with me."

"You know you've been banned by the big man from saying 'Spoonee' in public."

Mother ignored me. "I need a ride to his office.

Spoon and I have a date tonight; we're going to try a new restaurant that opened in Islamorada."

"I planned to invite the two of you over for pizza. Guess not." I made a sad face.

"Since Fab's driving, I told Spoon that we'd be there in five minutes, so you better step on it." Mother poked her in the shoulder. She turned in her seat to face us both. "I assured Kathryn that you wouldn't let her down, and you'd find a way to reunite her with her family. I can't imagine the hell they've been through. I also told her that she owes me lunch when her parents welcome her with open arms."

"If anyone's pushy enough to demand a sit-down with a stranger, it would be your daughter," Fab said.

Mother laughed. "Madison can be persistent. I love that you asked me to help with a problem and hope that you do it again."

"Our next get-together is going to be something fun, and soon." I stuck my head between the seats and kissed her cheek.

Fab swung into the driveway of JS Auto Body, the car repair business owned by Spoon, who ran it strictly by appointment only and for a select clientele with high-end autos. No one would suspect the man's bad-ass reputation, as he'd been tamed somewhat by the woman in the front seat. Spoon barreled through the door, a smile tugging at the corners of his lips as he jerked open the car door and swept Mother out and into his arms, whirling her around and laying a big kiss on her.

I got out and jumped in the front, then rolled down the window. "Knock it off, you two; the children are watching."

Mother laughed.

They both waved as Fab backed out.

I fished the copy of the police report the Chief had left for Fab out of her bag and perused it on the drive south. "Whoever it was went to a lot of effort to destroy the Chief's offices. They're probably disappointed the place didn't burn to the ground, but water can be just as damaging."

"I asked the Chief if he had a list of suspects, anyone to check out, and he had nothing. I inquired about the original partners, but he says that ended amicably."

"The Chief isn't the kind of man that cultivates enemies."

"I asked him about that, and he laughed it off, saying there was no one that came to mind." Fab grumbled at the car in front of her and skirted around the slow driver.

Traffic was light, and it didn't take long to get to Marathon. Fab turned off the highway onto a side street. Half a block down, she pulled up in front the Chief's old office. The windows had blown out, and the walls were blackened on the outside.

"The furniture and office equipment are replaceable." Fab stared at the building. "I asked him if he had his files backed up, and he grunted something unintelligible. I suggested that, in the future, he use Xander."

"We came and saw, and now what?"

"I already wrote this off as a waste of time, but then I remembered that store we like down here." Fab got out, phone in hand, and walked from one end of the property to the other, snapping pictures.

I picked a single key out of the cup holder and got out, unlocking the wood slab that had temporarily replaced the door and shoving it open. "It smells." I stepped back from the entry.

Fab poked her head inside and snapped a couple of pics. "The Chief said not to touch anything until the insurance company gets out here. He also said the owner was being super cooperative."

"That means everyone had good insurance." I stood back and looked at the second floor. "Was the Chief the only tenant?"

Fab nodded. "Get a good crew in here, and this can be cleaned up pretty quickly."

"Good luck to that if mold sets in." I peered over her shoulder at the smashed equipment on the floor in an inch of water. "I'll stand guard while you take more pictures; I'm not going inside."

"Me neither." Fab stuck her arm in the door and shot a video, then held out her hand for the key to lock up.

Waving and shouting, "Hello," a blonde woman ran across the driveway from the building next door. "Are you the insurance inspectors?" she asked, out of breath. She brushed past Fab before she could close up and stepped inside. "I've been curious to see the damage." She pulled a phone out of her pocket, walking around and snapping pictures. She started for the stairs.

"Hold on," I yelled. "It's not safe to go up there." The last thing we needed was someone getting hurt.

The woman grunted something. She had no intention of slowing down until Fab stepped in front of her and forced her to stop in her tracks.

"Who are you?" Fab demanded, ignoring the woman's question.

"I'm Robbie Lee." She pointed to the large neon realtor sign on the neighboring property. "Do you have a timeframe for how long the repairs will take? I've got a client interested, since I heard the current tenant isn't coming back." She gave us a toothy, predatory smile.

"Any clue how the fire started?" I asked.

"I wouldn't know anything about that." Her demeanor changed, now the picture of innocence. "I'm just doing my job, chasing a commission."

"You happen to see anyone suspicious hanging around the property?" Fab continued to block her way. "Before or after the fire."

"It wasn't unusual to see cars coming and going during business hours. Other than that, I never noticed anything out of the ordinary, but then, no one is in the office after six except by appointment." Robbie bent sideways and snapped more pics. "You didn't say how long the repairs would take."

"You should talk to the building owner and get any information you need from him," I said.

"We have another appointment and need to lock up." Fab motioned her outside.

Robbie nodded, acknowledging that she needed to leave, but didn't move. "Do you know the owner's plans for the building?" She shifted from one foot to the other, and only exited when Fab forced her to back up. She had to have noticed that we hadn't answered her questions, but she didn't press the issue. "I'll get with the building owner." She shuffled, not making eye contact, then pulled a folded business card out of her pocket and held it out. "Do you have a card?"

Fab pocketed the card. "You know, I keep meaning to reorder and keep forgetting." She unleashed creepy-girl smile.

Robbie did a double-take and smiled nervously. "If you're ever in the area… I'm off to get a cup of coffee." She waved as she walked in the opposite direction of her office.

We watched as she disappeared into a strip center.

"She's had too much coffee already," I said. "Did you notice her pupils were the size of dimes?"

"I had a couple of other questions I'd have liked to ask, but there was something off about her." Fab locked up and cruised the street before heading back to the highway.

Chapter Seven

Fab flew up the Overseas, managing not to honk at those going the speed limit.

My phone beeped with an incoming message. I pulled it out. "Xander emailed his report on Henry Beckett. He added, 'This one's elusive.'"

"My money's on you." Fab laughed. "You'll find someone to charm for an introduction or to look the other way."

"I need to stop by the office—" I grabbed the seat as a car swerved too close to the front bumper and roared off.

"Just great, a drunk," Fab said in disdain and took a shortcut over to the twin warehouses she owned. Ever since she updated the security system, all it required was scanning your index finger to make the gate roll back.

Out of the two buildings Fab owned, one had originally been used as office space for her and Didier, until for convenience sake, he moved into The Boardwalk offices. I'd talked my way into the use of a small alcove space with that coveted water-view that I loved.

After standing empty for a long time, the other warehouse was rented to Toady, who lived there in addition to using it as his office. He was also tasked with guard duty. It was his job to make sure no one vaulted the fence, and Fab made it clear she wasn't averse to intruders being shot.

She didn't bother with garage parking, and today, parked between the two buildings. We got out and hiked up the steps to the second floor of the building Toady occupied, and before we got to the top, the door opened and Xander beckoned us inside. Always in a good mood, his brown eyes danced with amusement.

The recent college grad had worked a deal with Toady for office space, since the young man had numerous projects and the need to spread out. The computer whiz hadn't even hinted at ditching us as clients, even though the majority of his time was spent on more lucrative projects. I knew that he was currently shopping a social media app.

Fab and I appreciated that Xander had a talent for legally digging up information. We were careful not to ask for anything illegal and banned all our associates from asking as well.

Xander ushered us into the wide-open space that encompassed the kitchen and living room—no expense had been spared in the upgrades by the previous owner. He flopped onto a stool at the island, which easily sat six and was currently used as desk space. The granite countertop was littered with notes and papers, which he smooshed into a pile.

He waved to us to sit across from him.

A door banged closed, and Toady tromped out from one of the bedrooms. "Hey, girlies." The old lizard had upped his game, thanks to Fab's influence, trading in his wife-beaters for tropical shirts. He grinned at us, the overhead lighting sparkling off his only tooth—gold, and front and center. He beelined for the refrigerator, reached in, grabbed a bottle of water, and held it up. Fab and I nodded. He crossed the room and set them down in front of us.

Toady was an "associate" of Fab's, meaning he took the jobs that came with a certain amount of danger. Nothing scared the man.

"I tried opening the file that you sent over on Henry Beckett, and no luck," I said to Xander and told the two men about Kathryn, her father, and what we knew about Colton Roberts. "If you could give me the quick version..."

"Billionaire. Somewhat reclusive. Not a whiff of scandal. Got his start with family money and parlayed that into a hefty ten figures for himself." Xander opened his laptop and scanned the screen. "He's CEO of Beckett Associates, a management company that repairs the images of high-profile folks."

"We could pay a visit to his office," I mused and looked to Fab for agreement.

Before Fab could insert her two cents, Xander laughed, and he wasn't amused. "He owns a sixty-story building in Brickell Plaza. His clients are referral only, and the more prominent the better. Another hurdle: getting past the security guards. If you're planning on a one-on-one, a cold call isn't the way to go. You'll be escorted off the property as a nutjob."

I turned to Fab. "You've been known to scale the sides of buildings."

"That was back when I lived for the adrenaline rush." She grimaced. "I still like action, just tamed down. Besides, Didier would kill me and then you. Because before I sucked my last breath, I'd tell him it was your idea."

I eyed Xander.

"More news you're not going to like," he said. "No way you're getting to him at his residence either. Lives on a private island off Biscayne Bay. Gates, guards, good luck."

"What we need is a Miami connection." I took out my phone and scrolled through my contacts. "Someone… with connections… that I can charm a favor out of and hope the payback isn't something I refuse to do."

"I know a guy," Toady said. "He comes with an 'f— with him at your own peril' reputation."

I set my phone down. "That sounds like someone who'd provoke a showdown, and I'd prefer a more low-key introduction."

"What did you find out about Colton Roberts?" Fab asked.

"Dead. Died in a car fire along with Kathryn Beckett." Xander hit a couple of keys on his laptop and turned it toward us. "Got the picture of Kathryn that accompanied her obituary announcement. Is this the woman you rescued?"

Fab and I put our heads together, and both of us nodded at the same time. "That's her," we said.

"Got a picture of Colton?" Fab asked.

Xander stood and leaned over her shoulder, pressing another key. "Here you go. It's his driver's license photo, and I did my best to enlarge it."

The problem with those photos was that they didn't show off a person's best side… more like a booking photo. Brown hair and eyes, boy-next-door appeal that was majorly deceptive.

Toady peered over Fab's shoulder and growled. "You get a lead on that bastard, give it to me. I'll pay him a visit and see that he's kibble for local wildlife." He brushed his hands together.

I shuddered, knowing the man's reputation and that he wasn't full of hot air. I wouldn't want to be on his radar. "I'm not suggesting murder, but hopefully Kathryn won't have to live her life with one eye peeled over her shoulder."

"Forward me the pic of Colton," Fab said. "We'll show it to Kathryn, and if she IDs him, then we'll pass it along to our cop connection."

Xander nodded and clicked away at his keys. "I think it's highly likely that Colton set up a new identity. Not sure how long he could operate using his real name when he's supposedly dead."

Fab's phone beeped with an incoming message. "If Kathryn makes a positive ID, then we need to commit this guy's face to memory and be on the lookout." She held up the screen. "If he approaches either of us, we shoot first."

"Shooting is too good for him," Toady grouched. "You two don't go looking for trouble on that front; I'm your go-to guy for solving this problem."

"I don't want you going to jail," I said adamantly.

"We haven't figured out how to orchestrate a breakout yet." Fab smiled at her friend.

Toady grinned and winked at her. If she asked, he'd do it, no excuses, no questions asked.

"I know someone who may have connections to get us an introduction to Beckett. He can definitely sic the law on Colton and keep us all out of trouble, and he owes me," I said with a conspiratorial smile. "You mind if I invite another guest to this party?"

"Invite away, missy."

I pulled out my phone and called Casio. "You in the area?" I asked when he answered, skipping all niceties.

"You wanting favors from me is getting to be a habit." Casio groaned but sounded amused.

"Please… this is an opportunity for you to make a dent in the pile I have with your name on it. Not that you're going to catch up anytime soon, but it's a start."

"Where are we meeting?" Casio asked.

I told him, and he paused and then said, "Be there in five."

"I didn't expect him to be able to get here so quickly, but works for me," I said.

"Casio's a good choice; he's sure to know someone." Fab got up and picked up the empty bottles, putting them in the recycle bin.

Fab and Toady hung back and talked about a car repossession case—another job that Fab had referred to the man.

I texted an update to Creole.

True to his word, Casio buzzed the gate in under five. Fab's phone dinged, and she let him in. He lumbered up the steps and through the door that Fab had left open, taking a mental head count when he stepped inside. "A meeting and I'm the last to arrive?" He stomped over to the island, moving a stool to the end.

"Drink?" Toady offered.

"Beer's good." Casio sat down.

Toady grabbed a beer and set it in front of him. "You want us to leave?" He pointed between him and Xander.

"No need." I turned to Casio. "I need someone to set up a meeting with Henry Beckett. So we're clear, I mean the billionaire out of Miami. Can you or someone you know make that happen?"

"Maybe." Casio gave me his best cop stare, and it was hard not to flinch.

"Stop that. I'm not one of your criminals." I squinted at him.

Casio smiled, which didn't calm my nerves. "I'll need to know the why, where, and what else is involved."

I pointed at Fab. "You tell him."

"Nice try, but I did the honors for the last explanation; time for you to step up."

That's a first. I frowned at Fab. "I'm certain you remember me calling about finding a girl on the side of the road and needing a doctor recommendation. Turns out she's Kathryn Beckett."

"Nice try," Casio scoffed. "Chick's conning you. Kathryn's dead. The Beckett family was devastated, and whatever this girl thinks she's going to get with this monster lie, I'm here to tell you, it isn't going to work."

I motioned to Xander to bring her picture back up. "This is the girl we picked up on the side of the road, unless she has an identical twin. If you can positively ID her, she needs to be reunited with her family."

Casio leaned forward and took a long look at the headshot. "The police need to be involved," he said adamantly.

"Agreed. But… not before she's back with her family. Kathryn isn't in any shape to deal with the police on her own. One step at a time."

Casio continued to stare at the picture. "You're certain?" I nodded. "Not even I could get past security at his office, not without an appointment or a warrant. Beckett plays golf on Wednesdays at a private club in Coral Gables, and afterwards, he eats in the dining room."

Of course, it would be private. "Can you get me a guest pass or whatever it takes to get in? It's important that he hears the news face-to-face."

"Agree with you there," Casio said.

"I gave brief thought to approaching him at his home or office but knew it had zero chance of success. After conning my way in with some untruths, I'd be told to beat it."

"Two things we agree on today." Casio downed his beer. "I've got a guest pass for the club that allows me to avail myself of the facilities. While Beckett knows me, he's not going to tolerate me invading his space. You'll have seconds to make your case, so you better practice."

"The sooner the better. Can we go this week?"

"I don't see why not." Casio heaved a long sigh. "There's no good way to break this news. I suggest that you bring Kathryn to this meeting, because once you break the news, he's going to want to see her. Waiting would be cruel and give him time to think it's a prank and shut you down."

Chapter Eight

Two days passed slowly, but Wednesday was finally here.

I'd updated Creole and Didier after the meeting with Casio. No one had a better suggestion as to how to deliver the news to Beckett. Both were confident that the man would be ecstatic once he was convinced it wasn't a prank.

I then ran the plan by Kathryn, who was adamant that it wouldn't work, but that was only because she feared rejection, no matter how many of us told her that wouldn't be the case. It took Mother to convince her she'd be safe waiting in the car. Mother had volunteered to come along to keep her company, saying that she was the best choice, since they'd already developed a rapport.

It was Fab's suggestion that we get something more suitable for Kathryn to wear, since Rude's housedress hung on her like a sack. Kathryn had insisted that the clothes she'd been found in, muddied and grimy, go in the trash. Unbeknownst to her, Mac had bagged them for the cops. Fab picked out a red sleeveless sundress and a jacket with three-quarter length sleeves to hide her bruises. I chose a pair of slip-on sandals, since her feet were still swollen and bruised.

Casio called the night before and confirmed that he'd meet us at the club.

Fab and I picked up Mother and arrived early at Mac's to pick up Kathryn. She was huddled in a chair, shivering, fear etched on her face. Mother talked quietly with her for ten minutes before she could convince her to stand, then put her arm around her and walked her out to the SUV. Fab and I heaved a sigh of relief. The two climbed in the back, Fab and I in the front.

The drive north to Miami was uneventful and quiet, and Fab stuck to the speed limit with no prodding from Mother. Kathryn stretched out on the back seat, head on Mother's lap, and fell asleep. The private club overlooked Biscayne Bay, and in addition to boasting an eighteen-hole golf course, it also catered to yachts.

Fab pulled up to the gate, and we both took notice of the two security guards. One was sitting on a golf cart, and the other came out of a small building, clipboard in hand. Both men were armed. Fab gave the man her name, and after a check of his list, the electric gate rolled back.

"It really is beautiful," I said, admiring the rolling expanse of perfectly manicured green lawn and abundance of tropical flowers.

"I perused the website, and they have every amenity." Fab spotted Casio's SUV and parked next to it. We were right on time.

Casio had gone over the layout of the club on the phone. Beckett lunched in the dining room at the far end of the terrace, which could be accessed from inside or off the greens. I was happy that Casio had agreed to accompany us and make the introduction. It was going to be awkward enough without barging up to the man.

My stomach was a mass of nerves. Mother's intuition must have kicked in, as she leaned forward and patted my shoulder. I sucked in a deep breath and sent her a weak smile, then got out and walked over to where Casio leaned against the bumper of his SUV, Fab by my side.

Casio straightened and patted my shoulder, uncharacteristic for him. "Heads up: Beckett has a short fuse and doesn't show it until he's erupting. So get to the point. In a nice way, of course. I'll be right there, in case you're in need of a friendly face."

"That's my job," Fab growled at him.

"I'm prettier than you." Casio grinned.

"You've got kids; you shouldn't be drinking in the morning," Fab said.

"Thank you, I needed a laugh," I said. "I'm assuming that they have a bar. This is Florida." One on every corner. "We got time for a quick one?"

"You getting sauced up would be a bad idea," Fab scolded with a smirk.

"Casio, no matter what happens, I want to thank you for arranging this today," I said as the three of us walked toward the clubhouse, which was the size of three mansions. "Without your assistance, I'm not certain how we would've managed to pull off a meet-and-greet that didn't include getting hurt or arrested."

"Don't think it will embarrass me to remind you of this little adventure the next time I need a favor." Casio grinned.

He pulled open the mammoth front door and steered us past the reception desk, winking at the young woman, who was on the phone. Instead of heading straight into the restaurant, Casio led us through a set of sliding glass doors, then veered right into an outside bar area that could easily seat fifty. "That's Beckett over there." He pointed to a fenced-off area farther down that held only a handful of tables. "He always sits outside on nice days."

"It's such a beautiful day, it would be my first choice." I glanced up at the baby blue sky, a cloud or two in the distance. "Beckett's got the best seat out here. He can watch his friends play golf or head out to the open water on their yachts and still have a modicum of privacy."

"Paste on a winning smile." Casio demonstrated, except that his made a person want to step back. "That goes for you, too." He tipped his head toward Fab. "Both of you go for friendly. He appreciates beautiful women without being a lech. If you feel an attack of nerves, know that once he gets over the shock of your news, this will go down as one of his best days." He led us across the patio, opening a small gate in the fence, and directly to Beckett's table. His approach caught the attention of Beckett and his two guards. Casio nodded to the three men. Beckett said something, and the guards, who'd stood, relaxed their stance.

"Beckett." Casio nodded. "This is Madison Westin, and she needs five minutes of your time."

His quasi-friendly stare turned to annoyance and was followed by an uncomfortable silence. "You'll owe me for this, detective."

"It will be just the opposite," Casio said, not backing down an inch.

Fab and I exchanged raised eyebrows.

Beckett waved me to a chair and tapped his expensive watch. "Four minutes."

I sat, and Casio stepped back and stood next to Fab, mimicking the bodyguard stance of the other two.

My inner voice said, Skip the 'nice to meet you' speech and get to the point. I subtly sucked in a calming breath—at least, I hoped it was. "This is about Kathryn."

"If this were a month ago, I'd strangle you right here," Beckett snarled. "Somehow, I've learned to deal with my grief better. If you're going to express condolences, just get up and leave now."

"Kathryn's alive."

Beckett laughed, and it sent a shiver down my spine. "An extortion attempt." He shot a death glare at Casio. "All of you, get the hell out of here. If you don't go on your own, I'll have you removed."

"Just listen," I pleaded, my anxiety on high. "I've got two more minutes." Beckett glared with such intensity, I took my phone out of my skirt pocket and brought up the first image—one I'd taken before we got in the SUV—and handed it to him. While he stared at the screen, I told him about finding his daughter on the side of the highway. I signaled to Fab, who handed over her phone; per usual, she'd snapped several more pictures.

"This looks…" Beckett fingered the screen. "I see a remarkable resemblance, but my daughter died in a car crash."

"Except she didn't." I went on to tell Beckett everything Kathryn had shared with us. "Your daughter probably does look different, but that's because she's been to hell and back and survived." Beckett's lips trembled, and he covered his mouth with his hand as he stared at the screen. "There were several reasons she didn't call herself—she didn't have the number, and she was afraid that since she wasn't the easiest of kids, you might not want her back."

"That's ridiculous," he growled and squeezed his eyes closed. "She was… and she wasn't. She was our most lively child growing up. You don't know how many times I regretted being critical of her."

"That's what Mother told her." Watching the riot of emotions racing across his face made me teary, and I swallowed it back.

"She was a great kid in so many ways, but a damn risk-taker. So many times, she scared years off her mother and me. When we buried her, a piece of us died." Beckett glared at me with an intensity that made me want to look away. "Are you absolutely certain?"

"I believe her, and so does my friend." I nodded over my shoulder. "And my mother. I know this is awkward, but I didn't know how to tell you other than blurting it out. There's no reason for her to lie. She'd be found out. But only you can decide if she's telling the truth."

"Where is she now?" Beckett looked around the room.

"Kathryn's asleep in the back of my car; my mother is with her," I said.

Beckett shoved his chair back and stood. "Take me to her."

"She's fragile," I said. "She's had some medical attention but needs more. She wasn't all that cooperative."

Beckett grimaced. "She never liked doctors."

"If by some fluke she's lying, we'll take care of her," I said.

Beckett motioned to Casio to take him to his daughter. The two strode out of the restaurant, followed by the guards. Fab and I broke into a run-walk to keep up with them.

As we approached, Fab remotely unlocked the SUV's doors. All of us hung back as Beckett flung open the door.

Kathryn had woken and was sitting up. "Daddy." She started to cry.

My mother got out on the other side.

Beckett turned and barked to his guards. "Get the car." He slid in next to Kathryn and gathered her into his arms, then reached out and closed the door. The remaining bodyguard slid over to stand in front of the door.

A black Escalade pulled up and parked. To my surprise, there wasn't any movement from my car. Beckett and his daughter were still inside, and the tinted windows made it impossible to see what was happening.

None of us said anything as the minutes ticked by. Finally, the door opened, and Beckett stepped out and reached inside, sliding Kathryn across the seat and into his arms. He carried her over to the Escalade, where the guard had the door open, and put her in the back seat. He turned back to me. "I'm going to have more questions. I can get ahold of you through the detective here?"

I reached in my pocket and pulled out my

business card. "Call anytime." I handed it to him.

Beckett nodded and climbed inside next to his daughter. The guard shut the door and climbed in front with his fellow bodyguard, and they left the parking lot.

"It won't take long for the shock to wear off, and you'll be hearing from Beckett," Casio warned me. "Any face-to-face meetings, take your bodyguard." He nodded at Fab. "Keep me in the loop. Email any new information that you get on that Colton character; the sooner we run him to ground and put him in jail, the better."

I thanked Casio profusely, and we all got in the SUV and followed him out of the parking lot, going in the opposite direction as we headed back to the Interstate.

Mother turned in her seat. "I want to hear what happened."

"Beckett's intimidating, and I was happy not to be the one breaking the news," Fab said. "It took him a few minutes to accept the news that Kathryn was alive."

"You timed your return just right; she woke up just before you got back to the car, which was good because she wouldn't have been able to suffer waiting," Mother said. "When we first left the Cove, Kathryn was such a bundle of nerves that I was relieved when she fell asleep."

"I'm happy that father and daughter were reunited, and soon, she'll be with the rest of her family," Fab said. "I was confident that Kathryn was telling the truth about her identity, but I admit to holding my breath when they first reunited. So glad it turned out her fears were for naught."

"You and me both." My nervous stomach was just starting to calm down.

No one was in the mood for chitchat, and we settled back. With light traffic, it was a fast trip home.

Once we passed the welcome sign, Mother broke the silence. "How about lunch at the Crab Shack?"

I raised my hand. "I'm all for getting sauced."

Fab licked her lips. I knew she was thinking of a martini, extra olives.

Chapter Nine

"Feeling better?" Creole kissed me, handing me a cup of my favorite brew as he slid onto the stool next to me. We faced one another, knees touching. He'd hustled me out to the kitchen, after we woke up and had gotten dressed, for a few moments of alone time.

Okay, I admit that I'd moped for a couple of days. Reuniting Kathryn with her father, although satisfying, had been an emotions-sucker. It didn't help that that cretin Colton was still on the loose. "You'll be interested to know that I'm interviewing an office manager this morning."

"I wondered why the dress. Looks good, babe." He leered and lifted the hem, taking stock of the gun strapped to my thigh.

I pointed my finger at him, which he bit. "Before you start, you know I don't like to leave the house half-dressed."

Creole laughed. "Try not to fill the position with a weirdo."

I saluted. "Normal, whatever that is, is overrated." I finished my coffee as Fab and Didier walked into the kitchen. I was the only lightweight downing one cup.

"Good, you're dressed appropriately." Fab gave me a once-over. She also had on a black dress. It was unclear whether she had any other color in her closet.

"Whatever you have planned—without requesting my back-up, I might add—I have a busy morning of my own." I turned slightly so I could slide closer to Creole, in case Fab decided to beat the heck out of me, as her glare would indicate.

The husbands grinned, always loving the drama. Not sure what they'd do if an actual brawl broke out.

Fab leaned across the counter. "Doing what?"

Didier handed her a cup of her preferred muck, and she took a long drink. Fab and Didier liked their coffee strong enough to wake the dead.

I leaned toward her, matching her stare. "I'm interviewing a paragon to run The Boardwalk office. You surely remember me being roped in by a unanimous vote."

"I have to apologize, cherie," Didier said. "I was certain you were stringing us along and never planned on finding anyone."

Creole laughed. "Thought the same thing, dude."

"I've been busy," I said in a faux-huff. "I'm on it now."

"How long is this interview going to take?"

Fab finished her coffee and handed the cup back to Didier for a refill. Great, she was going to be caffeined up and demanding we both be on our game. But for what?

Didier refilled all the mugs. Before he got to mine, I turned it upside down.

"I don't want to be rushed," I said.

Fab didn't roll her eyes, but she was clearly thinking it.

"I'm thinking if you find someone you think is right for the position, you should send them over and we'll have a go at the them," Creole said.

"That sounds swell. But probably not going to happen. If I find the right person, I'm snapping him or her up."

"Since my appointment is flexible, we'll do your meeting first," Fab said.

"I'm surprised the guys aren't asking what your job is, who's the client, and other pesky details." The guys weren't giving away what they knew. "I deduce that Didier knows, but I know that Creole hasn't been informed or I'd know. So enlighten us." I gave Fab a fake smile.

"I'm dropping off an envelope in Miami for Gunz." Fab waved off my response. "Before you start whining about how long the drive is, we've done it many times and it isn't."

"As long as you promise to be nice to the woman I'm interviewing and not scare her off."

Fab shook her head. "When am I not nice?"

The three of laughed and got a glare from her.

Didier turned Fab's face toward him. "I never want you going on a job by yourself. I don't want you to find your life on the line with no backup. We both know your cases take unexpected turns almost every time."

Fab wrapped her arms around him. "There was a time I wouldn't have given it a second thought, but those days are behind me."

Creole tapped his watch. "Time to go," he said to Didier and stood. "Call me." He leaned down and kissed me.

I waved as the two men walked out the door, and when it closed, I said, "We need to be at Howl's in a half-hour."

"That's a dump." Fab screwed up her nose.

"Some would say it has character." I ignored her snort. "If you can't behave, you won't be coming along if there's a next time."

The two of us grabbed our briefcases and purses and headed out the door. Fab drove out of the compound and over to the main highway and headed north.

"How did you find this person?" Fab asked.

"We have a mutual friend. Her name is Lark Pontana. She recently moved to the Keys to enjoy her inheritance from her grandmother—a double-wide on Highway One—and she needs a job. I requested her resume, and she sent back a file." I chuckled. "She included a professional version, a separate one that hawked her talents, three references, and a few pictures."

"You do know that if your hire goes south in any way, you'll never hear the end of it. I'm going to trot out a sad face and say, 'I tried to tell her.'"

"A stranger might believe your act, but not anyone that knows you." I decided to change the subject. "Bring me up to speed on your job for Gunz."

"For once, it's just what I said it was. I'm dropping off an envelope with a neutral third party."

"I wish I believed you." I turned toward the sunshine sparkling off the water as Fab curved to the north.

"If you behave yourself, lunch is my treat. We'll choose something waterfront."

"I need to get these lunch offers in writing, since something always comes up and I'm left starving to death."

Fab made an unsympathetic noise.

"Howl's is right up here." I pointed at the RV, boat, campground place it was part of. "If you feel the need to circle the place, be on the lookout—the folks have a tendency to wander around without looking where they're going." I bit back a laugh at her look of disgust.

Fab pulled up to a small cement building off to the side of the park entrance. A nude male mannequin holding a welcome sign stood next to the walk-up window. The chalkboard on the far side listed their menu items. A stack of folding chairs leaned up against the side of the building, and two men puffing on cigars occupied two others that barely held their considerable bulk. Under several palms in a gravel area were picnic tables. At one, a woman with long brown hair had pulled out a bench. She'd raised her sundress and was sunning her legs, a stiletto hanging off her toes and a golden retriever asleep on the other foot.

"Is that her?" Fab stared out the window.

I nodded. "Don't forget to be nice." I got out and closed the door on her disgruntled response.

Fab and I walked over. The dog lifted his head and studied us intently but didn't move. "Lark?" I asked. She nodded. "I'm Madison, and this is Fab."

"Can I get you something to drink?" Lark offered.

"We're good," I said as Fab and I slid onto the bench opposite her. "I read the file you sent over, and I'm impressed with your skills. Two of your references were from men I respect, and it went a long way to convincing me to set up this interview."

Her brown eyes were bigger than before; she appeared a bit intimidated.

"Another factor in your favor—you sold me in our email exchanges that you can run an office and not let three grown men push you around." I set a folder and pen on the table. "Now's the time to confess if you exaggerated your resume and your skills are non-existent, and we can part with no hard feelings. If I hire you and find out otherwise, I won't take kindly to being BSed."

"Not to worry. I didn't sell you a bill of goods." Lark laughed, her eyes dancing with amusement. "There are a couple of things I left off my resume. I'm a good shot, dead-on accurate with a bow and arrow, and can kick butt, thanks to my self-defense classes. Zach told me to mention those skills, as they might be a selling point with you."

"Lazzaro?" Fab practically screeched.

"You remember him? You two engaged in the horizontal hula at one time," I teased.

"You… you had a relationship with him."

"Long after you, and luckily it wasn't an impediment to our bestie relationship." Catching Fab off guard would be the highlight of my week, and I'd be reliving this moment. She knew that, hence the growl.

Lark watched the drama, wide-eyed.

I turned back to Lark. "Besides managing the Boardwalk offices, you'll be fielding calls for properties that me and my husband own. At first, you'll contact me for direction on how to handle things. Once you get it all figured out, you won't have to check with me, but that doesn't mean I want to be the last to know what's going on. Ticks me off."

"Got it." Lark's shoe bobbed up and down at a frantic pace.

I opened the folder, pulled out two one-page contracts, and handed them to her along with the pen. "It's a three-month agreement, and in that time, you need to prove yourself to your bosses. If you turn out to be full of yourself, you'll be fed to the alligators."

"What about Arlo?" she asked. The dog lifted his head and stared at her.

"No worries, we'll find him a great home."

Lark ran her finger down the page. "No bulling around on this contract." She scribbled her name at the bottom. I'd already signed both copies.

I handed her a business card. "On the back is the phone number for Mac Lane, the manager of my beach rentals. I'm going to have her contact you, and you two can work out a time that suits you. She'll give you the grand tour of Tarpon Cove and introduce you around." I turned to Fab. "Any questions?" Guess not, since she rolled her eyes. "I'll be at the office on your first day to get you started."

We all stood. "You won't be disappointed." Lark stuck out her hand.

"I don't want to be rude, but I don't shake hands."

"You know… good one. I can't tell you the number of times I've wondered where someone's hand's been and couldn't wait to wash with disinfectant."

I grimaced.

Fab choked.

Lark looked at her with a note of concern. "You don't have to worry; I'm going to do a great job."

We waved and walked back to the SUV.

"That interview was horribly unprofessional." Fab sniffed. "No real businesswoman would ever bring up the hula." She gunned the engine and hit the highway.

"I've got a good feeling about Lark."

Chapter Ten

It was a first, and surprised me, that Fab's job for Gunz was uneventful. It had been a fast and unexciting drive north, just as she promised. We parked in front of a mediocre office building in a seedy part of Miami, which lacked even a glimpse of the beach.

We took the elevator to the penthouse, which was actually the third floor. "What's in the envelope?" I asked, knowing there was a slim chance that she'd answer, and that was if she knew. "It costs Gunz a fortune to use you as a messenger chick."

"He trusts me."

Because something shady is going on.

The doors opened into a miniscule, dingy reception area, the woman behind the desk doing her nails and smacking her gum.

"I'm here to see Mr. Bart," Fab said, staring at the woman, who hadn't acknowledged her presence.

She poked her file in her beehive, which coiled up at least a foot off her head, and glanced up. "Delivery? Put it in my inbox." She waved to the corner of her desk.

"I need for him to sign," Fab said in an authoritative tone.

That wasn't true. I'd be interested to see how she played it off when the man in question put in an appearance.

The receptionist let out a long, aggrieved sigh, waved her fingers in the air, and stared at Fab, who didn't back down. After another sigh, she picked up the phone and used a pen to punch in the number. "Mr. Bart, there's a delivery woman here; she's got an envelope," she cooed. After a pause: "Told her. Claims she needs your signature." Whatever was asked, she gave Fab some close scrutiny and said, "It's hard to tell." She hung up and didn't say anything, instead studying a tray of nail polish that she slid over in front of her.

Due to the lack of signage, it was anyone's guess what kind of business was being conducted there. They either didn't have many clients or never kept anyone waiting, as there were no chairs.

A dumpy fifty-something strolled out in an ill-fitting suit. Once he got an eyeful of Fab, he ran his hand through his greasy hair and pasted on a smarmy smile that replaced the annoyance steaming out his ears. "Hey, hon, come on back to my office."

"Maybe next time. I've got two more stops for Gunz, and he's waiting for a call." She thrust the envelope at him.

I hit the button for the elevator, and the doors opened. I stood in the way to keep them from closing.

"You and Gunz—"

"Nice meeting you." Fab stormed into the elevator and punched the button for the ground floor.

I turned my back to the door. "Mr. Bart is in the business of what, exactly?"

"He's a loan facilitator."

"Code for loan shark. And you said that with a straight face." The door opened, and I didn't move. "Don't you think a word of warning would've been appropriate? I mean, before you dragged me all the way here."

"And subject myself to whining when you're only going to give in?" Fab cut around me and headed down the walkway, back to the SUV.

I breathed a sigh of relief that the Hummer was still where we parked it. "It was a red flag that I ignored when you hemmed and hawed about the job; I should've known that there was a backstory I wouldn't like." I hissed out my annoyance. "Since all of his jobs have to do with one family member or another, what's with this one?"

Gunz had been voted King, according to one family member, and they kept him busy cleaning up the messes they made of their lives.

"A cousin or some such—you know there's so many of them." She paused, noting my "hurry it up," glare. "Who can remember? He got in deep with a loan shark, and it was pay-or-die time," Fab said as she cut across traffic.

"I bet when you were blowing smoke in your husb's ear about this delivery job, you didn't mention one word about a loan shark. This little adventure could've gone south in a hot second."

"If Bart had touched me, he'd be dead and it wouldn't be pretty, and he knows that."

I turned away, leaning my head against the window. "This isn't the way back to the Interstate." I was ready to go home.

"I guess I need to remind you that I'm taking us to lunch."

"I'd prefer to wait until we get back to the Cove."

"It won't kill you to broaden your palate."

I groaned loudly with added emphasis, knowing that she already had a restaurant picked out. "Think simple food, and I'll be happy. I don't want to eat anything I can't pronounce."

Fab laughed.

As usual, I sat back in awe as she zipped through the streets, making turns without the benefit of GPS, and never got lost. Let's hope there wasn't a pop quiz, with the first question being, "Where are we?" She parked on a side street, the white sandy beach and waters of the Atlantic a half-block away.

There were several restaurants in this block,

and I hoped she'd chosen the one with the outdoor patio that overlooked the beach. "Another trick of yours?" I hissed, staring down the sidewalk, and returned the Chief's wave.

"Ladies," he said with a big smile as he approached.

Fab's phone rang. She looked down and took a step back to answer.

Tires squealed.

People screamed and ran.

I shoved Fab, knocking her phone out of her hand, then heaved my body into the Chief's, pushing him as hard as I could. We both tumbled to the concrete. My feet left the ground, and I landed on top of the Chief, my head buried in his chest. The sound of crunching metal filled the air, the noise ear-shattering.

After a brief silence, people started yelling.

Tires screeched again.

I lifted my head and stared into the Chief's eyes. "You okay?" My heart beat a wild rhythm as I looked around, noticing a couple of people with their phones out. I inched my way back to my feet and, once firmly on solid ground, stood and offered him a hand.

He ignored it and got to his feet. "How about you? You hurt?" His voice was calm, but concerned.

I shook my head. "I'm fine. You're the one that took a solid hit on the concrete."

He stared over my shoulder, then turned back,

looking the other way. "I hope someone got a description, something."

Fab, who'd jumped to her feet, joined us. "A black SUV smashed into the back end of the Mercedes over there, then collided with that pole." She pointed. It would have been hard to miss, since the bottom half had come loose from the ground. "The driver blew off down the street."

"An accident? Or…?" the Chief asked.

"Girlfriend here shoved me and you out of the way just as the SUV came out of nowhere, swerved across the road and into the back of the Mercedes, taking out the valet stand and jumping the curb. It then backed up into oncoming traffic, barely braking. Lucky my phone didn't break." Fab smiled at me.

"What the hell?" The Chief turned and stared at the dark blue Mercedes, which had ended up sideways in the street after the SUV made contact.

Fab took a tissue from her purse and handed it to the Chief, who sported a bloody gash on the back of his arm and had scraped the skin off one elbow.

The Chief stumbled over to the car and stood at the rear bumper, surveying the damage. He raked his hand through his hair. "Did anyone get a license number?" he yelled, loud enough, so that those had gathered to film the incident could hear.

"I didn't get a clear shot of the tag," one man yelled back.

"Cops are on the way," another yelled.

The Chief walked around the Mercedes, fingering the driver's side from front to back, his face a riot of emotions, moving from confused, what the heck, then angry.

Not one to be left out, Fab checked out the Mercedes, snapped pictures, and came back. "It took a pretty hard hit. I'm guessing that the SUV had steel bars on the grille. Chiefy's going to need a ride, and if we hurry, we can ditch him and leave him to whistle for a taxi."

"Dare you." I shook my head. "While you're thinking of a way to do just that, know that you'll never work for him again." Not that she cared.

"You don't want to stand around and wait for the cops to arrive either," Fab said. "For once, I'm an innocent party, and at this rate, we'll never get lunch."

"Hope you're enjoying your hissy fit. Here's some bad news, since it appears to have slipped your mind—we're witnesses."

The Chief walked over and joined us. "Can I impose on you for a ride back to town?"

"We were just talking about that and were about to suggest that very thing." I smiled sweetly and mentally applauded myself for holding still when Fab knocked me in the back.

"The cops are going to want to talk to you," the Chief said.

I smirked at Fab.

"Not sure how much help I can be," Fab said. "I only got a side view of the driver, who was wearing a baseball hat."

"The SUV made a sharp turn and headed straight for the entrance of this restaurant and your Mercedes," I said. "Since it's not a street that most people speed on, I'd guess you or your car was the target. You sure you haven't annoyed a person or two of late?"

The Chief jerked his head around and stared back out at the street.

Red lights flashed in the distance, headed in our direction.

"Thank you for pushing me out of the way." The Chief gave me a side hug. "I'm going to ask a few questions before the bystanders run off. You know they will as soon as the cops pull up."

"You better hurry." Fab pointed behind him at a group of people that were leaving; a couple of them were already a half-block down the street. "What you'll get from those sticking around are a bunch of different descriptions. Nobody yelled that they got a good picture, so good luck tracing the SUV."

"I'm thinking this wasn't random," I confided in Fab as the Chief walked over to a group of people that hadn't dispersed yet. "First a fire. Now a hit and run."

"The one time I'm not paying attention..." Fab was clearly annoyed with herself. "We are in his old stomping grounds. Maybe someone holding a grudge from his days as Chief of Police? Seems unlikely it's connected to his current business. Even if his venture down south wasn't amicable, why follow him up here?"

"If it was driver error of some kind and just an accident, why not pull over?"

"It seems like a trend these days. More often than not, people don't pull over after an accident, even though when they get caught—and they usually are—it means more charges being leveled."

Fab and I watched as two more cop cars blew up and parked behind the first two.

"Does the Chief have a love life?" Fab asked. "A disgruntled ex, maybe?"

I wasn't about to ask and would bet big that neither would she. "I've never seen him with anyone, but you'd think he'd be getting nookie; he's not butt-ugly."

Fab laughed. "This is the payback you deserve for your antics today: I'm going to tell the guys what you said and draw out the drama and relish every moment."

"If this wasn't random and Chiefy was targeted, how are we going to figure out who and where they might strike next?"

"We?" Fab smirked.

Two cops approached and separated us for

questioning. My answers were short and to the point, as I'd been reminded to make them on several occasions by over-priced lawyers. It would shock me if the Chief didn't have more questions, even if I didn't have answers for him. I'd suggest that the man watch his back. Although he'd probably already figured that out for himself.

Fab and I were finished being questioned at the same time, and she joined me.

I caught the Chief's eye. "Your baby going to need a tow?" I inclined my head toward the Mercedes. "I can take care of it."

He nodded and grinned.

I pulled out my phone and called Spoon, the go-to guy for auto repairs.

He groaned into the phone when he picked up. "What kind of trouble are you in now?"

I told him what happened. "You have a connection in Miami?"

"No worries. I'll make a call and have the car picked up and towed locally. If the Chief wants the work done here, then I'll send one of my men to pick it up."

"If someone is lucky enough to get one of your coveted appointments, they'd be crazy not to choose you to do the work. You're the best in the state."

"Flattery." Spoon sniffed. "You must need something else."

"Just a big thank you for always taking my calls."

"Some of your stuff entertains me." Spoon laughed.

"I'll have the Chief call you." We hung up.

"The Chief owes you now," Fab said.

"You can be the one to hold it over his head." I shook my head at her as though she'd lost her mind. "Why don't you run over and tell him to step on it?"

"What I'm going to tell him is that we'll be waiting on the patio, having something cold to drink," Fab said.

"Great idea. He's going to want to wait for the tow truck."

The restaurant manager seated us himself, and we got a corner table that gave us an unobstructed view of what was happening on the sidewalk. He let us know that drinks were on the house.

Chapter Eleven

I didn't tell Spoon to put a rush on the tow truck request, but thankfully, it didn't take forever for it to show up and haul the Mercedes away.

By silent consent, Fab and I passed on lunch.

Within minutes, the Chief made his way over to where we were sitting. "I'll take that ride." The paramedic had cleaned up his arm and affixed a large bandage.

Yay! But I kept that sentiment to myself.

Fab took the long way back to the SUV, bypassing her usual shortcuts. Once inside, she turned on the radio, which was code for she didn't want to talk. Fine with me. I leaned back in my seat as she flew down the highway, over the speed limit the whole way with not a peep out of the Chief.

As we were about to come up on the Welcome to Tarpon Cove sign, Fab turned off the music and flipped down her visor to look at the Chief in the mirror. "Where do you want me to drop you off?"

"My new office is good," the Chief said. "Has Henry Beckett contacted you since you reunited him with his daughter?"

"Hold on a second." I turned in my seat. "Did you sign the lease?" If so, Creole forgot to tell me.

"It's just a formality, as we're in agreement." He shot me a shifty smile, clearly amused with himself.

"Don't get comfy until you've signed on the dotted line."

"You hear from Beckett?"

"He called the day after and asked me to keep him updated." I was surprised by his interest. "He also grilled Casio, demanding information on his daughter's abductor. Casio told him what we both know—that there's pitifully little to tell. To my knowledge, Colton hasn't been located."

"This Colton character ought to fear Beckett more than the cops because he won't give up. He's a man that can make things happen."

"Interesting skill to have," I said.

Fab turned slightly and shot a smirk my way. She turned off the main highway, cut around the back of The Boardwalk, then shot down the street and turned into the parking lot of one of the four warehouses Creole and I owned.

I'd brokered a deal for the two of us to purchase three warehouses that sat side by side on a side street not far from The Boardwalk. We owned a fourth building a block away, and all the floors of that warehouse were rented to an eclectic group of tenants. Once the three new buildings were brought up to code, we'd leased two of them to a boat dealership, and the guys had moved their office into the first floor of the third.

The street side of the building was a drab, unassuming warehouse like the rest on the street. Around the back, the building had a limited view of the water. The guys had replaced the old shuttered windows with tinted, hurricane-proof glass garage doors. Next to those were the elevator doors, which opened to the outside, and the door into the stairwell. In the front was a paved patio area with a large table and numerous chairs.

Fab parked, and as we all got out, I took a car count. Everyone was there, including Mac, which surprised me, as I hadn't expected her and Lark to hook up so quickly.

Creole came out to meet us and pulled me off to the side as Fab and the Chief went inside. "Lark?" he said with raised eyebrows.

I looked around his shoulder and saw Lark and Mac sitting at the conference table in the middle of the room with Didier and Brad. "You nominated me to hire someone. Well…" I flourished my hand. "Lark comes highly recommended."

"Zach?" He sniffed.

"I'll tell you what I told her. She has three months to prove herself indispensable… unless she's a total fruitcake, and then I'll dispose of her sooner."

Creole flinched but wasn't deterred. "Lark

moved in a potted palm tree… named Fish. Sensitive fellow, or so I assume if I deciphered the cooing noises correctly. Almost forgot, no yelling in front of him. Him!" I bit my lower lip to keep back a laugh. "Then there's the dog."

"The office could use a little personality; it's a tad sterile. As for the dog, he's trained and most likely won't be peeing on the floor. Next?"

Creole shook his head. "You promised—"

"To find someone competent that could handle the office and not need supervision. If you give her a chance, you'll find she's easy to talk to and not easily offended. And the deal sealer: she laughed at my more outrageous statements."

Creole scooped me up and laid a big kiss on me. Setting me back on my feet, he folded my hand in his, and we walked into the building.

"I was just telling everyone how you saved my life," the Chief said as we joined everyone at the table.

I nodded at Mac and Lark, who had clearly become fast friends already.

"Madison's amazing. She arranged for a tow truck, and it didn't take all day." The Chief winked.

Creole gave me a side-eye stare, then looked around the table, asking, "Anyone get a call?"

"You know how it is when the cops are badgering you with one question after another," I said with all the drama I could muster. "You're on the spot, and you have to come up with something that sounds truthful."

Fab and I smirked at one another.

The guys laughed. Brad shot me a thumbs up behind Creole's back.

The Chief related the events of the hit-and-run incident, putting his own flourish on what happened.

Lark asked everyone what they wanted to drink and raided the refrigerator, handing me a bottle of water. "Mac and I decided to meet up today. She gave me the tour around town, and we ended up here. Sorry, I didn't know that the guys didn't know I'd been hired. They'd just finished interviewing me again when you drove up."

"I hope they didn't interrogate you and now you're quitting." I laughed.

"It won't be long before we'll realize we've grown on one another." Lark lit up with a smile.

Creole pinched my leg.

"You got any questions, come to me," Brad told Lark, passing her his business card. "I'm the early one, since I take my daughter to school, so I'll be here Monday to let you in."

"So Chief, you got a girlfriend?" Fab asked.

He squinted at her.

"Good question," I chimed in. "How about anyone with a grudge? Can you think of someone that would want to run you over?"

"No to all three," the Chief said adamantly.

"Dated any crazy chicks that didn't want to hear 'See you, it's been fun?'" I asked.

No snap answer had everyone staring.

"I dated a woman for several months, but she broke it off weeks ago because her friend told her that I was dating both of them at the same time. She didn't believe me when I swore that I wasn't."

"Dated as in take her out to dinner and have a conversation? Or just sex?" Fab asked.

Didier said something in French, which Fab ignored. Creole laughed. I'd get a translation later.

The Chief didn't answer the question directly. "We dated, broke up, and two weeks ago, she showed up at the office in Marathon and wanted to forgive and forget. The girlfriend fessed up that it was all a lie. I told her that a relationship with someone who didn't believe me wasn't going anywhere and that we'd moved on and it should stay that way."

"How did she take it?" Fab asked.

"She slapped me and stormed out. Never saw her again."

"I'd have one of your cop friends run a check on her—see if she's still in the area and find out where she was today," I suggested. "Do you know what kind of car she drives?"

He shook his head.

"If she checks out, you need to think of someone else who might want you maimed or worse. You can take me and Madison off the list." Fab flicked her finger between the two of us. "This could've been a case of mistaken identity, but I doubt it."

Chapter Twelve

I wanted a day off, but no such luck. The door had barely closed, the guys leaving for the office, and before I could slide off the kitchen stool and make a run for it, Fab cornered me and, in an imperious tone, commanded, "Try to look presentable."

"So sorry." I made a sad face. "I'm already booked. Doing nothing. You had an opportunity to bring up whatever's on your agenda when the guys were here to give their yea or nay, and no peep out of you, so you're out of luck."

"They already know and gave their approval." Fab smirked.

I stared her down, surprised that Creole hadn't said anything.

"I'm telling the truth." She held up her right hand.

"What's in it for me? Skip the 'goodness of my heart' part." I downed the last of my coffee, maneuvered around her, and put the mug in the dishwasher. I turned back and leaned against the counter.

"I've got a meeting this morning with a new client, and even with me choosing a neutral place to meet, there's still a better than even chance of the unexpected happening." Fab flashed a smile that would have most doing a double take. "You'd feel bad if something happened to me and you'd declined to lend your bodyguarding skills."

"What a bunch of drivel." I almost laughed at her look of annoyance. "You're the one who can kick butt with one hand tied behind your back. My kicking skills are negligible. Now, if you're looking for someone to put a bullet in someone's butt, I'm your girl." I formed guns with my fingers, and shot up the room, complete with sound effects.

"Are you done?"

I nodded.

"You've got ten minutes." She pointed down the hall.

"I'll remind you that you said 'presentable,' so I'll need a half-hour." I headed for the bedroom, mentally planning my outfit for the day.

I showered and stood in front of the mirror, giving the black dress I'd chosen, with its full skirt and fitted top, a once-over. I strapped my Glock to my thigh, grabbed my purse and briefcase, and met Fab in the hallway.

"Tell me about this client of yours," I said, sliding into the passenger side of the SUV. "Start with how you got the call. I want to make sure it's not some weird cold call you're responding to."

"New rule: Clients have to be referred. The client, Jennifer Charles, was referred by Fern Wallace, Gunz's Aunt Somebody-or-other. Remember her?"

I nodded and squirmed in my seat, remembering the man who'd been living in her attic and tumbled through the ceiling. "Grey-haired oldster that nicknamed Gunz the King. Last we saw her, Gunz had fixed up her crumbling house, and she was all sass and attitude about it." The upside to Gunz's cases was that he stressed safety first, which wasn't the case with the rest of Fab's clients, who didn't think anything about hanging her backside out to dry.

"Fern made the initial call, saying she figured that since we said to call anytime, so what the heck, she'd find out if we were full of it or not."

"Is this a freebie?" I guessed not, as Fab's nose scrunched up. "Just a little surprised that Fern didn't route this request through Gunz."

"The case deals with a custody issue the client would like cleared up."

"You're not a lawyer."

"I made that very clear and said that I wouldn't be offering legal advice of any kind. Mrs. Charles, who didn't want to disclose the details over the phone, assured me that she requires an investigation in case she ends up in court. Her goal is to be well-informed and not caught off guard."

"Where's this meeting taking place?" I asked, surprised when she turned into Jake's, a dive bar that I owned in the middle of town.

Shortly after I came to town, I bought out the bar's namesake and, defying expectations, didn't run the business into the ground. The opposite, in fact—it now had a healthy bottom line.

"I offered to come to her home or office, but she shut that down, suggesting a neutral place." Fab slowed going by the lighthouse, the ownership of which was contested—she thought it was hers since she had it hauled there and offloaded without asking, and I claimed ownership since it sat on my property.

"Now that Gunz has moved—" He'd needed more room and rented one of the floors in the first warehouse I'd bought… after I'd extracted a promise that he wouldn't be doing anything illegal. "—letting it sit empty will invite trouble. If you don't want to go to the trouble of finding another renter, you could give my gift shop idea a moment's thought."

Silence. She'd come around when she had to shoot a squatter or two.

She rolled by Junker's. The old gas station had had the grease scrubbed from the walls and floors and been turned into a garden antiques store that catered mostly to other dealers. I theorized that Junker would rather spend his time chasing finds and offloading them in bulk.

He had no patience for selling one piece at a time.

Jake's sat at the back of the property. A quick car count before Fab pulled around to the back said that the "beer for early lunch crowd" had arrived. She parked at the kitchen entrance.

We went through the back door and cut through the kitchen, where Cook whistled and waved as we continued down the hall and into the bar.

Kelpie, our pink-haired bartender, was busy dazzling her customers with the impressive display of lights she had wrapped around her chest as she gyrated back and forth, bent over in one of her bikini tops that gave the best view of her assets. Today, she'd paired it with a fringed cowboy skirt.

"Bossaroo." She gave me a two-handed wave over her head.

The men that filled the bar stools turned and momentarily looked my way, then returned their attention to Kelpie's chest.

I waved back, mine sedate in comparison.

Kelpie turned her attention to Fab. "You got someone waiting on your behind." She pointed to the deck.

"You go ahead, and I'll order us drinks," I said. "If Mrs. Whatsername wants anything, stick your head inside and yell."

Kelpie cut in, "She only wanted water."

"I'll take our non-alky regulars," I told her.

"I figured, since it's not even noon o'clock." Kelpie stuck her finger down her cleavage, and the lights started to blink furiously. It was hard not to stare, as evidenced by every man at the bar.

"Since I know you can do six things at once, update me. The cops been here lately?"

"The owner hates when that happens. She also insists on a call when it does, but nobody's perfect."

I sighed. "How about a yes or no?"

She grinned and handed me a tray with my drinks on it. "Nopers."

"Spread the word that we're going for a no-cop-call record."

"You're forgetting that it's good for business. Sure, it clears out the joint, but when they come back, they're stacked ten deep."

I shot her a lame smile. I knew that was the rationale, but I still didn't like it. I walked out to the deck, shut the door, and served the drinks.

Fab made the introductions. There was an air of unhappiness around Jennifer Charles, a non-descript woman in her forties with a dark-brown bob, wearing a colorful spaghetti-strap tent dress.

I slid into a chair next to Fab.

"Fern assured me that I could trust in your discretion," Mrs. Charles started.

Fab and I agreed.

"I have two children that were adopted a year

apart, and I need you to find their birth certificates," she said. "They were in the safe before my husband, Donald, died, and now I can't find them."

"I have someone on staff that I use and trust—he'll be able to research the information for you," Fab said. "Do you know where the children were born?"

"I thought that they were both born in Miami but wasn't able to find a record of their birth certificates there. I can't imagine that anyone would forget to file them. I also thought that was where the adoptions were finalized. Now I'm not sure of anything."

"Why not contact the adoption agency you used?" I asked.

After a short pause, Jennifer said, "Donald handled everything. He was a controlling man and saw to all the details himself."

"It's a matter of searching all the county records, but it should be easy enough to get what you want," Fab assured her.

"There's one other thing. One far more important to me..." Jennifer hesitated before continuing. "I'd like you to find the birth mother. When you do, make sure that she has no plans to take the children away should she find out that Donald's deceased."

"One mother?" Fab asked. Jennifer nodded. "Once she's signed away her rights and it's been formalized by the court, I'm fairly certain that she can't win custody back just because your husband died."

"I need to be certain."

"Was this a private adoption?" I asked.

"Donald used a lawyer that specialized in adoptions. When we started talking about starting a family, Donald insisted that we do genetic testing first, and I failed." Jennifer swiped at the tears leaking from the corners of her eyes. "My husband wanted perfect children, and the lawyer assured him that this woman had been given a clean bill of health and the test results were what he required. Donald also wanted the same mother for both children and made that clear from the start. Her eggs and his sperm were used."

I handed her a napkin.

Jennifer blew her nose, took several breaths, and looked up. "Shortly after my husband died, I found a file in his safe. He had copies of my and the birth mother's health records. That's how I found out about my failing grade. He covered all the bases on his lies—all this time, I thought I had fertility issues and that the doctor was giving me shots that could reverse my condition. It turns out they were contraceptive shots. Early in our marriage, I suffered a miscarriage, and I now wonder if it was induced."

"You've been through a lot," Fab said in a sympathetic tone. "This might be a situation where once you have copies of the birth certificates and assurance that everything was done legally, you shouldn't invite trouble by confronting the surrogate."

Jennifer shook her head. "I need the reassurance. I can't live my life wondering, looking over my shoulder. I thought about leaving the state, but my family is here and I don't want to deprive my children of an extended family."

"Once the adoption is final, the records are sealed," Fab told her. "I'll certainly do an exhaustive search, but I can't guarantee that I'll be able to find the woman."

"That means the surrogate won't be able to find you either, which should give you peace of mind," I said.

Jennifer pulled a piece of paper from her pocket and handed it to Fab. "These are the names that were in the file. The first is the name of the lawyer my husband used. No way do I want him finding out that I'm having anything investigated. I've had contact with him several times over the years, and every time, he gave me the cold shivers. The two women's names are unknown to me. Perhaps one of them is the surrogate."

"I can't give you a definitive estimate of how long the investigation will take, but I'll keep in touch with updates," Fab said.

Jennifer nodded.

Fab opened her briefcase, pulled out a file, and

handed a contract to the woman, along with a pen. "This details my services and what you can expect from me. I'll need you to sign before I get started."

Jennifer settled back in her chair and read the contract. It didn't take her long. She signed, keeping a copy for herself and handing the original back to Fab with a check. She stood and shook hands with Fab, then acknowledged me with a nod. "I look forward to hearing from you." She opened the deck door and left.

When the door closed, I said, "I get that she needs the birth certificates. But confronting the surrogate?" I could think of fifty ways that could go bad, and fast. "What do you know about Jennifer Charles?" I already knew the answer. "You need to run a background check and know what you're dealing with. Even then, I wouldn't give her the personal information of any of the people on that list." I nodded at the piece of paper, which Fab stashed in her briefcase along with the file.

"I'll add her name to the list and forward it to Xander," Fab reassured me.

"Another name to add to the list would the husband. How did he die? I'm surprised you didn't ask."

"I hoped that you'd ask, since that kind of snoopy question always sounds friendlier coming from you."

I laughed. "You haven't concerned yourself

with being friendly in the past. Keep in mind that there are children involved."

"Unless Jennifer Charles checks out, all she's getting is certified birth certificates."

My phone dinged. I read the message.

Fab stared, with "Who?" on her face.

"Mother's on her way to the Bakery Café."

Fab nodded.

I stood and cleaned off the table, taking the tray back inside.

"Where's my manager?" I asked Kelpie.

"Doodad will be in later, don't ask me why. I did ask, but he told me to mind my own business. He's always here, so a few hours isn't a big deal… unless it is." Kelpie quirked her head.

"Just means that you have to keep the hoodlums in line by yourself."

"If I had my way…"

"I know," I groaned, then laughed, waved, and followed Fab to the kitchen.

Chapter Thirteen

We arrived at the Bakery Café with a minute to spare. Mother had claimed a table on the covered patio; she wasn't enamored of our favorite seats on the sidewalk, having no interest in people watching.

Mother waved.

I hugged her and sat down.

Fab and Mother whispered together before sitting.

I pushed the menu away, as I had it memorized. The restaurant was a favorite of everyone in the family. The server came by and filled our glasses with iced tea from the mammoth pitcher that Mother had ordered.

"You two look really nice." Mother smiled, having given us a once-over before we sat down. "A new case?" she asked Fab.

While Fab relayed the events of the morning, a person in jeans and a hoodie—and to complement the outfit, a slim jim in hand—caught my attention. They were hovering around the driver's side of the Hummer. I jumped to my feet, kicking the chair back, which caused several people to turn and stare. "Someone's attempting to steal my SUV."

Fab was on her feet in an instant and followed me as I raced out to the sidewalk.

Noticing that the person was smaller than me, I launched myself at the would-be thief, grabbed hold of their arm, and spun them around. To my surprise, a young girl stared back, wide-eyed and frightened. I gripped her shoulders and gave her a hard shake, and she dropped the bar. Fab kicked it under the SUV. "What the hell are you doing?" With a shock of recognition, I realized I'd seen her several times before—she and her little brother regularly panhandled at the gas station Fab preferred, their cross-eyed mother always slumped against the side of the building, brown bag in hand.

She jerked against my hold. "I, uh..." She continued to struggle. "I have to steal this car or he'll kill me."

"Not going to happen," Fab barked. "You and whoever 'he' is are going to jail." She looked around.

I loosened my hold, and the girl used the opportunity to jerk away and run. Several steps later, I caught up, grabbed her by the back of her hoodie, and brought her to a halt.

A pickup screeched to a stop, a shot rang out, and the girl screamed, grabbing her arm and tumbling to the ground. The truck squealed off.

I dropped to my knees and cradled her head. "We need to get you to the hospital." I waved Fab over, and she helped me get her to her feet and into the back seat. I slid in next to her, not trusting that she wouldn't jump out into traffic.

Her cries turned to sobs, and she attempted to talk, but it came out as incoherent mumblings.

Fab waved to Mother and rushed towards her as she came running, purses in hand. She and Fab exchanged words; then Fab slid behind the wheel. "Madeline's going to take care of the check and meet us at the hospital."

The girl wailed.

I wiped at her face with her hoodie. "I've got a one-time deal for you. You're going to answer every question I have, starting with why you were attempting to steal my car. If not, I'm handing you over to the cops and you can enjoy jail."

She coughed and hiccupped. "Please..." she whimpered.

I only had a few minutes before we arrived at the hospital. "What's your name?"

"T... Tessa Hunter."

"Your mother? Do you want me to call her?" I asked.

"Karla Hunter." Tessa shook her head vehemently. "She'd only show if it meant she could sell me again. I'll tell you whatever you want to know, but please, don't turn me in. I'll leave town."

"Where's your little brother?"

"Timothy's going to be upset if he never sees me again."

Fab took a couple of shortcuts to the hospital and parked at the emergency room entrance.

I opened the door and helped Tessa out. "I'm going to cut you a break and not say a word to the cops about your car-theft attempt. Promise me that it's the last one you'll try to steal." Tessa nodded wildly. "You're going to be asked, by more than one person, and your story is that we were talking and you got shot at. No need to mention anything about my car."

Tessa leaned her head against my chest and sobbed. "T… thank you."

Fab ran inside and came back out with an orderly pushing a wheelchair. He got Tessa seated and ushered her inside with me right on their heels. Fab went ahead to talk to the receptionist.

Mother flew through the door and jetted to my side.

I bent down and whispered to Tessa, "You mentioned someone killing you if you didn't get the job done, is that who shot at you?"

A nurse sprinted down the hall, cutting off any answer, and wheeled Tessa away.

The three of us followed.

The nurse turned and raised an eyebrow.

"Sisters," I answered the unspoken question. "This is her grandmother." I pointed to Mother, who raised her brows.

Mother tugged on my arm and slowed me down. "You can't help everyone," she whispered. "Do you need to be reminded that she's a car thief… or a wannabe one anyway?"

"I already offered her a deal, and I'm not going back on my word."

"You make me tired." Mother sighed.

"Tessa's underage. It stands to reason there's an adult behind this scam."

"That's why you should let the cops handle this." Mother trotted out a tone suggesting I was being obstinate. "They'll be here any minute, since I told the manager we were taking her to the hospital."

Mother and I came to a stop outside the exam room where Fab waited. We peered through the glass, and saw that the nurse had transferred Tessa to a bed. A doctor rushed into the room.

"Although today's the first time we've officially met, I feel like I know this girl," I said. "I've had a few encounters with her at the Quik Mart."

"I thought she looked familiar," Fab said.

"Tessa and her little brother are regulars there, holding up an 'I'm hungry' sign. Oftentimes, their mother's around, but sometimes not. It wasn't that long ago that, on my way inside, I overheard Tessa's brother say he was hungry and her answer that they hadn't made enough money to eat yet. Then she added, 'You know how she gets when we don't bring in enough cash.'"

"Let me guess—you gave her the money she needed and then some," Mother said.

"What would you have done?" I asked testily.

"The same thing."

"Didn't you also save her from arrest once?" Fab asked.

I nodded. "A month or so ago, when I went in the Mart, the clerk was screaming that she stole food and he was calling the cops. I stepped up and paid. She ran out, and by the time I got outside, she'd disappeared. I looked for her after that but didn't see her. I wondered what happened to her and hoped she'd found something better than panhandling but worried that she'd been arrested someplace else."

The doctor left. An attendant rolled another bed into the room, transferred Tessa, and wheeled her to the elevator.

The nurse came out. "Tessa's on her way to surgery, and it'll be awhile. Waiting room is down the hall."

Mother stared over my shoulder and groaned. "Here comes Kevin, and he doesn't look happy."

"He never looks happy," Fab said.

Kevin Cory was a local sheriff's deputy who lived at The Cottages, snuck in by my brother. He somehow almost always drew the short straw when it came to getting calls where Fab and I were involved. He strutted down the hallway with an all-too-familiar "what have you done now" look on his face. Personally, I preferred the surfer boy persona that he adopted on his days off. "You left the scene of a shooting?" he crabbed.

"Sorry. We should've called 911, but we knew that a call had already been made and we were close to the hospital. So we rushed Tessa straight here so she wouldn't bleed out and die." No way would I admit that I had questions I wanted to ask before the cops got their hands on her.

Mother stepped forward. "It was my fault. I thought about staying behind to wait for you to show up, but my worry got the better of me."

Surprisingly, Kevin didn't lecture her.

"There were several eyewitnesses, and they all agreed that a shot rang out and then the girl started screaming. One of your admirers miss and hit an innocent bystander?" Kevin asked, unleashing his sense of humor, which no one found funny.

Mother glared at him.

"We were bystanders." I circled my finger. "Tessa and I were talking…" I told him the story that we'd agreed on.

"What about you?" Kevin barked at Fab.

"I was several steps behind and didn't see anything," Fab said.

"That's a first," Kevin said, an eyeroll in his tone. "Don't go anywhere." He strode over to the nurse's station.

We continued to stand in the hall in front of Tessa's room. It didn't take long before he was back. "Tessa Smith is in surgery and will be released tomorrow if there are no complications. Since she's underage, a real family member—not some phony sister or grandmother—will need to show and sign her out." He glared.

"Not knowing what the rules are, I only said that so they'd help her," I said. "I didn't sign anything."

He softened his glare. "What do you know about the girl?"

"Honestly, not much." I ignored his skeptical look. "I believe she's local, as I've seen her around town with her mother and little brother. She was in so much pain that she could barely speak. She did mention being afraid of some guy, but that was all she said. Father maybe? I don't know. I hope a family member wouldn't shoot at her."

"These days, you never know," Kevin grumbled. "Do you think she was the target, or was it you?"

"I haven't annoyed anyone of late that they'd want to shoot at me," I said, and turned to Fab.

"I've been well-behaved lately. Just ask my husband." Fab smiled sweetly.

Mother and I laughed.

"Since it will be hours before Tessa's lucid enough to speak, I'll be back in the morning. In the meantime, I'm going to follow up on the contact information she gave the nurse."

Given she'd used a false last name, I'd bet that any information Tessa handed over was fake. "Try not to scare her." Kevin's lips quirked in an almost-smile. "I'm hoping that you arrest someone soon and this doesn't turn out to be a random nutjob on the loose."

"If I have more questions, I know where to find you." Kevin strode away.

"I'm guessing you're going to wait until she's out of surgery." Mother pulled out her phone.

"I'm not confident that anyone's going to show up for her," I said. "I'd like to make sure she's okay. I'm not pressing charges in the hopes that she gives up car thieving."

Fab and I walked down the hall to the waiting room. We exchanged raised eyebrows when we heard Mother giggle.

Mother caught up with us. "I'm going to meet Spoonee."

"Mother, stop with the bedroom talk in public."

"He's a good husband. He promised me a cigar and a glass of Jack whiskey."

"Here's something else that will make you happy—you can call our husbands and update them. Tell them we'll be home pronto-ish." I hugged Mother.

"You can trust that I'll only add a little flourish." Mother grinned.

While Fab walked her out, I went in search of

a nurse to get some questions answered. I found out that the surgery wouldn't take long and it was one with few risks. Fab came back and found me in the waiting room.

We didn't have an overly long wait before Tessa had been wheeled back to her room. We took one last peek at her and told the nurse we'd be back in the morning.

"Can I get a ride?" I asked Fab.

"You're lucky I'm going that way."

Chapter Fourteen

I wanted to stay in bed all day, feeling emotionally drained from yesterday, but Creole had an early morning meeting and hauled me into the shower with him. He left first, and I finished dressing and joined everyone in the kitchen for coffee.

Creole held out a glass of green muck and a coffee mug. "Your choice."

Wrapping my arms around my stomach, I unleashed an impressive barf noise. Fab gave me a thumbs up for the performance. "For the first time, I don't trust you. There's probably something equally disgusting in the mug. To be on the safe side, I'll make my own." I slid off the stool, but before I could take a step, he wrapped his arms around me.

"You can trust this one." He handed me the mug.

"Cherie." Didier shook his head. "Kale's a great way to start the day."

"Yeah, okay." I sniffed the contents of the mug before taking a sip.

"Casio called while you were getting dressed," Creole announced. "He reached out to one of his partners still on the force for information about Colton. Beckett's been burning up his phone, demanding to know if Colton's been arrested—not being able to locate him is not acceptable to the man."

"Let Beckett unleash his resources," Fab said.

"Why would Casio tell you and not call me directly?" I asked.

"He intimated that he'd run out of favors." Creole laughed.

"I'll call him." I sighed. "He's not going to be happy. You know as much as I do, and I've got nothing new to add. If I did, I'd be hot on the phone."

"Your helpful husband, wanting to be rid of Casio, passed the phone off to me," Fab said in a disgruntled tone. "Casio attempted to grill me on the location where we found Kathryn. I told him he needed to take a drive out there, and that even with an address, good luck."

"Beckett's probably frustrated that Kathryn can't tell him anything either. Based on what she told me, she doesn't know where the heck she was being held," I said.

"If Colton is smart, he's long gone," Creole said.

"Since you two have an open morning," Didier said, "Creole and I will take you to breakfast."

My phone rang, interrupting an answer, although Fab had slid closer to Didier and smiled up at him.

Kevin's name popped up on the screen. Too early for him—it wouldn't be good news. I pushed my phone across the countertop at Fab. "It's for you."

Fab glanced at the screen and shoved it back. We engaged in a faux glare-off until it stopped ringing.

Creole had seen Kevin's name and told Didier; they both laughed.

It started ringing again.

I sucked in a deep breath and answered, hitting the speaker button. "Good morning, officer."

"Where's Tessa?" Kevin barked.

All eyes turned to me, and I shrugged. "At the hospital, I assume. When Fab and I left last night, she was out of surgery and sleeping it off."

"You'd be wrong," Kevin snapped. "Tessa disappeared early this morning in the middle of shift change. Her sudden departure made me think of you."

Creole leaned over to speak directly into the phone. "This is Creole. And Didier's here. Our wives have alibis. If you're suggesting that they helped her sneak out, they didn't," he said in a clipped tone.

"I wouldn't have helped Tessa leave, not until she was released by a doctor and certainly not without having somewhere to go," I managed to say in a calm voice, even though my worry for the girl had ratcheted up.

"If you see her, you need to call me. I need to speak to her." The line went dead.

"Now what?" I shoved the phone away. "Maybe her mother showed up and snuck her out, since I'm certain they don't have the money to pay the bill."

"Not everything is your responsibility," Fab said, as though I needed reminding.

Maybe I did. "Raincheck on breakfast," I said to Creole. "I want to—"

Creole wrapped his arms around me. "It doesn't surprise me that you want to help the girl. Just be careful."

"I need to change." I slid off the stool. Creole put his arm around me, and we walked back to the bedroom.

He closed the door and drew me into his arms, giving me a big kiss. "You be careful."

"We need to sneak away for some alone time."

"Soon, we're going to have a big house all to ourselves." He kissed me again and left.

I changed into a different top, a fuller one to cover the Glock I strapped to the small of my back, and slipped into a pair of sandals. No telling if it was going to be one of those days. I grabbed my purse and met Fab back in the kitchen.

"You know you can't help someone who doesn't want it." Fab finished her second cup of coffee.

"I don't want Tessa disappearing into the wind without me ever knowing what happened."

"You've got a full schedule today." Fab trotted out her sneaky grin.

"I'm sure it'll be a swell day."

"Sarcasm is so unbecoming." Fab shook her finger at me.

"Not sure I agree." I noticed her smirk before she turned away. "You're not pitching a fit about driving me around to look for Tessa, and that's what we'll be doing, so you must have something on your agenda."

"Xander got copies of the birth certificates Jennifer Charles requested. I'm meeting her to hand them over."

"That was fast."

"I'm sure she's going to want certified copies, and those have been ordered. The good news is that she and the husband are listed as mother and father."

"Why not email the docs? Wouldn't that be more efficient?"

"I suggested that, and having them delivered by someone other than me, but she wasn't going for any of my good suggestions."

"I suppose this is where I graciously offer to go with you?"

"I'm prepared to drag you."

I laughed.

"You want to hear an interesting tidbit? The

dead husband was murdered, his body found on the side of the road. No suspects."

"That's really creepy."

"Dude was a lawyer with a law firm that specialized in family law and that included adoptions. Apparently, it's a lucrative field, as he left his wife and kids with an impressive net worth."

"Why not get her adoption questions answered by someone in her husband's firm? Surely they handled the case." I squinted at her. "Did you get the name of the surrogate?"

"Xander's working on it for me. Well, not him... one his secret sources, who costs a fortune."

"First off, you're not to ask Xander the name of said source and get mixed up in the middle of whatever Mr. Illegal Source is doing." I ignored her frown. I already knew that I sucked the fun out of everything. "Second, handing the name over to your client is a bad idea. There's no good reason that she needs it, and you don't know her well enough to know what she plans to do with the information."

"You're going to be happy. I'm telling Mrs. Charles that the adoption was legal, and that since she's listed as the mother, the surrogate wouldn't have any legal standing. I'll stress that all the appropriate paperwork was filed and the original file is sealed, protecting her and the birth mother. I'm going to suggest, in a nice way, that she be satisfied and move along."

"I'd feel better if you told me that you got a background check on the woman and she hasn't been a frequent visitor to the looney bin."

"Mrs. Charles doesn't have a criminal record and also has a clean driving record."

"Was she a suspect in her husband's murder?" I asked, knowing the cops would look at her first.

"Love that Xander always anticipates these questions and had the answer. She and the kids were at a birthday party for one of the daughter's classmates."

"Happy to hear that." I slid off the stool and smoothed down my skirt. "Once we're finished with your client, I want to do a slow drive by the Quik Mart. I don't think Tessa would go back there, but you never know."

Fab handed me my purse and briefcase and led the way to the SUV. She pulled out to the highway and turned south.

"We going to the client's house?" I peered out the window, wanting to catch a glimpse of the water.

"We're meeting her at a coffee place on the main highway. And before you start, it's one of her choosing."

"Did you at least suggest the Bakery Café?" I made a face.

"I did, even though I didn't think they'd want to see us back so soon after yesterday. Mrs. Charles preferred this place because she's familiar with the location."

"Where does Ms. Charles live?" I asked.

"North in Palmetto Bay."

"And she's coming down here?"

The drive was a short one. Fab turned down a side street and then into the back entrance of a postage-stamp-sized building that advertised coffee. The parking lot had space for six cars, and currently there was only one.

"I know my part: smile, and if shots ring out… well then, game on."

"Behave," Fab admonished.

We got out and stepped gingerly down a gravel path that ran along the side of the building. The client was sitting in one of a handful of webbed chairs that had seen better days.

Mrs. Charles looked up and smiled as we approached. "Coffee?"

"We're not going to be here long, as I have another appointment." Fab smiled back.

The two of us unfolded chairs and tried for a level spot before sitting.

I inclined my head toward the client.

Fab reached in her briefcase and handed Mrs. Charles an envelope. "These are not certified copies, but as I told you on the phone, those'll be mailed to you direct from the county recorder."

Mrs. Charles opened the envelope and pulled out the paperwork; glancing over it, she smiled with a sigh. "What about the surrogate? I agree that I don't want to create a situation that would lead to contesting the adoption or extortion of some sort."

"The file was sealed."

Mrs. Charles pulled a card out of her pocket and handed it to Fab. "I have another job for you. I'd like you to make a few discreet inquiries into my husband's old law firm."

"What kind of information are you looking for?" Frustration seeped into Fab's tone.

"I'd like to be reassured that every case the firm handles is legal."

Really bad idea.

"If you start digging around into the legalities of their cases and they get wind… If they're on the up and up, they might laugh it off. If not, you could end up like your husband—dead, with no suspects; your children orphans."

Mrs. Charles flinched.

I was surprised by Fab's directness but wanted to clap.

"Couldn't you look into it discreetly without anyone being the wiser?" Mrs. Charles insisted.

"I'll have my associate do a records search, and that's as far as I'm willing to go," Fab said adamantly. "I have a husband and children to think about."

"I understand and look forward to hearing from you about what you find." Mrs. Charles stood, and the two shook hands.

"How many children?" I asked as we watched

her walk back to her Mercedes.

"A bunch." Fab smirked.

"Our husbands have expressed a desire for eleven each for that football team," I reminded her. "Are you thinking about getting started?"

Fab shook her head and laughed. "Twenty-two kids. That's not going to happen, and I'll let you tell them."

"You want to make a little wager?" I rubbed my fingers together.

Fab didn't roll her eyes, but close. "What?"

"Snooping into the law firm… Knowing you, you already had Xander do a check. My reward for being onto you is next time, coffee's on you."

"Xander ferreted out a few interesting tidbits. At first glance, they look great, but do a little digging, and they're pushing out more adoptions than any other firm."

"And?" I asked.

"Xander found articles that said one of the partners was investigated on baby-selling charges, but nothing came of it."

"That's some good connections."

Mrs. Charles had loitered in the parking lot, garnering both of our attention. She finally backed out and hit the highway going north.

"Another bet? Mrs. Charles knows exactly what's going on in that law firm, or has a good idea anyway. Why she wants you snooping around is a mystery to me."

"I'm going to relay what Xander told me and

hope that satisfies her. If not, she can find someone else to do her snooping. That investigation has trouble written all over it. My days of putting myself on the line for my clients is over."

We waited until Mrs. Charles's car faded in the distance before we got back in the SUV.

"Expect to have to block her number; she's not going to be easily deterred."

Chapter Fifteen

Before Fab could hit the highway, I informed her, "I'm hiring your services, since I know you don't have anything else on your calendar for the day." I was surprised that she didn't counter with made-up appointments. "Find Tessa. If anyone can seek her out, it's you."

"Where do I send the bill?"

"Freebie, babes." I smiled at her. "Take me on one of those secretive treks of yours where you cruise the streets looking for bad guys."

Fab waited patiently for two ducks to cross the highway. Both of us flinched when it was clear that a couple of cars weren't going to slow down. They hadn't used up their nine lives yet, as they made the trek without losing a feather.

"It's possible Tessa is with her mother," Fab mused. "Hopefully, they have a place to sleep and aren't living on the street."

"The woman is a drunken cretin. It was clear that she used her kids to make money for booze," I said in disgust. "If panhandling is their full-time gig, then their home life is probably grim."

It took a few minutes to arrive at the Quik Mart. Fab cruised past slowly, turning on a side street before pulling in and cruising the lot. She circled twice before exiting out the back and through a residential neighborhood.

I kept my neck craned.

"You do know that if we find Tessa, you have to call the cops," Fab reminded me. "Doing otherwise could get you locked up."

I sighed heavily. "We both know what will happen then. If the mother can't show some kind of stable lifestyle, Tessa and her brother will be put in foster care. And unless she's sent to a locked facility, she'll be gone in a couple of hours. I'm basing that on the fact that she was gutsy enough to sneak out of the hospital. She's going to be something as an adult, and I don't mean that in a good way unless she gets the chance to turn her life around."

"Her best hope is if she's got relatives that will step up." Fab turned into familiar territory—The Cottages was at the far end of the street. "This is my next best idea."

Mac was loitering on the side of the road, talking on her phone. She waved wildly when she spotted the SUV.

Fab coasted up alongside her and rolled down the window. "We're looking for a young girl." Fab gave Mac a vague description.

Mac stared at her, waiting for her to elaborate.

I leaned forward. "The panhandler that hangs out at the Quik Mart with her little brother."

"When you find her, is she moving in with

me?" Mac asked in a skeptical tone.

"I haven't forgotten how amazing you were with Kathryn, and I've got something huge planned for you." I spread my arms as wide as I could and not smack Fab.

Mac squinted at me. "I'm thinking you just came up with that huge plan but know you'll come through with something good." She half-turned and pointed to an empty lot, catty-corner, one block over. "Your little friend is camped out behind the dumpster. I've seen her come and go a few times this morning. Figured she'd get caught when a car pulled up and cleaned out their trunk. Since the dude didn't linger, I'm guessing she managed to stay out of sight."

"I'm impressed." I smiled at her. "Nothing happens in this neighborhood that you don't know about."

"Got to stay one step ahead." She shook her flamingo-slippered foot.

Fab raced the engine. The two women laughed. She cut across the road and parked in front of the dumpster. If anyone was peering out their window, they might think we were tossing trash.

I got out, rounded the SUV, and yelled, "Tessa. Get out here."

Nothing.

"If I have to come in after you, you're not going to like it," I yelled.

Fab grinned at me.

Tessa crawled out from underneath the dumpster, which had me cringing, surprised there was enough room in the tight space. She rolled to her feet and attempted to brush the dirt from her shorts and scraped-up knees. "Jeez, you're loud."

"Don't you dare run," I grouched. "Get over here." I wanted to hug her and check out the arm she was holding, grimacing in pain.

"Someone might see me." Tessa started to cry, tears rolling down her dirty cheeks.

Fab patted my arm, so I'd calm down.

"We're not going to let that happen," I said in a quieter tone and opened the back door. "You hungry?" I noticed her shiver and pulled a beach towel out of one of the duffel bags we kept in the back.

Fab handed her a package of tissues.

"You going to turn me over to the cops?" Tessa whimpered, wrapping herself in the towel and wiping at her face.

I helped Tessa into the back seat and got in after her. I avoided answering her question, as I didn't know what to do that would end well for her. "As far as the cops know, you're a victim. I didn't say one word about attempted grand theft auto." I touched her uninjured arm gently. "How's your shoulder?"

"It hurts like the devil. I had my last pain shot in the middle of the night, and it's worn off."

Fab flipped down the visor and stared at me.

We traded a look, and I knew she was reminding me not to get involved. Too late.

"Why did you leave the hospital?" I asked.

Fab sat idling, also wanting to hear the answer.

"My mom showed up." Tessa blew her nose. "I overheard her on the phone, telling Colton she'd meet him for the swap and not to forget the cash. She's nuts, asking him for more money. He's terrifying." She covered her face with her hands and started to cry again.

Fab and I both reacted to that name with a grimace.

Fab broke the gloomy silence that had descended and asked Tessa, "What do you want to eat?"

"Hamburger, fries if I can have them," Tessa said in a pitiful tone, blowing her nose on the end of the towel.

I winked at Fab, knowing burgers would be her last choice. "You can eat what you want and as much as you want." I smoothed her hair back from her cheek, noting that she was painfully thin. "I promise you that Fab and I are going to help you and you're not going back to your mom."

"Do you think you could get my little brother?" Tessa asked in a hopeful tone.

Another question I couldn't answer directly. "First, we're going to feed you." I wanted to give Tessa all the assurances she needed, but I couldn't do it on my own and would have to enlist others to help. "Then we're going to have a long talk about your life and how you got to this point, and then we'll help figure a way out for you."

Fab pulled into Roscoe's drive-thru—everyone in the family's favorite, and hers too if she'd fess up. Fab and I encouraged Tessa to order whatever she wanted, and she got two double burgers, fries, a chocolate shake, and an apple pie. It would break my heart if she ate it all. Fab and I ordered iced teas.

"We eating here?" Fab asked, handing the bags over the seat.

I handed them to Tessa and put her shake in the cup holder. "Go ahead and eat," I encouraged her. "Let's go to the Boardwalk offices." There was ex-law enforcement available there to give good advice without the threat of locking up me or Tessa.

Tessa tore apart her bag, wolfed down one of the hamburgers, and started on the fries, not hindered by only having the use of one arm.

Chapter Sixteen

Fab zipped through the streets and over to the far side of the Cove, rocketed into the driveway and around the back, and parked.

I dug the pie out of the bottom of the bag and handed it, along with what was left of the shake, to Fab. The rest, I wadded up and tossed in the trash can. I got out and motioned to Tessa, who nodded and scooted across the seat. Once she had her feet firmly planted on the asphalt, she looked around. "Where are we?"

"You're safe here. The outside suggests a nondescript warehouse, but inside is three floors of office space."

Tessa was intrigued as she watched Fab whip out a lockpick and open the door.

Lark greeted us, shotgun in hand.

Tessa yelped and jumped behind me.

"We're going to have to set rules on who you can and can't shoot," I said to Lark, who appeared chagrined and laid the rifle on her desk.

The guys were sitting at their desks, watching the unfolding drama and smirking.

"My bad. I figured you'd knock or something."

"Boring," Fab told her.

I ushered Tessa over to the conference table, took what was left of her lunch from Fab, and set it in front of her. All eyes were on me. "This is Tessa," I introduced. "Raise your hand when I call your name. Creole, my husband. Didier, Fab's husband. My brother, Brad, and new manager and gun-toter, Lark." The guys nodded.

Lark waved wildly as she marched across the room to the kitchen, snatching up a roll of paper towels and setting it in front of Tessa. "If you want something else to drink, the refrigerator is full. We're low on snacks, even though I offered to hop to the grocery store."

Fab kissed Didier and sat on the corner of his desk.

Creole closed the space between us and hooked his arm around me, kissing my cheek. "Is this the car thief?"

"Technically, no," I responded with a shifty smile.

Fear flooded Tessa's face and only minimally subsided when Creole winked at her.

Brad laughed. "Mother called, gloating that she had a big story, and I almost didn't believe her, but once she mentioned you two were involved, I changed my mind. She went on to detail yesterday's adventure. Glad to see you're okay." He nodded at Tessa.

"Madeline called and wasn't happy that I already knew." Didier laughed. "Then she wanted to know if Creole knew. I told her he did, and she ended the call with an aggrieved 'Okay.' Next time, I'm going to claim ignorance and let her be the bearer of whatever the news is, no matter how many times I've heard it."

"We didn't discuss this before," I said to Lark, "but since you worked for a PI, you should know that anything that's said in or out of the office is need-to-know."

"I'm not a blabber." Lark zipped her lips.

I pointed to Fab, and she updated everyone on our morning. Sort of. She was light on details when it came to her client.

Tessa finished her pie and shake, gathered up the trash, and I tossed it. She rested her head on her arms, and her eyelids fluttered.

I rubbed her back, and she smiled faintly. "Good time for a break."

Fab, who'd been on her phone, hung up, and it rang minutes later. After a few curt responses, she hung up. "That was Blunt. The doctor," she added, since the guys didn't know who she was talking about. "He checked, and Tessa was going to be released today. So she should be okay without further care. He's on call if we need anything."

"Then I can stop feeling guilty about not insisting that we go straight back to the hospital."

"A kind heart is not a defense for harboring a

runaway," Creole said.

I nodded, grabbed a bottle of water, and took a seat outside. I needed to drink in the sunshine.

Fab appeared at my side and took a seat. "You're going to figure out something."

"One of these days, I'm going to run dry, and then what?"

"You worry too much."

An hour later, Lark whistled loud enough to wake the dead. "Tessa's awake," she yelled from the doorway.

"Question-and-answer time." Fab grabbed my arm, hauling me to my feet.

I sat opposite Tessa and gave the girl a sympathetic smile. "You up to answering a few questions?" She nodded tentatively. "Last time I saw you before yesterday, you and your brother were panhandling at the Quik Mart. I'd like to hear how you graduated from panhandling to stealing cars."

Aware of all the eyes on her, Tessa grew wide-eyed and shrank a little.

"The guys look like thugs—" Only due to the scruffed-up state they had going for them today. "—but you can trust them with your life. I have, and they've always come through."

"If you need a reference, I have a six-year-old," Brad joked.

The guys laughed, and Tessa noticeably relaxed.

"How old are you?" Creole asked.

"Fourteen.

She didn't know Creole well enough to know how much her answer angered him. I imagined the rest were mad as well but didn't look around to check.

"My brother and I worked different locations around town, but the Quik Mart made us the most money. Some days better than others." Tessa unleashed a big sigh. "One day, this guy shows up and pulls my mom aside, and they have a long talk. The whole time, the two of them are staring at me. Made my skin crawl. Later that same day, he showed back up with a fistful of cash, and that's when I found out my mom had sold me."

"Was that man Colton Roberts?" Fab asked.

Tessa lowered her head and nodded.

The guys exchanged raised eyebrows, recognizing the name and knowing the cops would like to have a chat with him about Kathryn.

"Then what happened?" I patted her hand.

"I didn't want to go with him. My mom slapped me hard and forced me into Colton's truck, threatening that I'd never see my brother again if I didn't behave. Before she could slam the door, my brother ran up, crying, and jerked on her pantleg. She hauled off and kicked him, and he landed on the pavement. I shoved her out of the way and ran past her, hugged Timothy, and whispered for him to be good and do what he was told and I'd be back. Which was a big lie. I knew chances were slim that I'd ever see either of them again."

"Fab and I are going to help you. Not exactly sure how yet." I smiled weakly. "We never break our word."

"You've done a lot already. I don't want to get you in trouble."

"Don't worry about us. Getting out of troublesome situations is a specialty." I winked at Fab and didn't bother to figure out who groaned.

"What happened when you got back in the truck?" Fab asked.

"The door barely closed before Colton threatened to beat the hell out of me if I made any attempt at escape. He only had one rule—to do what he said, when he said, or he'd break my bones. It was a silent drive to his house out in the middle of nowhere, which creeped me out as much as not knowing what he had planned for me."

"It's remote out there, all right." I grimaced.

"He took me to a run-down house and jerked me out of the truck onto my butt in the gravel drive. Told me not to bother screaming cause no one could hear me. He laughed, and I thought I'd be sick. I told myself before he dragged me up the step that I'd do everything he told me and look for a way out."

I got up, walked around the table, and sat next

to her, putting my arm around her. "Time for a break? You want something to drink?"

"I'm good," Tessa said shakily. "It feels good to tell someone what it was like to live out in that creepy place with a psycho. And I'm doing it for my brother, hoping you can rescue him from my mom before she sells him."

"I want that, too," I said sincerely.

"That night, and more after that than I can count, I slept on the couch and he kept one of my arms cuffed to a chair. Then, one day, he hauled me outside and showed me how to use a slim jim on a junky old car he had sitting next to his truck. Once I got the hang of it, he timed me with a stopwatch. If I didn't best myself, he'd whack me with a stick." Tears ran down her cheeks. "It didn't take long before my butt and thighs were black and blue. But I got faster."

I grabbed a paper towel and handed it to her.

Tessa wiped her face and sat back. "If Colton found out I was telling you about him, he'd kill me."

Fab jumped off the corner of Didier's desk and took the seat across from Tessa. "No worries that that awful man will ever hear a word of what we talk about. We're going to use what you say to help you."

"I'll take that drink," Tessa said.

Lark jumped up and waved her over. "Come pick out your own." She told Tessa that she was going to suggest getting a soda machine. "More room in the fridge."

"Colton told me I was a star pupil." After picking out a soda, Tessa crossed the room and sat back down. "Had a great career ahead of me. I thought 'only if I don't end up in jail' but kept that to myself. He took me to a restaurant for my final test. He timed me while I unlocked all the cars. I was to keep my face hidden in case there were cameras he hadn't seen. I caught on quick. I didn't have a choice or I'd never sit down again… comfortably anyway."

"If you have bruising, there's lotion in the bathroom that will help," Lark said.

Tessa shook her head. "After a handful of whacks with that stick, I followed his instructions to the letter. A couple of times, he gave me a pass because he knew I was trying, but it happened so seldom that it would've been stupid to count on him looking the other way any other time."

I started mentally ticking off the names of a couple of guys I could sic on Colton.

"Did he ever touch you sexually?" Fab asked in a low tone, but everyone heard.

"He freaked me out one night when I thought he wanted sex. Laughed in my face, telling me I was too scrawny for his tastes. So relieved." Tessa laughed humorlessly. "After that, I got in the habit of eating just enough that I wouldn't pass out. Besides, he had someone else. Kept her locked in the bedroom. I only know because I heard her crying a few times. I made the mistake of asking once, and he slapped me so hard, I hit the wall. Never asked another question that didn't pertain to a job. I felt sorry for the woman, but there was nothing I could do."

Fab mouthed Kathryn, and I nodded.

"When did you start stealing cars?" Fab asked.

"The day after I aced unlocking all those cars, he ordered me into his truck. I hoped briefly that he'd return me to my mom, but he didn't, and after that, I didn't allow myself to think about life before Colton. He drove to a fancy neighborhood, pulled up across the street from a big house, and ordered me to boost the car in the driveway and follow him." Tessa finished off her soda and crunched the can under her foot. "The first time behind the wheel scared the heck out of me, and then I thought it was fun."

"Colton had you driving without a license?" Fab asked.

"I wondered what would happen if I got pulled over but was afraid to ask. The drop-off for the car was always a short drive away, usually a parking lot. I'd leave it and get in Colton's truck. He was proud of my skills, boasting several times that I'd stolen pricey autos, and once telling me the cars were worth more than I'd see in a lifetime."

"It's not a profession you chose willingly; you were doing what had to do to survive." I'd heard enough and knew that Tessa needed a break.

"How about a shower and some clean clothes?"

Tessa nodded shyly, her cheeks turning pink. "I don't have any clothes," she mumbled.

"See that woman over there?" I pointed to Fab. "We'll let her figure it out. Trust me, she's good at it and will love it."

Fab smiled at her. "I've got a sundress that will look perfect on you."

I stood and held out a hand to her. "We're going to Fab's for a change of clothes and to come up with Plan B."

"Wife, I'd like to speak to you," said my disgruntled husband, crooking his finger.

"I don't want to get you in trouble," Tessa whispered.

"No worries about him; he's a softie," I whispered back. I motioned to Lark, who bounded up out of her chair and over to the table. "Will you help her to the car?"

"You betcha." Lark grasped Tessa's hand in hers.

Fab handed Lark the car keys.

I waited until the two left the building. "Yes, dear." I turned and faced down Creole's annoyance, Didier standing next to him with the same disgruntled expression.

"What you're doing is illegal." Creole stared me down. "The cops want to talk to her, and you should let them handle it."

If he expected me to squirm under his scrutiny, it wouldn't be today. "You're right."

That surprised him. "But before I ring up the cops, Tessa needs a lawyer." Said lawyer could make that call.

Creole groaned and turned to Fab.

Fab threw her hands up. "Don't grouch at me. I'm not the do-gooder here, not by a long stretch." She jabbed her finger in my direction.

Didier tried, but I saw a glimpse of a smile before it disappeared.

Creole pulled his phone out of his pocket and tapped the screen. "Good! I have a bail bondsman on speed dial and that friend of a friend of some cousin that can get me a jail visit right away."

Everyone else laughed. Creole and I engaged in a glare-down.

"Just give me a couple of hours, and if I can't concoct a workable plan, you can call the cops." I flashed him a cheesy smile.

Creole gave me an exaggerated eyeroll.

"We'll see you later." I hurried to catch up to Fab, who'd already beat me to the door. How did she almost get out of the building without me noticing?

"Sooner than you think," Creole bellowed.

I heard the guys laugh.

Chapter Seventeen

During the short drive back to Fab's, Tessa nodded off in the back seat. Once inside, Fab took over as hostess and showed Tessa to a guest bathroom and where she could find anything she could possibly want, and that included an oversized fluffy bathrobe. While Tessa showered, Fab went into her closet and came out with a knee-length navy dress with a design of white flowers, a woven belt in her other hand.

"Very cute. Who knew you had anything with color in your closet?" Ignoring her turned-up nose, I offered, "I have shoes."

"You have flip-flops," Fab said with a snort.

"They're perfect if Tessa isn't the same size as one of us."

"Madeline demanded that I buy the dress, with the same snarky comment about introducing color into my wardrobe. I bought it with no intention of wearing it, and now I'm glad I did."

"Tessa's in the process of finding out what I already know—staying here is the best."

Fab scooted around me and headed down the hall to the other side of the house. I stopped in the kitchen, pulling an aluminum tub out of the cupboard and filling it with ice. My plan was to sit outside, soak up more sunshine, and enjoy the breeze that rolled in off the water.

The front door opened. "Honey, we're home," Brad boomed, coming through first, Creole and Didier behind him.

"Let me guess, you three figured out it's hard to eavesdrop from miles away?" I almost smirked.

"We took a vote, and it was unanimous that we should be here," Didier said. "Where's my wife?"

I pointed down the hall. "She's making sure Tessa gets the most amazing shower experience she's ever had." I slid onto a stool and let the guys have control of the kitchen. They knew what everyone liked to drink. Just as I was about to share my idea of sitting outside, it started to rain.

"You need to find out if she's got any family besides that mother of hers." Creole slid onto a stool next to me and took the beer Brad handed him.

Didier dragged out a couple more stools from a nearby closet. The island was mammoth and easily sat eight.

"Strongarm one of those lawyer friends of yours to represent Tessa so she doesn't end up where she doesn't want to be," Brad said, sitting opposite me.

"We need some more information from Tessa before I make any calls," I said.

"I'd like to know how your SUV got targeted for theft," Creole said.

Tessa walked barefoot into the kitchen, freshly scrubbed with a sparkle. The navy dress was a good choice. Her sandy brown hair was pulled into a high ponytail.

Didier whistled. Tessa blushed.

Fab led her over to the counter and got her a water.

"We don't want you to feel ganged up on," Creole said. "But I've got a couple of questions about who decided that you'd steal my wife's SUV."

"I thought it was your car," Tessa said to Fab.

"It's mine." I unleashed a long sigh aimed at Fab. "It's impossible to wrestle the keys away from her."

Tessa laughed, then sobered. "Every time we went out to steal a car, he'd show me a picture of it, usually in someone's driveway, and then we'd hit the road. This time, the picture was taken out in front of his property. He grumbled all the way to town that the owner was trouble."

"Maybe he was shooting at you," Fab said, looking at me.

Tessa worked her lower lip, hesitating. "I got the feeling that stealing your car was connected to something that happened a week ago, maybe two—I'm not sure exactly how long. He was on his computer and went into a rage. Jumped up, tied me to a chair, and banged out of the house for what seemed like hours. I wondered what was going on but had the sense not to ask. When he got back, he was still angry and threatened again that if I attempted to escape, he'd kill me and go get my brother."

The guys' faces were filled with fury.

"When was the last time you saw your mom?" Creole asked.

"This morning." Tessa shuddered. "She didn't give a fiddle that I'd been shot. Never even asked how I was doing. Instead, she stood at the end of the bed and called Colton to ask what she should do with me. I ran into the bathroom. She came after me and attempted to tie my hands with an old scarf. I kicked her in the stomach as hard as I could. She howled and bent over, and I ran."

"Where was your brother during that?" Brad asked.

"My mom brought him with her, and he was asleep on the couch. He can sleep through anything. I wanted to take him with me but knew I'd never get both of us out of there. If we were caught, I didn't figure anyone would believe my story, and she might have me arrested."

"You're fourteen?" Creole asked. Tessa nodded. "We're walking a fine line here."

"I promised…" I said.

"Do you have any relatives in the area that we

can contact?" Didier asked. "Other than your mom?"

"I have a grandmother that lives here in the Keys." Tessa smiled faintly. "I don't know where; it's been a long time since I've seen her. We used to visit all the time, and then Mom and her got in a fight and that was the last I saw her. I asked about her several times, and Mom finally threatened to slap my head off if I mentioned her again."

"What's her name?" I asked.

"When I was younger, she was Blanche Hunter; then she got married, and I never met him. Mom said she married a Frenchy. I didn't want to provoke her by asking what was wrong with that, since she was already angry."

I looked up and smiled at Fab and Didier. "Absolutely nothing. They're swell people." I winked at the couple.

"Part of the problem was Mom swore Grandma liked her dogs better than her."

"Blanche?" I said, and Tessa nodded. "Big dogs?" Tessa shrugged. "I bet I know your grandmother. Maybe. If I'm right, her name's Blanche Bijou."

"Last time I saw my grandmother, she told me I could call anytime, and she'd come get me. Mom found the number, ripped it up, and threw it in the street. Rather than cry about it, I told myself that it didn't matter because I didn't have a phone."

Brad leaned into the counter and smiled at her in that dad way he'd developed for soothing his daughter. "There isn't a problem too big for my sister. This is going to work out."

"I know what you're thinking, wife, and you need to slow down." Creole pulled out his phone. "I say we get the Chief over here so he can pave the way with his connections and make sure that you and Tessa stay out of jail."

Tessa gasped.

I reached over and hugged her.

"Mention that Tessa has a brother," Fab said to Creole.

Creole slid off the stool and went outside, phone in hand.

"I'd offer you junk food, but this house stocks only healthy stuff." I made a choking noise that had Tessa laughing. "I could easily rustle up a vegetable."

Tessa wrinkled her nose. "I'm good."

"How does pizza sound?" Fab whipped her phone out. Tessa licked her lips. "I'll place an order for everyone's favorites, and we'll get it delivered."

"Don't forget a salad for the health nut." I laughed at Didier's growl.

Brad focused his attention on Tessa, asking her about school, and found out she hadn't been in a while but that when she had, she'd liked it and was a good student. The more the two talked, the more Tessa relaxed. His dad skills were coming in handy.

Creole blew back through the door. "You need to find out if the Blanche you know is Tessa's grandmother. Otherwise, according to the Chief, Tessa will end up in the system."

We both already knew that, but I wasn't accepting that as an option.

"If you've got her number, I could call her," Tessa suggested tentatively, looking scared.

I pulled out my phone, found the number, and handed it to her. "Press here when you're ready." I pointed.

Tessa stood and followed Creole's example, but instead of going outside, she wandered over to the couch and sat facing the patio.

I heard her ask cautiously, "Grandma?"

"I hope this works out," I whispered, and everyone nodded.

Tessa turned, a huge smile on her face. "It's her." She nestled back against the cushions and talked in an excited tone.

"Well… good for Tessa. At least one thing has gone her way," Didier said.

"The Chief has a meeting, or he'd come over," Creole said. "He's friends with the sheriff and knows he'd want to be in on any discussions."

"I don't agree," I said in a hiss. "Sounds more like an ambush. We need an attorney."

Fab and I nodded in agreement—one lawyer needed now. She picked up her phone, and without having to ask, I knew that she was calling Tank, AKA Patrick Cannon, a lawyer we had on speed dial, who'd agreed to do our jobs or find another lawyer who was more qualified. She talked for a few minutes, explained what we needed, and hung up. "He's on the way over."

Who knew you could meet a good attorney, jailed due to a misunderstanding, during a visit with another inmate? Lucky for us, his visitor bailed on him, and Fab had boldly sat down and chatted him up.

Fab handed me another bottle of water and sat across from me. "I've been thinking about that cretin, Colton. He knows Tessa's alive and has to know she left the hospital. His nightmare is that she's on the loose and he can't control her. We need to keep our eyes peeled. You can bet that he'd snatch her up again if he could get his hands on her. And then follow through on his threats."

"Now that we know she's Blanche's granddaughter, that's the best place for her to go if the woman's agreeable, and I bet she will be," I said. "She lives south of the Cove, and Tessa's not likely to be spotted down there."

"We need to find the mom, broker a deal for the brother, and ship that b— off to Alaska." One look at Fab, and you knew she was working out the kinks in her plan.

Didier wrapped his arms around her from behind. "You're not to do anything illegal."

I raised my hand. "I volunteer."

"Not funny," Creole growled.

"What would be ideal is to get the mother to sign a custody agreement," said Brad, who'd been through a custody fight of his own. "If she's as money-grubby as we think, she'll jump at the easy cash. Guaranteed she'll be back with her hand out, but a legal document would force her to court. She'd have to hire a lawyer, and she wouldn't have the money."

"Your best bet is to find out where the mom and brother are panhandling and make a generous offer for him," Didier said.

Tessa came back over, a big smile on her face, and handed me the phone. "My grandmother wants to talk to you."

"Blanche, this is Madison Westin."

"I remember you from that dog fiasco. I can't thank you enough for what you and your friends did for me. I'll do whatever I can for my grandchildren, but I'm telling you now that my daughter is worthless and she'll do whatever she has to to make sure that I'm not in their life in any way. I do love them, and I'm willing to fight."

"I've got a lawyer on the way over, and he's going to look out for Tessa's rights," I assured her. "He can take care of the custody issue and make sure that everything's legal, so your daughter can't come back and snatch the kids away… at least, not without hopping through a lot of hoops."

"Tessa told me what she's been doing to keep

her brother safe," Blanche said, sadness in her tone. "She's smart as a whip, and if we can get her away from my daughter, she'll turn her back on any kind of criminal activity."

"The lawyer just walked in," I informed her. "After their meeting, I'm going to drive Tessa to your house. If plans change for any reason, I'll call you. I'll also call to let you know we're on our way, so you won't have to worry."

"I'm not going anywhere."

I hung up and turned toward where Tank loomed in the doorway, a man behind him with a stack of pizza boxes and two shopping bags. Brad intercepted him and put everything on the counter.

Creole cornered Tank in the entry, and the two men talked.

Fab insisted on food first. Legal discussions could wait. She introduced Tank to Tessa and directed everyone to the kitchen, gently pushing Tessa to have first choice. As usual, more food than an army could eat had been spread out on the island. Everyone filled a plate, grabbed a drink, and sat at the dining room table.

The guys joked and laughed. The tension eased off Tessa, and she ate heartily.

After the table had been cleared, Tank settled his considerable bulk on one of the couches, legal pad and pen balanced on his crossed leg. He motioned to Tessa. "Creole filled me in on the details of what's been going on, but I'd like to hear it from you."

"I'm not sure where you want me to start," Tessa responded hesitantly. "When Madison caught me trying to boost her SUV?"

Tank brushed his hand across the lower half of his face. My guess was to cover a smile. I suspected that he hadn't gotten the whole story from either Fab or Creole.

"I want you to go back a little further." Tank smiled encouragingly. "Start with the last day you panhandled."

Tessa revealed facts about her life that we hadn't heard before. She and her brother lived in a pay-by-the-week motel when her mom could afford it. And when she couldn't, they slept on the beach. "I didn't mind the beach, but my brother hated it. I did my best to pocket some of the money so we always had enough to pay rent, but sometimes I couldn't do it."

Fab and I exchanged a nod. We knew all about the fleabag motel on the main highway just south of town that Tessa was talking about. Like me, she was probably wondering if the little brother was still there. I hoped he wasn't alone, living amongst drunks. If they'd moved out, from Tessa's description, I knew the alcove that they used to hide out on the beach. It would mostly protect them from the elements but not encroaching water.

Even though I'd never met Tessa's mom, I'd seen her a few times. She was a pitiful excuse for a mother and did very little, if anything, to protect her kids. Her need for alcohol superseded everything. I suspected Tessa was the one looking out for her brother.

Tessa went on to add a few more details, and everything she said was unsettling. Fourteen. She sounded much older. Life on the streets had forced her to grow up fast.

"On the way over, I spoke to a local sheriff's deputy, Kevin Cory, who was assigned your case and informed him that I was your lawyer," Tank told Tessa, whose eyes grew round as saucers. "I arranged with Kevin to make you available for an interview. It won't be today," he told the relieved girl. "No charges have been filed against you, and I assume they won't be."

"They won't," I said.

Tessa smiled weakly.

"You don't have to worry about being arrested for the attempted boosting. You're being treated as a victim, and as such, they'd like to talk to you so they can make an arrest and close the case. I will share that it's Kevin theory that Madison was the intended target."

"If I get a theory, I think we both may have been targets," I said.

Tank turned his stare on me and nodded. "I asked Kevin if a missing persons report had been filed on you, Tessa, and it hasn't, which we can use to our advantage. As I'm certain all of you know, because Tessa is underage, certain laws have to be followed."

"Madison's worried about Social Services involvement," Creole said.

Tessa's face drained of color.

Brad grimaced, remembering when he'd had to deal with them. His lawyer paving the way had made it easier for him.

"Their involvement is inevitable, so I made a quick call to a friend that works for the agency; she'll be showing up anytime now." Tank glanced at his watch. "The two of us will escort Tessa to her grandmother's. That's where she'll stay until a court decides otherwise."

"What about her little brother?" Fab asked.

"Do you know where he's at?" Tank asked Tessa. She shook her head. "Once we locate him, my friend with Social Services will call in the cops. They'll escort her to pick him up, and he'll be taken to your grandmother's."

"If we could both stay with my grandmother and not have to leave, we'd be really good," Tessa said softly.

I'd do whatever it took to make sure she could enjoy her teenage years.

"If your mother decides to fight the placement, she'll have to wage her own court fight and, prove that she cleaned up her life and can provide a suitable place to live. Even if she manages to do all that, once the court hears that she sold you, they'll never return you or your brother to her care. By the time she gets all the court orders satisfied, you'll be of age and can make your own decisions."

"You think maybe I can go to school again?" Tessa asked hopefully.

"Of course. What was the last grade you finished?" Tank asked.

"Sixth."

"Another thing that will go against your mom," Tank said in disgust.

Two years to make up, but if she was as smart as I thought, she could accomplish that in no time. "You're a bit behind, but I know just the person to catch you up. He's a bit eccentric, but he's got kid rapport, and if you want references, I've got several kids you can talk to." I smiled reassuringly at Tessa.

"You're being too nice." Tessa grimaced.

"If I'd known anything about your situation, the first time I saw you, I'd have done more. Not exactly sure what that would've been, but Fab and I would've come up with something. Huh?" I nudged Fab with my foot, and she made a face.

Tessa laughed, and it sounded good. "You were always generous. Now you've saved my butt twice."

"You want to pay me back?" I asked, and Tessa nodded enthusiastically. "Enjoy your life as a kid." My phone rang, and I looked at the screen. "How long before your friend gets here?" I asked Tank.

Tank looked at his watch. "She should be here soon."

I stood and crossed to the island, where I could keep an eye on anything new that unfolded. "Hey, grouchy." I almost laughed. "Madison Westin. Thanks for not ducking my call." Doc Blunt came with an attitude, but so far, he'd never turned down a request for help.

"Casio warned me you'd be calling again. Didn't expect it to come so soon."

I updated him on Tessa and told him that I'd given her a couple of aspirin, but they were barely making a dent in the pain. She hadn't complained, but I'd seen her wince several times.

"Ah yes, the chick-a-rune that skipped out of the hospital, leaving everyone in an uproar and asking one another, 'Where the hell did she go?' Once security went over the tapes and realized she left of her own volition, they grumbled about her cutting out on the bill. I told them to get over it; she probably doesn't have two nickels."

"It's a long story. She might share some of it with you if you manage a little bit of sunshine."

Blunt snorted. "You're drunk. Where do you find these people?"

"I've been asked that a lot and don't have a good answer," I said. "Get the hospital to discount the bill and send it over, and we can get a Go Fund Me started. I don't want them sending the cops or siccing collections on her."

"Gossip that trickled through the grapevine—

and you'd be surprised how accurate it can be—is that she's underage and homeless. She might just qualify for a grant. I'll talk with the Finance department."

"That would be incredibly sweet of you."

"Don't tell anyone. I don't need it getting out," Blunt grumbled. "Give me the address where I need to go."

I scrolled through my phone and read it off. "It's south on the Overseas, just on the outskirts of the Cove. Blanche Bijou is Tessa's grandmother and runs a dog rescue. To be on the safe side, give us an hour." I hung up and went back to the living room, sitting on the armrest next to Creole. "I've got a doc paying a house call to your grandmother's place to give you a quick check and help manage your pain," I told Tessa. "A little warning: he comes across as a grouch, but he's a softy."

"Is there anybody you don't know?" Tessa asked.

"Between me and Fab, we've got it covered." Fab and I exchanged grins.

Creole's phone rang. He walked outside and wasn't gone long. "That was the Chief. I brought him up to speed. The sheriff is expecting a call from you," he said to Tank. "He wants Colton Roberts put away for a long time."

"That's nice of Chiefy." I tried not to laugh.

"One of these days…" Creole shook his finger at me.

Chapter Eighteen

The social worker showed, and after a brief conversation with Tank and Tessa, they got into Tank's SUV and headed out to the highway, Fab and I behind them.

"It was nice of you to give Tessa clothes," I said. "And the cute backpack."

"You know how I love to boss people around and tell them what to wear." Fab laughed. "On a more serious note, I brought up a pic of that motel on my phone and showed it to Tessa, and she confirmed it's the one they stayed at. I called and got the manager—chatty woman—and told her that I was trying to locate the kids."

"Did you impersonate law enforcement?"

Fab ignored my question, which meant it was a definite maybe. "Karla left owing money after the manager threatened to call the cops and have her tossed to the curb. She hasn't seen her in two weeks."

"Since Karla doesn't have the money to blow town, you can bet she's around somewhere, panhandling. I just hope we find her before she sells her son."

We followed Tank to Blanche's. The houses

out there came with acreage, and almost everyone had animals in fenced-off pastures. He turned into the u-shaped driveway and pulled up in front of the single-story white farmhouse with a wraparound porch. The screen door flew open, and an older grey-haired woman came running out and bounded down the steps.

It was heartwarming to sit back and watch as Tessa jumped out of the car and ran to her grandmother. They hugged for the longest time. A grey-haired gentleman came out of the house and stood on the porch, smiling at the two. Blanche put her arm around her granddaughter, beckoning to the man, and he joined them, enveloping them in a hug.

The social worker and Tank sat in the car, giving the three a few minutes before getting out. They all went into the house. Tank had already told Fab and I that Blanche had paperwork to sign.

"Cute porch." I admired the handful of rocking chairs on the porch to one side of the front door. All were piled with pillows. "We might as well make ourselves comfortable and greet grouchy Blunt when he gets here."

Fab and I got out, made our way up the stairs, and sat down. The wooden screen door opened, and a German Shepherd stuck his nose out. He spotted us and came out, holding the door for his lookalike friend. Both ambled over for a sniff and a head rub, then laid down.

It wasn't long before a beater Mercedes pulled in. Blunt got out, black bag in hand.

"I'm surprised that thing runs," Fab said.

I chuckled and went to meet him.

Tank shot out the door and rumbled over, and I introduced the two men. "You two have shifty appearances going for you." I bit back a laugh. "He looks like a thug, but he's a lawyer," I told Blunt. "And you both make house calls."

"Don't plan on needing your services anytime soon, but should the need the arise, I expect a discount." Blunt eyed Tank like he was a roach that had wandered up.

"Same here," Tank grunted and led the man into the house, giving him the latest on Tessa.

The door opened again, and the same grey-haired man as before came out. Up close, he had a kind face, and warm brown eyes. "Anton Bijou," he introduced himself, then pulled up a chair opposite us and sat down. One of the dogs got up and moved, lying on his feet. "Thank you for bringing Tessa to us. I promise you, we're going to take good care of her."

"Tessa was excited to see her grandmother again," I said.

"We're going to do what we can to find her brother."

"You're in luck; here sits a world-class PI." I waved my hand at Fab. "I know the case is top priority for her."

Fab turned so Anton couldn't see her smirk.

"We promised we'd look for her brother, and we intend to keep that promise."

I squealed when a gigantic Maine Coon took a flying leap from the banister and landed in my lap. While I tried to catch my breath, he made himself comfortable and stretched out, filling up the chair. "How's the animal rescue business going?"

"Blanche can't take as many dogs and cats as she'd like, as there's always a funding issue." Anton's serious look turned to humor, and he added, "She recently took in two goats. The previous owners failed to check with their HOA, and after the neighbors got wind of it, they were ordered to get rid of them or else. Which I assume meant a court fight."

Fab had taken her phone out and continuously tapped the screen. I attempted to kick her, but she moved out of the way. "Except for a phone listing, Blanche and her rescue have no social media presence. Having one in place would go a long way to get people interested in donating."

"Blanche and I were just talking about that. I suggested that one of us should get up to speed on our computer skills, and I really meant her." Anton chuckled. "My computer skills are basic and not quite up to snuff."

"It would be a good way to keep funds coming in to run the place without placing added stress on your budget," Fab insisted.

"I'll mention it again." Anton didn't seem

convinced the conversation would go anywhere.

"I've got a better idea," Fab said. "I'll have my associate, Xander, call and talk to you about it. He's a computer whiz, and it would be easy for him to set up a website and get you signed up on some social media sites. I'm certain that he can have it practically running itself. Since I'm already a donor, I'll make it a gift."

I smiled at her, thinking it was a great idea. "Xander's your man. People love pictures of dogs and cats, and I'm sure the goats will also be a hit. It'll spur folks to donate, and there might be some that will want to offer forever homes for the animals."

Blunt blew out the door, which came within a breath of hitting the shingle siding. He nodded to Anton. "I checked Tessa, and she's doing well, all things considered. I gave her a shot, which knocked her out. She'll probably sleep through the night. I'll call in a prescription and stop back by tomorrow to check on her."

"What do I owe you?" Anton reached for his wallet.

Blunt waved him off. "Don't worry about that. I'm looking into a grant that I'm fairly certain Tessa will qualify for, which will cover her medical expenses." He turned to me and asked. "How's your other friend?"

"We were able to reunite Kathryn with her family," I said. "They live up in Miami. I'm certain she's seen a doctor by this time."

Blunt nodded. "That's what she needed—to be surrounded by family."

"I'll walk you to your car," Fab said.

"On the way back, grab a business card," I said to her.

"I wish Tessa had called us sooner," Anton said.

"She would have but didn't have a phone or your number; Karla found it and tore it up." Anton's face filled with anger. "Also, she's a great big sister, and before she'd have done anything to jeopardize her brother, she'd have to have been certain that she could get the two of them away from their mom."

Fab came back and handed a card to Anton. "Anything Tessa needs, call."

I'd finally insisted that we had to get more professional business cards and had Xander design one, which Fab gave the okay to.

Tank and the social worker came out on the porch. Blanche behind them, and she sat next to her husband, who clasped her hand.

"Either of you know the whereabouts of Karla?" Tank asked Fab and me.

I shook my head.

"Based on Tessa's description, I was able to call the motel they were staying at, and she moved out two weeks ago," Fab told them. "When we find Timothy, who do we call?"

"Call me or Tank," the social worker said. "I'm going to file a police report so they'll be on the lookout. If they find him first, they'll know to contact me, and he'll be brought here." She and Fab exchanged cards. "I'll be in touch with Tank about the court hearing, which will award you temporary custody and get the ball rolling." She nodded at Blanche and Anton.

"Anything you need, call; we're happy to help," Fab said, and she and the woman exchanged a nod.

"Keep me updated," Tank grunted.

The two hustled back to the car and out of the driveway.

Fab turned to Blanche and told her about the social media idea. "I'll have Xander call tomorrow."

"You saved my operation once before, and now you're back, helping again, and this time bringing me my sweet granddaughter." Blanche got teary. "I'm worried about my grandson and what will happen when my daughter finds out they're living with me."

"Not sure if you remember, but I'm a licensed investigator," Fab said to Blanche. "Madison and I are in agreement that your daughter can't have gone far. We'll find your grandson."

"On the off chance that Karla shows up here, call the cops," I said. "Even if she manages to get a ride down here, the threat of jail and she'll run. Tank is a good lawyer; he'll get you legal custody. Her only option after that, if she wants the kids, is to get her act together, and that will be a long road." My phone dinged with a message. I pulled it out of my pocket. "My husband." I smiled at the screen.

"Anything you need… questions, call," Fab told the couple.

I got a dirty look from the cat when I moved him off my lap. "Next time, I'll bring a treat," I whispered, as though he'd understand, and gave him once last head-scratch.

Fab and I walked back to the Hummer with a wave.

I took out my phone as soon as I closed the door and called Creole. "You cooking?" I asked when he answered.

"Didier and I figured that it was your and Fab's turn in the kitchen." He laughed.

"So mean of you two, thinking we can't pull it off. Just wait, we've got it covered." I hung up. "We need to call in a to-go order."

Chapter Nineteen

I spent the morning on the little patio off the bedroom, catching up on paperwork. I'd made a list of all the places we could check for Timothy, and it was short. Out of options, I called my bar manager, Doodad, and asked him to put out feelers amongst his street snitches and reimburse himself for the cost out of the till.

And where was Fab? She was clearly up to something—she'd showed signs of it before the guys left the house earlier and had been quiet ever since. Why was I the only one to notice?

As though reading my mind, she banged on the bedroom door loud enough that I could hear it through the slider I'd left open. I made a bet with myself that she'd be out here in under ten seconds and started counting. She cut it close—nine.

"I've got a job and need you to go along. I'd appreciate no whining."

I frowned at her for the sheer amusement, thinking that an annoying whine would be perfect right now. Her barging in was par for the course, but there was still something off about her that I felt I should question. "How should I dress for this fun foray you have planned?"

Fab gave my skirt and top a nod of approval.

I stood and went back into the bedroom, slid into a pair of sandals, and strapped my Glock to my thigh, then followed her out to the SUV.

Once on the highway, we hit a red light, and a hotsy sportscar pulled up alongside and revved his engine. "Please, oh please, ignore him."

She laughed, and when the light turned green, she let him roar off.

I wanted to wave. "Now's a good time to share a few details about this job of yours."

"The Chief called and asked me to check out an address, report back, and send pics."

"Your being vague is highly suspicious. I'd prefer it if you'd beef up the deets."

"You know how these jobs are."

"Could you be vaguer? Dumb question, because the answer is yes." I was tempted to snort, but the big-nostril thing that Mother had threatened was a deterrent.

Fab turned off the highway, and onto a concrete strip surrounded by gravel. Grabbing her phone out of the cup holder, she rolled down the window and snapped away as she coasted by a warehouse building with an office off to the side of the loading dock and no signage. She circled the block and parked across the street in the parking lot of an office complex that was for sale, then leaned between the seats and pulled a pair of binoculars out of a bag on the floor.

I was afraid of the answer but asked, anyway. "How long are we going to sit here?"

"A few hours. Long enough for me to record the comings and goings."

This was going to be boring, since so far, not one other car or truck had passed us. "The word 'stakeout' slipped your mind?" I said in a snappish tone and attempted to slug her in the arm, but she jerked back and I ended up grazing her shoulder.

"If I'd been totally honest, you wouldn't have come. Honestly, neither would I, so evasive was the best course." She smiled cheekily. "Hurry up and do nothing sucks, but with the two of us here, we can entertain one another."

"What? A little song and dance?"

"The bright side…" Fab screwed up her face, sporting a demented look. "I'll make this up to you."

"Where are the snacks and drinks?" I peered over the seat and ignored her aggrieved sigh as I looked for and found the usual insulated soft cooler. I turned back. "What's this case about?"

"The Chief's new client recently purchased this business, which distributes fitness equipment. His warehouse supervisor found a suspicious crate and brought it to him. Inside was a cache of pills. They were sent to be tested and came back as ecstasy with a street value of half a million."

I made a shocked face.

"Besides the client wanting to know what's going on, he also wants to know if the delivery trucks match up to the manifest."

"I get that the client is always right, even when they aren't, but wouldn't it be better to have a person or two on the inside? Once the delivery truck backs up to the roller doors, anything could be offloaded, and you're not going to know squat sitting out here."

"I suggested just that to the Chief, and he agreed but added that the client specifically asked for it to be done this way."

I gave an exaggerated phony yawn, which brought on a real one, which I milked. "You've got a limited amount of time before I kick your butt out of the car, and then you can sit on the asphalt all day if you'd like while I go home and put my feet up."

"Good luck implementing that plan," she said with a smirk.

Sitting and doing nothing wasn't her forte either, and I bet myself she'd get bored sooner rather than later. At least, I hoped so. I grabbed up my phone, clicked around, and checked out the latest drama on social media.

I looked up often enough to know that only one truck offloaded and left, and after that, it was quiet. It was creeping up on three hours, and I'd had enough and was about to tell her just that when she cranked the engine and pulled back out on the street. She took another turn around the block before she hit the main highway.

"I didn't tell Didier about this job."

"Why? There was no reason not to, and now you've created unnecessary drama with the husband." I shook my head. "I'm not going to say anything, but if Creole asks, I'm not lying. The biggest reason is because there's no reason to lie. The client's bad idea was a waste of our time and his money."

"The business needs to be staked out at night."

I heard the excitement in her tone and bit back a groan. "I'm going to tell you again—what this job needs is someone on the inside. Anything else is a waste of time." I knew that wouldn't dissuade her from whatever she was planning. "Good luck getting past Didier. I'm not volunteering to go along. I'm married to an ex-detective and probably wouldn't make it out of bed." That stunt wouldn't be worth the ensuing drama. "You're on your own. If you drug Didier, be prepared for divorce."

"You're so dramatic."

"I'm also hungry." I picked up my phone and texted Creole the same sentiment.

He texted back that he'd be cooking.

We rode home in silence. I knew Fab well enough to know that she was plotting how she could pull off the late-night stakeout.

We walked in the house, and the guys were in a good mood, laughing it up in the kitchen, drinking beer. I slipped down the hall and came back in a t-shirt dress and bare feet. Creole handed me a margarita, and we toasted.

I was happy to see that shrimp tacos were on the menu. Creole was outside grilling, and Didier mixing up a concoction that would go on the tortillas. The side dishes were finished and waiting.

We sat outside on the patio. Over dinner, Didier asked what we'd done all day. Fab gave a benign run-down of the day—albeit a true one, but not a word about Plan B. One would think she'd ditched the idea, but I knew her better.

I had a hard time joining in the conversation when I knew that Fab was planning something that would turn dangerous if she uncovered anything.

"If you clean up, I'll do it the next two times," Creole said to Didier.

Didier grinned at him. "I'll go for that deal."

Creole stood, swept me out of my chair and into his arms, and carried me down the hall to the bedroom. He closed and locked the door, setting me on the bed.

"When is our house going to be ready to move in?" I slurred a bit, having sucked down a couple of margaritas, and was happy that I hadn't ask for another.

"Two weeks." He pulled my dress off and replaced it with my favorite football jersey, which was once his, then pulled back the sheet and laid me down, getting in.

"I've got our bed ordered. It's big, but not football-field-size." I rolled away, doing three turns, and there was still room before hitting the floor.

He pulled me back and rolled me over so we were nose to nose. "What's going on?"

"What? Where?"

"I know there's something up with you, and how do I know that? You've barely said a word all night." Creole shook his head in amused disgust. "If you don't start talking, I'm going to break out advanced interrogation methods."

"I can't." I'd closed my eyes, and now peeked out under my lashes. "It would be such a violation of friendship."

"What the hell is Fab up to now?" Creole grouched, not as irate as he could be. "It better not involve you."

"I'm thinking getting somewhat tipsy has saved me, or she'd have figured out a way to spirit me away."

Creole kissed me and said against my lips, "Whatever's going on, I can probably fix it. Unless it's a felony that you've already committed; then we'd have to pack quick and go on the lam."

I sighed. "You know the boring-ass job she did for the Chief today?"

"So he's the client; Fab left that part out. I was waiting for Didier to ask, but he was caught up in her flirting." There was an eyeroll in his tone.

"Fab's annoyed that she wasn't able to make a big discovery and thinks the reason is that any and all illegal action probably goes down at night. She didn't say that she was sneaking out tonight, but I know her and I'd bet she's planning how to get out of the house and get a look, leaving her husband none the wiser."

"Does she even know that something's going down tonight?"

I shook my head.

"I'm going to take care of this little problem, and your name will never come up." He reached over, grabbed his phone, and made a call. "We have an encroaching water problem on the patio, can I get your help?" After a pause. "Okay, thanks." He got up and pulled on his jeans.

"I'm surprised he bought that story."

"You think you're the only sneaky one." Creole leaned down and kissed me. "I'll be back." He left through the patio door.

I lay there and stared at the ceiling, hoping that when Fab was caught, she wouldn't plot payback. Once she got over the disappointment of missing out on all the sneaking around, she'd be happy that her plans had been derailed. I wasn't going to sleep, only closing my eyes for a few until Creole came back and shared what was about to happen.

The bedroom door slammed shut. "You ratted me out," Fab shrieked as she flicked on the lights and stormed across the room. "Wake up." She gave me a hard shove.

It really was a nice dream—tropical island—and it faded as soon as my eyes opened. I rolled on my side and squinted at the clock. Why was she on a rant at three in the morning? "Can't this wait until it's sunny outside?" Where was Creole?

I guess I said it out loud, as she said, "As if you don't know," flinging her arms in the air. "This is all your fault." Wrapped around one wrist was a silk tie.

I flicked at the ends as she waved it in my face. "I can honestly say that I don't know what you're talking about."

"Didier did this to me." She shook her arm around wildly.

I laughed when I realized what he'd done. "You're going to have to give him a few tips on how to secure you better so that next time you won't be able to untie yourself."

"You're annoying."

"I'm not at my best at this hour. If you could wait until I get a few more hours' sleep and down some coffee, I'll be perkier." I started to roll over and stopped. "Where's Creole?"

"Those two decided that they would stake out the warehouse and neither of us were invited," Fab hissed in annoyance.

"You didn't follow them? That's right, you were tied up. How long did it take you to get free?"

Fab ignored my questions. I bit back a smile, knowing that meant it took longer than she wanted to admit. "Didier hid the keys, including the spares."

"Good for him. Most times, your need for excitement overrides your good sense," I admonished. "You should have asked him to go along, play PIs, and have sexy time in the car… and if you're going to take my suggestion, take your own car."

Fab fought hard not to laugh.

"Not sure why you'd want to go traipsing around in the middle of the night. The Chief didn't ask you to do it and wouldn't dare. I don't think I've seen Didier hit someone, but there's always a first time."

Fab laid on the bed and yakked in my ear until I dozed off. A door slammed in the distance, and my eyes flew open. Fab was gone. It was five in the morning, and the bedroom door was standing open.

I bundled into a robe and traipsed out to the kitchen. Both men were standing at the island. Not happy was a good description, but no smoke coming out of their ears. I slid onto a stool and waved to Fab to ensure that while she was making coffee for everyone else, she wouldn't forget me.

"Something went down last night, but we have no way of knowing exactly what," Creole grouched.

"Four men showed in a pickup truck," Didier said. "They got out, one pushed up the roll-up door, and they disappeared inside. Less than an hour later, another truck showed up, offloaded a crate, and split. Half-hour later, maybe longer?" he asked Creole, who nodded. "Several cars and an SUV showed and didn't stick around long. After that, the original four locked up and were gone."

"You can bet whatever went down was illegal," Fab said, earning herself a glare from Didier.

"Now what?" I asked.

"The Chief will need to talk some sense into his client. The cops need to get involved, so everyone will be arrested and the owner doesn't end up in jail," Creole said.

"You're calling the Chief tomorrow and quitting," Didier told Fab in a no-nonsense tone.

"Don't blame him. Going back last night wasn't his idea; he didn't even know," Fab said.

Didier inspected her wrists and rubbed them. "First thing tomorrow, I'm getting a pair of handcuffs. There will be a next time, and I need to be prepared." He scooped her off her feet, throwing her over his shoulder, and disappeared down the hallway to their bedroom.

I launched myself at Creole, who caught me in his arms. "You're the best."

Chapter Twenty

I've been kidnapped.

Creole handed me the sheet of paper as I slid onto a stool. He was dressed in jeans and a button-down, his briefcase sitting on the end of the island. "If you're wondering why your friend isn't here."

It was Fab's signature alright, and I wondered where the lovebirds had jetted off to. No wonder it had been so quiet around here after all the action of just a few hours ago. "Do you think we should call the cops? Round up a search party?"

Jazz and Snow trooped into the kitchen and wound themselves around Creole's legs, meowing "feed me and do it now," ratcheting up the volume, as though they weren't accustomed to regular meals. He gave in to the pressure and split a can of cat food between the two.

He turned his attention back to me, a huge smirk on his face. "I say we wait until we get a ransom note." He laid a big kiss on me. "Do you think you can stay out of trouble on your own?"

"It'll be good practice."

He laughed, then picked up his briefcase and disappeared out the door.

I left the cats wolfing down their food and went to retrieve my laptop, then came back to sit at the island. It was rare that I ended up in this big house by myself. It needed a dog or something. I laughed, imagining the reaction I'd get to that suggestion.

I got busy sending emails to my managers, demanding to know where their weekly reports were. I wondered how long it would take them to realize I'd never requested a report and get back to me, pointing out the obvious. Or would they come up with something entertaining, a monsoon or some such? Good thing they all had a sense of humor, and once their initial annoyance passed, they'd figure out that I was amusing myself at their expense.

My phone rang. I looked at the screen, groaned, and pushed it away. The funeral boys, or Diggers as I called them behind their backs, wouldn't be calling me unless they couldn't get ahold of Fab, and it must be one of their emergencies. I was relieved when it stopped ringing; I wasn't going to feel guilty about letting the call go to voicemail. The relief was short-lived, as it started ringing again.

"Good morning," I said in a cheerful tone that I wasn't feeling.

"I wouldn't be bothering you unless…" Raul sounded short of breath. "I did call Fab first."

Dickie and Raul were the owners of Tropical Slumber Funeral Home. The two men never suggested that a client dial back whatever weird idea they had for a final send-off and go with sedate. "Why not shock everyone in attendance" always seemed to be part of the theme.

"No bother at all. She's out of town for… a couple of days." I made up the latter since the note didn't say.

"You're probably not aware that Dickie and I have come up with yet another new marketing strategy, and it's debuting today." Da-da-da in his tone. He chuckled.

Rolling my eyes was rude, but he couldn't see me, so I made it overly dramatic.

"Our newest offering is a birthday funeral. Our first one is in a few hours. Dickie and I were going over the details and started wondering if anything could go wrong. We finally agreed that since we had no clue what to expect, we should have security. That's the reason for the call."

"Which of you came up with this latest idea?" I asked. That was a tad snarky, and I was relieved when he laughed.

"You sound like Dickie. It's a constant struggle to come up with new ideas to stay competitive."

Had the deceased died on his/her birthday? I didn't ask, figuring that I was about to be invited to the party. I plastered on a stupid smile, as though we were face-to-face.

"A young woman called," Raul continued. "She'd gone to a funeral-themed party and wanted one for her thirtieth celebration. She thought a funeral home would be the perfect setting. The other party was held in a backyard with fake props, and she thought it was too pedestrian."

Can't have that.

"Another fun element: it's going to be a surprise for the guests. They're being bussed here and won't find out it's a birthday party until she pops out of the coffin," Raul relayed, excitement in his voice.

"Like a Pop Goes the Weasel thing?" I asked. If Fab were here, she'd make a face and kick me.

"Exactly."

"Do the guests think they're attending a funeral?" Fake funerals. Now birthday funerals. I'd want to beat up the not-so-dead guest of honor. "You have a reason to think there might be trouble?"

"I didn't ask, but I'd think it would dilute the surprise. As for trouble, you know how these events can easily get out of hand—a cross word here or there and fists fly. Or worse." Raul sighed. "There will be an open bar and a few toasts, and that can add to the drama. Thank you for the rental of your bus. We paid extra to have your driver run the guests back to their cars should anyone want to leave early."

The short bus had been purchased to haul Cottages guests around town for a little sightseeing. Those trips should last all of five minutes, but Rude led the trip and made up stuff as they rolled down the road. I suspected that most of the riders were drunk when they boarded and didn't care, as long as it was outrageous. And that was Rude's middle name.

Bus rental. My driver? That better make it into the report, since this was the first I was hearing of it, or I'd be reminding my employees who was boss. I glanced at my screen. Hmm… no texts, so my ruse hadn't been figured out yet. "What time? I assume casual dress." I ignored my inner voice, which was screaming, Just say no.

"If you'd feel more comfortable hiring someone to come along, we're more than happy to cover the cost."

Who? But I didn't ask. I wondered if I could get any takers for a birthday funeral. Maybe if I suggested they gun up. "No need to worry; I'm an accurate shot." I heard him suck in his breath and added, "I don't usually shoot to kill."

A nervous laugh erupted, and Raul got off the phone with, "I'll text the info."

I stared at the phone, shaking my head. "I forgot to ask if I should bring a gift." I laughed, realizing I was talking to myself and waiting for some kind of answer. I scrolled through the contacts in my phone, and most ended up in the "best not take a chance" column. I'd call Mother, but this was hair salon day. I sent my brother a text: I'm calling. Don't tell Creole.

"What are you up to?" Brad asked in a quiet tone when he answered.

"Time to pony up on one of the multitudes of favors you owe me."

Brad groaned.

"I need Creole to come home, but he'd want to know why before he came, and I can't tell him. Of course, I'll be rolling you under the bus later over it."

"Do I get a clue?" Brad didn't balk at setting up his friend and business partner.

"Nooo... You'd let the cat out. If Creole gets a whiff, he won't come home."

"Must be a good one." Brad laughed. "You're on. With the condition that I get to hear the details and be the one to spread it around the family."

"There's something a bit off about a family that enjoys narking on one another." Family dinners were the favorite venue for these activities.

"Don't answer your phone or, better yet, turn it off. It's very probable that he'll be calling in a few to find out what's up."

"You're my favorite brother. To hell with the other one."

We hung up.

True to Brad's prediction, my phone started ringing before I'd made it down the hall. I'd left it on the counter so I wouldn't feel bad about not answering, knowing it would increase Creole's urgency to get home. I hustled—showering and changing into a sleeveless black dress with a fitted top and flared skirt to cover my Glock. I chose some low heels. If I needed to run, I'd have to kick them off, since I hadn't perfected running in heels.

"Madison," Creole bellowed, slamming the front door.

I hustled down the hall.

Creole swept his eyes over me from head to toe and whistled. "What are you up to? Brad said the contractor next door was giving you a problem. Talked to the man, and he didn't know what I was talking about. Now Brad's not answering his phone."

I took his hand and pulled him down the hall to the bedroom. He eyed the black suit pants and dress shirt on the bed but didn't say anything. I pushed him down and stood in front of him.

"I need you on a job. And I knew if you got the details ahead of time, you wouldn't bother with an excuse, you'd laugh me off. So… not having a backup plan, I decided to morph into Fab and use my brother to get you to come home." I knew he was waiting for the punchline, clearly not believing me. I told him about the call from Raul. "You know you don't like me doing a job by myself."

He shook his head in disgust and grouched, "Did you enjoy your con job?"

"Kind of." I nodded. "Being all sneaky perked me up after the call from Raul."

I tried not to squirm under his hard stare. He

kicked off his shoes and stormed into the bathroom. Surprisingly, the door closed so quietly, I barely heard the click.

I slipped out to the kitchen. Although he hadn't said it, I knew from his actions that he'd be accompanying me. I'd owe him big.

Ten minutes later, Creole came out dressed in what I'd laid out, accessorized with a shoulder holster. He extended his hand.

I slid off the stool and went to his side. "You're going to need a jacket."

"No, I'm not. These funeral birthday well-wishers are going to know that they can get their asses shot off if they start any trouble."

I grinned up at him. "You're so sexy."

"You'll be receiving a list of my demands later, and everyone better be met with no whining."

"Yes, sir." I saluted.

Chapter Twenty-One

Creole swept me off my feet and slid me onto the seat of his pickup. He quizzed me on the drive to the funeral home about how these inane jobs usually went down. "Why didn't you just say no? As hard as it is for you, you know you could have used the lack of notice as an excuse."

"Because... neither Fab nor I ever say no. They hid Fab when she was on the lam from the cops. Then stepped up and hid both of us when we were hiding from criminals."

"Did they put you up in one of the viewing rooms?" Creole screwed up his nose.

I squirmed at that visual. "They have a really nice apartment upstairs that they keep for guests. They're great hosts."

"Let's not vacation there." He pulled into the driveway of Tropical Slumber Funeral Home, which had morphed from a drive-thru hot dog stand into a full-service operation for all your weird funeral needs, and then some. If you couldn't come up with a bit of outrageousness on your own, they'd built a museum on the opposite side of the parking lot, showing vignettes of all the services they offered.

He helped me out of the truck, enveloped my hand in his, and led me over to the red carpet that ran straight to the front door. The hearse was sitting next to it, shined up and on display. "How do they keep it clean? Tire-mark free?"

"I asked once and forgot the answer." I didn't want to admit that I was only half-listening. "Promise me, babes—" I tugged on his hand. "—that you're going to be nice and not scare anyone, even though you were hornswoggled?"

"We'll just have to wait and see." Creole winked.

The front door opened, and Raul filled the doorway with his bodybuilder physique, decked out in basic black, dark hair slicked back. Dickie, the pale beanpole, stood behind him, similarly decked out. They both looked surprised to see Creole, but their greetings were friendly.

"The birthday girl is due to arrive any minute." Raul motioned us inside.

Creole checked out the entry and said, "About that… you and I need to have a few words." He crossed to the main room, giving it a once-over, and the two men stood in the doorway.

I bypassed my usual plastic-slip-covered chair by the door, moving closer to Creole so I could eavesdrop and also talk to Dickie. "How are you holding up?" I asked the man who dressed the dead. Raul handled the business end. "I know you're not fond of debuting a new trick."

"There wasn't anything for me to do, since no

one's actually dead. I try to be supportive when Raul wants to try something new. When the woman called and pitched her idea, I thought it was weird but kept my misgivings to myself. I've got my fingers crossed." Dickie held up two long, reed-thin digits and wiggled them around. "They're also crossed that you won't have to shoot anyone." He shot me a smile.

I assumed that was his attempt at humor and nodded. I didn't ask if he was happy not to be holed up in his workspace; he'd told me once it was an art to get the dead looking just right, and he loved his job.

"Where's Fab?" Dickie asked. "Raul was worried when her phone went to voicemail, since she always answers."

"Didier took her away for a couple of days of alone time," I confided.

Creole was done grilling Raul, shooting one question after another at the man until he looked a bit worn. Raul gave him a tour of the room, opened the door to the patio, and explained the setup.

Dickie had propped the front doors open, giving us a clear view of the comings and goings in the parking lot, and Creole sidled up to me as a white limo rolled up. We stood at the back of the entry area.

The driver got out and swept around to the other side, opening the door. A fairy princess in shades of blue and yards of glitter tulle stepped out. The band of flowers across the bodice matched the ones in her hair, and there was a wand in her hand.

Raul and Dickie greeted her.

"Birthday girl's got flair." I took my phone out of my pocket, snapping a couple of pics and frowning that I hadn't gotten closer.

"It's time for you to shine. Show me the tricks. Where to sit. Best place not to get shot." Creole grabbed my hand. "Knowing you, you have a favorite place to take in the action."

I nudged him toward the main room, pointing to the back row, which was the best place for a quick getaway without getting tangled up in the guests. "Since I'm lead on this job, you're backup—"

"Nice try." He shoved me into a chair, dropped down next to me, and put his arm around me, anchoring me to his side. "When did sedate, quiet funerals go out of style?"

"That's old school." I shook my finger at him. "No eye-rolling."

"I'm going to have a few words with the birthday girl." Creole stood. "If you make a run for it, I'll be hot on your trail."

My cheeks turned pink, and I tugged on his hand. "Please don't scare her."

"Don't worry, sweetums." He patted my cheek. "I'm going to be on my best behavior. At least, to start with." He was clearly amused with himself, stepping aside when the Princess entered the room.

Raul made the introductions and motioned for the two of them to follow him up to the front. The curtain behind the podium had been opened, and the sun glistened off the green grass. The three disappeared behind a large screen that had been rolled out. I could hear voices but had no clue what they were talking about.

The roar of an engine caught my attention. I leaned sideways, looking out the front as the bus pulled up to the door, another limo behind it, and both vehicles filled to the maximum. The doors opened on the bus, and I lost count as people trooped down the steps and clustered into groups. All eyes were on the exterior of the funeral home, and most weren't happy when they realized where they were.

Several people spoke at once, asking what was going on. Dickie, who'd gone outside upon their arrival, answered evasively.

Creole reappeared and stood guard at the entrance to the main room, staring grimly as the guests filed by, most giving a double-take at his weapon.

I snuck a few photos while no one was paying a bit of attention to me. I couldn't wait to send them to Fab.

A blonde in a low-cut skintight dress slowed in font of Creole and ran her finger down his chest. He pushed it away. I squinted at him and lifted my skirt, a reminder I also had a weapon.

He smirked. A brunette stopped, fished through her purse, and handed him a card with a wink, then continued up the aisle to sit with her friends.

Creole waited until everyone was seated, then closed the door and moved to the podium, tapping on the microphone. "Welcome," he said in a stern tone that had more than a few heads snapping up. Several women ogled him appreciatively. "The owners of this establishment want you all to enjoy today's festivities, but know that if a single one of you gets out of hand—arguments, fights—you run the risk of being shot." That garnered a few gasps. "A bullet to your backside can kill you, but only after you suffer immense pain. Any questions?"

Total silence.

"Thank you for listening and enjoy yourself." Creole walked back down the aisle to a ripple of voices all around him.

"Well done," I whispered as he sat down next to me. "In their moment of confused bereavement, you scared the devil out of them."

Creole grinned and pulled me close.

"What's the birthday girl going to say about you being a party pooper, laying down the law to the guests?" I asked.

"Princess loved the idea, and so did Raul. She wanted me to pour it on like they were naughty boys and girls," he growled in my ear.

I laughed into his shoulder. "You did a good job."

A pop song that I didn't recognize came through the speakers, signaling the start of the festivities. If I'd bet on Pop Goes the Weasel, I'd have lost. The drape rolled back, and a coffin was rolled out. The guests reacted with exclamations of shock. "Oh no. What happened? But I thought…"

I shuddered at the thought of going for a ride inside a coffin… with the lid down. Open or closed, no thanks.

A thirty-something man in a black suit and photo collage tie rose from the front row and strolled up to the mic. "Welcome everyone. Just a reminder: Let's not give killjoy a reason to shoot any of us." He glared Creole's way but didn't make eye contact. He then motioned to two young women, who stepped in from the patio, trays of champagne in their hands, and handed out glasses to the guests. He held his in the air. "Let the party begin." A jazzed-up rendition of Happy Birthday filled the room. Most looked around in confusion. The lid of the coffin opened, and the Princess sat up and waved to her guests. With a few exceptions, they gasped.

The man at the microphone strode over and scooped her out, setting her on her feet, and she took a bow. He turned to the audience and started clapping, and everyone joined in. Then he grabbed his glass, made another toast, and once everyone emptied their glasses, led them in a rendition of Happy Birthday.

The two servers raced around the room, refilling the glasses. One by one, the guests filed up to the microphone to wish the birthday girl the best day ever.

Creole whipped out his phone and leaned over, whispering, "I'm going to start making my list, because it's going to be a long one."

I batted his phone down. "So mean."

"I worked a side deal with Raul that he's going to share with Dickie. Don't want anyone claiming ignorance. Should I ever need a place to lie low, it's agreed I can come knockin'. I told him you talked up the accommodations, and once he got over the shock that I knew they'd hid you two, he agreed. Also let him know that for my final shindig, I want a tricked-out funeral—Cadillac version."

"Stop," I admonished. "You're not dying anytime, ever."

"The nice part about today's party is that we'll be here max two hours. Princess confided that they had another shindig to attend."

Creole and I sat in the back and watched the festivities unfold, listening to all the toasts and well-wishes. Creole got more than a few furtive glances from the guests, mostly the women. One guy stared from across the room in a challenging way, and Creole shot him a demented smile and put his hand on the butt of his revolver. The guy snapped his head in the other direction and never looked back.

Once the well-wishes wound down, Princess and her suited friend moved the party outside to the open bar and buffet.

Creole checked his watch. "Another half-hour and the limo and bus will pull to the end of the red carpet. Princess wants to make her departure memorable and have her subjects follow her on foot. Then off they'll go to the next venue, and we're out of here."

"Do you have plans for later?" I asked.

"You bet I do. You're looking hot, so I'm taking you to your favorite seafood joint for dinner."

"I should be taking you. I'm in awe at how you handled this soiree and laid down the law so nothing got out of hand. Which, by the way, is a first."

Chapter Twenty-Two

The lovebirds were back and indulging in a late morning.

I was hiding from Creole out by the pool, under an umbrella, my feet kicked up in a double chaise. The Chief was burning up his phone about some issue regarding his lease that Creole had failed to clarify. His idea of a perfect plan was to shove it off on me. No thanks. I reminded him that he had an office manager, and he griped that she was "new."

"But qualified." He ignored me.

Eventually, Creole tracked me down, which I figured he would. He'd printed up a list of demands/favors, depending on your point of view, that he set on the cover of my laptop. Before I could peruse it, he laid a big kiss on me and left. "Have a nice day," or some such, floated back. My powers of deduction from the male laughter that followed indicated that he and Didier were beating it out the door together.

Item number one: deal with the Chief. To that end, I picked up my phone, and when Lark answered, I asked, "Do you know how to play hard-ass?"

Lark giggled. "You betcha. Just when I got my bow and arrows hung on the wall." After a pause, she said, "I can improvise."

I didn't ask if the guys knew about her "artwork." Let it be a surprise. "Find out what's chewing on the Chief's rear and get it taken care of. And do not take any guff."

"I'll lie in wait and follow him into the elevator for a chat."

"Sounds good." I hung up, smiling, wondering if the security camera would pick up that bit of fun.

Number two: Rent out the third floor of the warehouse. He'd mentioned in an irky tone that it was taking longer than he expected, and I said, "I'm happy to shovel it back on you." He changed the subject.

Numbers three through ten were listed as "to be determined." I don't think so. I didn't agree to ten anything. My fault. I knew better than to not specify the number of favors up front.

Fab's phone rang from behind me, announcing her arrival. She answered with her patient tone, which she only trotted out for a client.

My phone rang, Tank's face popping up. "Got an update for you," he said when I answered.

"Can't wait." The lawyer never wasted our time with good news.

"Tessa handled herself like a trooper when questioned by the cops," Tank related, clearly pleased. "She was able to give decent enough directions to Colton's place—first turn-in after the alligator sign. When the cops got out there, he'd packed up and left. In a hurry—whatever he didn't want, he left on the floor. Unfortunately, there weren't any neighbors to question."

"Were they able to get anything useful?"

"Fingerprints were lifted from several places. They have yet to be identified, but I'm hoping that in addition to his, they find Tessa's and Kathryn's."

I wanted this to be over and his behind in the pokey. "That means Colton is in the wind. We all need to keep an eye out."

"Always a good idea to be on the lookout. Colton didn't waste any time hitting the road. And unless he's stupid, arrogant, or both, he won't be hanging around. The property had cameras everywhere, and if he's able to remotely access them, he knows the cops are onto him."

"I'm hoping that they stay on the case and it doesn't get pushed to the bottom of the stack," I said.

"If we could find Tessa's mother, she might have information that could be useful."

"Unlike Colton, Karla doesn't have the resources to go very far," I said in exasperation. "She's also got a young boy slowing her down, if it's her plan to skip." I told him I'd checked her usual haunts and didn't spot the two.

"Tessa told the cops all the places they'd

panhandled. Heard back already that they checked them, and nothing. Although they said they wouldn't give up."

"Fab just deigned to grace us with her presence." I chuckled at her frown as she sat down across from me. "I'm putting you on speaker."

Tank hurriedly caught Fab up on what we'd talked about. "If you find the woman, don't approach her, and call me before you call the cops. That way, Social Services can be on the scene, and the boy won't be carted off to foster care."

"Thank you for all you've done and continue to do," I said.

"The Bijous are a great couple, and I like them a lot. The kids deserve a break."

"We'll keep in touch." After the usual pleasantries, we hung up.

"You've got that scowl on your face that suggests whatever you're about to tell me, I won't like," I said to Fab.

"Birth Certificate Mom is calling, even though she's got everything she needs. Makes me wonder why she's determined to dig up trouble."

"If you don't give her what she wants, she'll probably hire someone else." I moved my legs so Jazz could jump up.

Snow had claimed part of Fab's chaise before she sat down.

"Xander located the surrogate, Tanya Coleman. She's late twenties, single, and doesn't have any children of her own. I'm going to talk to her and get back to my client, and that's the best I can do for the woman."

I knew what Fab was about to ask and offered instead. "I'd love to go along." I smiled sweetly. Fab nodded, only slightly amused. "I'll go change my clothes and gun up."

"How am I going to question this woman without raising more questions?"

"You're going to take a deep breath." I demonstrated. "This is not one of those situations that you're not going to be able to pre-plan. Casually check her out and friend her up. You might not have to say much of anything. Just get a feel for her and, with what you already know, pass along enough info for the client to call it a day. Hopefully, she'll give it up and focus on her kids."

"Here's something I won't be passing along to my client. Turns out that that partner in her husband's firm who was investigated for baby-selling before is back under investigation."

"You need to be firm with your client and tell her case closed. If the law firm's doing anything illegal, and you go digging around and they find out… who knows what lengths they'll go to shut you up," I warned her, hoping she was listening.

"I just got out of trouble with Didier. He told me if I scare him by sneaking out again, he'll kill me and then leave me." Fab grimaced. "He said if I need excitement, he'll take care of it."

"You've got the second-best husband."

Fab didn't need to say anything; her look of "you've lost your mind" said it all. "Go get dressed."

On the way back to the bedroom, my phone rang, and it was Lark.

"Mr. Harder wants to speak to Creole. I told him I could handle any issues, but he wasn't having it," Lark said in an annoyed tone.

"No one calls him that; he still goes by the Chief."

"Not for me. When I called him that, I got a glare. I stopped short of telling him to stuff it. Mac said I don't have to take any business off anyone, but I figured I should wait until I've been around a while before telling him to get over himself."

"I'll talk to him." I sighed. "Mac's right; you don't. I'll make it clear to him and anyone else that didn't get the message that you're the one that will be dealing with any issues."

Not in the mood to talk, I texted the Chief. Appointment out of town. That was a lie, but he didn't know that. How about tomorrow?

My phone rang again. I glanced at the screen and groaned. The Chief. I picked up. "I hear you're being a pain in the backside to the new office manager. She better not quit."

The Chief snorted. "I'm dealing directly with Creole."

"Except it's been shuffled to my desk. Taking into consideration our special relationship, I hoped to get whatever ails you taken care in a timely fashion."

There was total silence. I looked at my screen. Still connected.

"So tomorrow then?" I said.

He grunted. "What's happening on my case? I tried calling Fab, but no answer."

"She just got back to town. I'll have her call you."

"I'll be in the office tomorrow, aside from a lunch appointment."

"See you then." I hung up before he could ask more questions and threw the phone on the bed, along with my laptop.

I went to the closet and put on a full skirt and t-shirt top. I strapped my Glock to my thigh and slipped into a pair of tennis shoes. Checking myself in the mirror, I made a face; the shoe choice wasn't totally ugly, but not cute. But I had to be prepared for "run for your life." I shoved everything I thought I might need into my briefcase and grabbed my purse.

Fab had changed and met me in the kitchen, coming from her side of the house.

"The Chief wants an update on the fire in his previous office," I told her. "I thought that once you checked out the crime scene, your involvement ended."

"No one wants to hear that you don't have an answer for them. I'm not the only one without a lead; the cops don't have any either. He should be burning up their phones instead." Fab whooshed out a breath of annoyance. "I'll call him later."

"Now would be better, so he doesn't call me and start in about wanting answers I don't have either." My phone rang for the umpteenth time. "I'm turning off my phone."

"Then people will call me, and I'll just hang up."

I looked at the screen before answering. "Hi, Blanche. Hope everything's all right."

"We invited Xander for breakfast. It was nice to have a new face at the table. He's such a smart young man. Tessa hung on his every word when he talked about computers; she's eager to learn, and he was patient with her. Anton and I were a bit lost." She laughed.

I'd forgotten I'd called Xander and hired him to set up a website and social media profile for Sanctuary Woods—Facebook, Instagram, and an easy way for people to donate. I told him to let me know when it was up and running, and I'd make a large anonymous donation to get things started. They needed an infusion of cash, and it needed to keep coming so more dogs could be rescued.

"When Tessa's ready, I've got someone that

can tutor her and her brother and get them up to speed so they can go to school next term," I said.

"That would be great. Tessa will be happy to hear that. And we'll all be happy when Timothy's found." Blanche's voice was heavy with sadness. "Another reason for calling is that Tessa has another place you might look for her mom. It would go a long way to assuage her guilty feelings if she had a part in finding her brother. I explained to her that Karla's an adult and responsible for her criminal decisions and that she had plenty of other options but turned her nose up at everyone in favor of the bottle, but I don't think she believed me." Blanche called for Tessa and handed her the phone. "It's Madison," I heard Blanche tell her.

"Hi," she said in a softer tone than usual.

"We're still on the lookout for your brother," I said. "Your mom isn't at any of her usual places, but don't worry about us giving up—that won't happen. I hear that you might have a new location for me to check."

"You know who might know..." Tessa lowered her voice. "Sam, the owner of the Quick Mart... She did stuff with him when we were short on money. I'm not sure if he'd help, since he probably doesn't want anyone to know how well he knows her. I know because I saw them once."

Fab looked at me, and we both grimaced.

"If this Sam person knows anything, I'll find

out," I assured her. "I'm positive that we're going to find Timothy soon and get the two of you reunited. In the meantime, soak up all the love from your grandmother."

"I'll try."

"I'll keep in touch."

Chapter Twenty-Three

Fab whipped into the driveway of the Quik Mart. "Do you want me to come in with you?"

"You call and give the husbands an update; that will keep us out of trouble for the next hour or so." I got out and stuck my head back inside. "Don't frame it as though I'm strong-arming the owner of a convenience store." I went inside and up to the cashier. "I'd like to speak to Sam."

She picked up the phone, and I couldn't hear what she said, but a door behind the counter with a small one-way window opened and a short, dark-haired, rotund man came out and around the counter.

I skipped introductions, deciding in that moment to go for direct. "I'm looking for Karla Hunter and hoped you had a forwarding."

The mention of her name zapped the friendly expression off his face, and he turned belligerent. "I don't know who you're talking about." He took a step back and started to turn.

I had to be quick before he ensconced himself back in his office. "Skinny drunk woman who panhandled with her two kids in front of your store for months on end."

He retreated another step. "Her." He nodded. "She left a couple of days ago, and I haven't seen her since."

"Too bad you don't know anything. I thought, since you were trading alcohol for sex, that you might have info for me."

His head whipped around. "You need to keep your voice down," he hissed and motioned for me to follow him outside.

"Since you can't be helpful, I'll be forced to give your name to the cops. Maybe you'll remember when questioned by them."

He stepped to the side and lowered his voice. "If I knew something—"

"This about locating a small child."

His eyes skittered around, and he pasted on a phony smile and waved to a couple of customers entering the store.

"If you were forthcoming, there wouldn't be any need to call the cops or say a word about you knowing the woman. In fact, no need to mention your name at all. I don't imagine that it would be good for business to have the cops crawling all over this place." Sam and I both knew he'd be the talk of the town if his extracurricular activities were to become public. It was unlikely the extra attention would be good for his bottom line.

"Karla confided that her abusive ex was back in town, threatening her, and asked for help. Shifty fellow showed up here a couple of times. I thought he was young for her, but what do I know? After his last visit, she was visibly upset." Sam shifted from one foot to another. "I... uh... had a friend give Karla and the kid a ride to my store in Homestead." He rattled off the intersecting streets. "There's a storage room around the back. I told Karla that she and the kid could stay until she found something else."

Aren't you a swell guy? "Don't tip off Karla, or I'll share what I know." I didn't think he'd done anything illegal, but he didn't seem to know either. I glanced over my shoulder, then cut around the side of the building and across the street into the neighborhood.

A minute later, Fab rolled up and stopped the SUV alongside me.

"Your exit plan was a good one," Fab said as I climbed in. "Sam watched until you disappeared out of sight. I waited until he went back inside before leaving."

"It was a split-second decision. I was about to walk back to the Hummer and changed course mid-step. I didn't want him giving a description of my ride to anyone. It's bad enough that we're constantly on alert. Why invite trouble?" I told Fab about the conversation with Sam and kept what I thought of the man to myself, though I'm certain she guessed.

"Send Tank a message that we're on our way to check out this new location. Tell him to be ready if we call." Fab picked my phone out of the cup holder and handed it to me. "Would be interesting to know if Karla was eager to skip town because she knows the cops are hot on Colton's trail or if she's afraid of him, since Tessa got away."

"Karla has to know that she's also in felony hot water if Tessa told her story to the cops." I sent the message and added that we'd call either way. "If Sam tips off Karla, he'll find out that I'm not kidding about outing his relationship with her."

Fab turned onto Highway One, where the traffic was light in both directions. "I wouldn't worry about that. He's not going to want to mix it up with the cops, not with kids involved. As for Karla, she's short on options, and if I were Sam, I'd want her gone."

"The sooner we find Timothy, the better."

"So you know, I had a conference call with the guys and told them we'd be robbing convenience stores today and they were to have dinner ready when we got home."

I laughed and picked up my phone. "I haven't gotten a call or text, so Creole must be okay with the plan… or he knows you're a good storyteller."

"First there was a long, rude silence and then laughter. I think it was Brad who broke the mood. Then I gave them a brief rundown of what we were really doing."

It was a beautiful sunny day, which made me wish I was still at home, where I could run down the sandy strip and drag a floating chair into the water.

Fab turned off the highway and drove like she knew right where she was going. "This place shouldn't be hard to find." A block later, she pulled into another Quik Mart.

"There's Karla." I pointed to the side of the building, where the woman leaned up against the wall, Timothy sitting next to her, watching people pump gas.

"We'll circle the store and find a place to park."

"I say we hang back and keep an eye on her every move. I'm not certain whether she'd recognize my SUV and make a run for it." That was a drama I didn't want to watch unfold.

Fab pulled around the back, into the parking lot of a neighboring strip mall, and found a place where we could watch the two. She pulled out her phone and called Tank. The conversation was short. "Tank already contacted his social worker friend, and they're headed this way now. Said she'd call the cops."

"I hope Timothy's not scared, being carted off by strangers."

"I don't imagine that it's ever easy, but surely she knows what she's doing and can calm his fears." Fab reached over the seat and grabbed a duffel bag off the floor, retrieving the binoculars.

We didn't have long to wait. Fab pointed out Tank's SUV as he pulled into the parking lot. The man must have had a lead foot, like Fab, as he showed quicker than I thought possible. He parked off to the side. No one got out of the car.

Five minutes later, two cop cars rolled up, parked, and officers got out of both. The social worker got out and walked over to them, and they had a short chat. While the cops arrested Karla, who went without a glance back to see what happened to her son, the social worker knelt in front of Timothy and talked to him. He nodded a couple of times, and she led him over to Tank's SUV. The two got in the back seat.

"I'm happy that was uneventful as arrests go; only one person took notice of what was going down," I said.

"Or the rest had outstanding warrants and didn't want to attract attention," Fab said with a smirk.

I put my feet up on the dashboard, knowing it was a surefire way to irk Fab. "I need a beach break. Toes in the sand."

Chapter Twenty-Four

Before Fab could speed down the Overseas to her next stop, I demanded a double shot of caffeine. After a quick run through the drive-thru, she raced south and, due to light traffic, whipped down the highway and turned off in Marathon.

"While we're down here, I'm stopping at the Chief's old office and taking a couple of pics. I'll forward them, telling him I hung out for hours. My hope is that he'll stop burning up my phone."

It amazed me that the Chief kept hiring her for jobs and she kept accepting. It didn't seem that long ago that he'd have liked to put both of us in jail. Her more than me. "Try the real estate office again. Hit up the broker with all your questions; it's possible she's got an update or someone else in her office will have information."

"Her name?" Fab snapped her fingers.

"If I worked for you, I'd quit."

Fab laughed.

"It was on the sign." We were both terrible at remembering names, and in my defense, I wasn't making an effort. "Report back that you hit up the other businesses in the area and call it a day.

Remind the Chief, as he's done to us in the past, to 'let the cops handle it.'"

Fab pulled up in front of the burned building and parked. Someone had been called out to nail plywood over the windows.

"Well, this has been fun." I got the behave stare, which from her only made me smile.

Fab got out and snapped a couple of pics—proof she'd actually been here—then started towards the real estate office.

I jumped out and yelled, "Slow down; I'm not missing out on the fun." I hustled to catch up.

"Robbie Lee is the broker's name." Fab pointed to the sign.

"I'm going to hang by the door and watch you work your magic."

Fab opened the door and waved her hand. "After you."

"Like I don't know that trick." I took a step back. "No way am I letting you stand behind me and make me the frontwoman." I watched in amusement as she huffed, then marched up to the reception desk. The two women there, who'd been talking, were now staring.

"Robbie Lee." The forty-something handed Fab a business card. "How can I help you?"

"I'm looking for the security business that used to be next door," Fab said. "Do you happen to know where they relocated to?"

"No one's been around since it burned down." Robbie shook her head sympathetically.

"I hired the… Mr. Harder to upgrade my security system. I guess I'll just have to wait until he contacts me. He wasn't hurt or anything?" Fab's tone injected an appropriate amount of concern.

"It burned down in the middle of the night, and luckily, there was no one in the building at the time," Robbie assured her.

Fab's phone rang, and she sent the call to voicemail. "Thank you." She waved.

Ready for a quick exit, I had the door open. As soon as we got outside, I said, "I don't remember everyone's name, but faces… That wasn't the woman who bounded over to the Chief's business that day and introduced herself as Robbie Lee."

"Not even close. The other one was younger by a few years… and twitchy."

"Should we mention to Robbie that someone's impersonating her?" I asked.

"Most people would immediately call the cops. I don't want to waste time being questioned about a brief meeting that was unremarkable."

"Put that in your report to the Chiefster. Beef it up. You know… you spent hours and this is what you got." I could tell that Fab was mulling over my suggestion. "I can't remember if I asked him if he was banging any crazy broads."

"Madison Westin." Fab's hands flew to her hips. "I'm going to tell on you… to… someone.

And if you do ask, make sure I'm standing right there."

We both laughed.

"I hate to finger an innocent woman, but let's face it, she's not acting like one. Impersonation and all. I've been your tagalong long enough to know that. We'll compare notes and run the description by the Chief—see if he has a lightbulb moment." I jumped in the SUV and waited while Fab took one last walk around the building.

"I'm going to tell the Chief that some cases don't get solved and to get over it," Fab said as she got behind the wheel.

"Be sure that you word it just like that."

Fab entered another address into the GPS and pulled out of the parking lot.

"Now what? Off to talk to the surrogate for your stalker client, Jennifer Charles?" I asked. "I understand her wanting the birth certificates. She has them. Hunting down the baby mama is ridiculous. And a red flag."

"I was already irritated when she called and told her she got what she wanted and now she needed to let it go. Also told her that if anything happened to the surrogate, I'd turn information about her and the husband's law firm over to the cops." Fab blew out an irritated breath.

"What did she say?"

"I was prepared for an argument, but to my surprise, she backed down. Said that I was right and thanked me for my services. She couldn't get off the phone fast enough."

"I hope you got paid."

"I get paid up front. Learned that lesson early on."

I grimaced, knowing that if that weren't her policy, we'd be chasing deadbeats. "You want my opinion?"

"No." Fab pulled up across from an all-white four-unit apartment building and parked at the curb. "I'm here to make sure that Jennifer Charles won't be able to track down or contact this woman on her own."

I wondered how she planned to accomplish that but didn't ask.

Fab stared out the window. "The blonde hefting boxes into the back of the Jeep is the one I'm looking for—Tanya Coleman. She matches the picture Xander sent."

"She's also pregnant." I stared over her shoulder. "She shouldn't be lugging boxes. Let's go be friendly and offer our help, and you can sneak in any questions you feel compelled to ask. And then what?"

Fab ignored me and crossed the street. I was right behind her. She introduced herself to the girl, surprisingly not using a made-up name, then stepped in front of Tanya and lifted the boxes off the handcart. After a little rearrangement by Fab and I, we got them in the Jeep.

"Do you have any more?" Fab asked.

Tanya nodded. "But I can't—"

"Nonsense, lead the way." Fab waved me back and followed her into one of the bottom units.

It surprised me when she didn't come right back out. I took up a post at the rear of the Hummer, leaning against the bumper. If I'd had on a watch, I'd be tapping the face, as though that would make Fab hurry. Finally, the two came out of the apartment, talking like old friends. Fab had two boxes in her arms, which she loaded in the back of the Jeep, then motioned me over.

"Congratulations on the baby." The girl smiled at me, rubbing her stomach.

I pasted on a lame smile and mimicked her, rubbing my own stomach. It would be fitting to hear screech marks after Fab's bold trick. "Thank you," I mumbled.

"I confided to Tanya that you were thinking about giving your baby up for adoption." Fab smiled conspiratorially. "Lucky I was able to get her name from a friend of mine who works at the law firm."

"We sign confidentiality agreements and aren't supposed to utter a word about the program. To anyone," Tanya shared, worry in her tone. "Fab wanted me to tell you my experience, but I don't want my name ever mentioned."

Tanya's shy smile at Fab made me feel wretched. "Understood. I'm just feeling a little nervous. It's such a big decision."

"Have you passed your physical and completed all the testing they require?" Tanya asked. I shook my head. "They have strict standards, wanting only the healthiest girls for their elite program. Since you're already pregnant, if both of you are healthy, they can place your baby in a good home. The fee you get won't be as high, though."

"You've done this before, and it's all legit?" I asked, covering my shock at the nonchalant way Tanya talked about her baby.

"I don't understand all the legalities, but my lawyer has assured me that it's all on the up and up." Tanya smiled. "My plan is to have at least three more babies, take the money, and move to California, which has always been my dream."

"They treat you well?" I tilted my head at Fab, conveying, Help.

"Like a queen. The reason I'm moving is because I'm far enough along that I qualify to move into the mansion at the beach. I'll be waited on hand and foot until the little one arrives." Tanya patted her stomach.

"You've put my fears to rest. No worries about me saying anything," I put my finger across my lips.

"Are you sure you have everything?" Fab asked Tanya, and when she nodded, Fab closed up the back of the Jeep.

"I just need to grab my purse." Tanya turned to me. "If we see each other again, we'll pretend it's our first time."

"Absolutely." I waved.

Fab hooked her arm in mine, and we walked back to the car.

Once we were both inside with the doors closed, Fab said, "If you haven't guessed already, Tanya is a professional surrogate. Apparently, it's a lucrative business." She held out her cell phone and showed me a picture of Tanya's lawyer's business card. "If you pass the extensive medical testing, you get a bonus."

"It's surprising that it's all legal."

"The adoption agency, Tanya's lawyer, and Mrs. Charles's husband all work out of the same office. How's that for cozy?"

"I'm happy that this case of yours is over."

"Stopping by was a good idea. Now that I know Tanya's moved out, I'm going to tell Jennifer Charles that she's moved out of state. I gave Tanya tips on how to keep her whereabouts to herself unless she wants to share. Not wanting to scare her, I told her that in light of her profession, a low profile would be safer and was happy when she agreed."

"The only people I want showing up at my house are the ones I invite."

"Agreed."

Chapter Twenty-Five

"Next stop: Boardwalk offices," I said and ignored the face Fab made. "We've both got business with the Chief, and afterwards, we can take the guys to lunch."

"Not your worst idea."

"When you turn off the highway, drive slow so I can look for 'for sale' signs."

"You're going to acquire so many properties that you'll always have one excuse or another for not backing me up on my cases."

"I don't know why we can't partner up and own the entire block." When I didn't get a response, I asked, "If you weren't doing investigations, then what?"

"First Didier and now you're asking me the same question, and I still don't have an answer." Fab appeared to be thinking about it. "Didier told me to think about it, that I might come up with something that excites me more."

"I imagine Creole and Didier tire of wondering whether we're going to get hurt on any given day."

Fab had raced up the Overseas and was now turning off to take the back road to the office.

I turned in my seat and stared out the window. Even if no one else agreed, I liked the idea of buying up all the old buildings that ran along this street and giving them a much-needed facelift.

Fab passed Spoon's Auto Body, and as usual, it was impossible to see that there was a thriving business behind the barbed-wire fencing. She slowed, going past the two warehouses that she owned, and all was quiet.

I kept my eyes out as we passed the first warehouse I'd bought and all was quiet. Reaching the building the Boardwalk offices were in, Fab pulled into the driveway at the far end and around to the back and parked facing the building, both of us taking inventory of the cars parked nearby and recognizing them all, except one—a ratty sedan.

I reached out, grabbing Fab's arm, and pointed at a female facedown on the pavement. Crawling to her knees, face turned away, she tried but couldn't make it to her feet. My attention snapped to a woman pushing a wheelchair, the Chief was in it, and slumped sideways.

"That's, uh… the phony real estate agent." Fab stared over the wheel. "What the heck is she up to?"

"I'm betting this has to do with the Chief's namesake? You know, his little friend," I said in answer to Fab's what the heck are you talking about now look.

Fab grimaced. "Stop. If he's given it a name and you tell me, I'll shoot you."

"Explain that one to Mother." I drew my Glock. "We've got to stop whatever her name is before she gets away with the Chief." The woman made a beeline for the sedan, jerking the wheelchair from side to side. It was surprising the Chief didn't tumble out.

"Let's hope he's still alive." Fab drew her Walther.

We got out and crossed the parking lot. The woman turned. She squealed as we bore down on her and drew her own weapon. "You're not stopping me now." She unleashed a high-pitched scream.

As we approached, I realized that the other woman, bent over and sucking in raspy breaths, was Lark. "Drop your gun. Now." I aimed at the woman. "Anyone dies here, it's going to be you."

The Chief's head rolled to the side, his eyelashes fluttered, and he rocked side to side, almost tipping over the chair. The woman grabbed the back of his shirt as the chair tipped precariously. She hauled off and smacked him a good one to the side of the head. "You and I both know that we're meant to be together, and now there's a baby," she gritted. Spit flew, landing on the back of his head.

"Baby?" Fab whispered.

"No… no… not true." The Chief switched to a back-and-forth motion.

Lark lurched to her feet, grasping her midsection. "Bitch kicked me in the stomach," she shrieked.

The woman turned, waving her gun at Lark. "You're the bitch. How dare you try to come between me and my baby's father?" she screeched.

The Chief moaned, "No," over and over. It wasn't clear if he was denying impending fatherhood or saying it was fine with him if we shot her.

"Stand back, and no one gets hurt," the woman demanded loudly, then rammed the chair into the side of the sedan, the Chief's head making contact with a loud thump that made me wince. Her hand shot out, and she jerked on the door. When it wouldn't open, it sent her into a frenzy, and she kicked the door panel several times.

Lark backed up to the building.

"Guess the bashed-in passenger door was a little more mangled than she realized." Fab inspected the twisted metal from where we stood.

The Chief jerked around in a frenzied motion.

Fab nudged me and nodded toward the Chief—both of his wrists had been tied to the armrests. Suddenly, one came loose, and the Chief used the momentum to rock for all he was worth.

She must have drugged him, or she couldn't

have gotten this far with him. And it must be pretty strong stuff, or he'd have upended that chair already. Good luck getting away in that state. I didn't see the woman giving up at this point.

"I love you," she screamed, wrapping her fingers in his hair and attempting to tug him back into an upright position. He yelled. She dropped his head and fisted the back of his shirt, stopping him mid-lunge. Her gun fell to the pavement, and she bent over to get it.

"Leave it," Fab roared, "or I'll shoot."

I knew Fab wouldn't risk shooting a woman that might be pregnant. If she was, then she must be early on, since she wasn't showing at all.

The woman jerked upright and glared. In an abrupt move, she spun the chair on a dime and made tracks down the driveway.

"What the..."

"I'll flip you to see which one of us chases her down." Fab flipped an imaginary coin in the air. "You're up."

"Then you get to call 911 and get the paramedics out here to check on Lark and the Chief." I put a bullet in the trunk of the only palm tree to grace the front of the property—if it died, I would sue the woman—at the same time, roaring, "Stop." That fell on deaf ears.

Lark groaned and clutched her middle. "I'm going to barf," she moaned.

I squeezed my eyes shut. Hearing it was bad

enough; I didn't want to witness it firsthand. Fab turned away, also fine with missing the action.

The office door flew open, and Creole filled the doorway, weapon in hand. "What the heck's going on?" he roared. From his vantage point, he was unable to see the crazy broad about to turn into the street, screeching at the Chief about happily ever after and doing her best to keep the rocking wheelchair upright.

Didier and Brad emerged behind him, both with weapons drawn.

I hurriedly told the trio what was going down. They gave a unanimous snort of disbelief.

"Cops and ambulance on the way," Fab yelled. "Hustle. She just jetted out into the road."

Heads craned.

"Didn't get a good look at the Chief, but something's wrong," she told the men.

I reholstered my weapon and broke into a run.

"Hold up," Creole shouted.

I knew he'd catch up, and he did, running up alongside me. "Do we get to shoot her?" he asked.

"Better not; she might be preggo."

Two cop cars squealed up the street, lights flashing, cutting off more questions, I was sure, starting with, "How do you know?" They hemmed in the woman taking her half out of the middle of the road. We skidded to a stop at the end of the driveway.

Not to be deterred, she made a hard right,

losing control of the chair and catapulting herself and the Chief down a ravine. Good thing it was weedy. The downside was it had a couple inches of water running through it and smelled. She stood, hands on knees, and sucked in a breath. "You don't understand; we're in love," she screeched at the top of her lungs. "We're fated."

The deputies had drawn their weapons. Whatever they said, she shook her head.

"We're getting married." Her ranting was hard to make out and getting weaker.

One cop approached her slowly, and she threw herself back into the sludgy water next to the Chief's chair, now tipped on its side. The smell must've gotten to her, as she jumped right back to her feet and climbed out of the ravine, crossing the bank to a grassy patch, where she beelined for the road and made a run down the middle of the street.

A car backing out of a driveway clipped her leg and sent her flying.

Fab and Didier joined us, and we watched as the cop ran to her, bent down, and gave her a cursory check. She attempted to fling her arms around his neck. He patiently pried her hands off and cuffed her.

The four of us stepped onto a grassy patch as an ambulance approached and slowed. Another cop arrived and jumped out, running over to have a short conversation with the driver, who continued down the street. They parked and hopped out, bags in hand, and ran into the street to attend the woman.

"Brad's with Lark. She hasn't gotten sick, so no cleanup," Fab said. "Lark made the mistake of asking Whack-job what was wrong with the Chief and where she was taking him. Whack-job responded with a kick to the stomach with the ugly boot the woman's sporting. It hurts like the devil, if you want to know, and Lark's annoyed that she got caught off guard."

"Anyone want to bet that Whack-job is an ex of the Chief's? Banging partner, perhaps?" I asked and got no takers. Creole and Didier smirked. Another ambulance pulled up, and the paramedics went to help the Chief.

It took some muscle, but the first set of paramedics managed to wrestle the kicking, screaming woman to her feet and onto a stretcher.

"Good thing we arrived when we did or Whack-job would've hauled the Chief out of here, and then good luck finding him," I said in disgust, watching as the woman continued to scream and flail as she was being strapped down.

The other paramedics finished untying the Chief and helped him to a sitting position on the bank. They loaded him on a stretcher, and he was put inside the second ambulance.

"Interesting that the Chief didn't mention the woman." Creole looked to me for verification.

"Not a word."

"I'm going to go check on him." Creole kissed me on the cheek, then ran to the ambulance and hopped in before the doors closed.

"I just made an executive decision. I'm calling the company that installed the fence at my other building and getting one installed here. I should've had it done already," I lamented to Fab. "Where did Didier go?"

"Back to check on Lark." She nodded at the receding bumper of the first ambulance. "I'm guessing there goes the Chief's arsonist. Another case I can close."

"In order for Whack-job to show up here, she had to have been stalking him. Let's hope she doesn't make bail and show back up." Another cop car rolled into the driveway. "What did you do, report this as a five-alarm crime?"

Fab shrugged.

Kevin Cory got out of his patrol car and surveyed the property before walking over to us. "Which one of you wants to go first?"

I started from when we arrived and didn't cut corners relaying the events.

Fab nodded in agreement.

"I don't know if Fab mentioned when she called in, but the man in the back of the ambulance that just left is the retired Chief of Police from Dade and plays golf with your boss."

Didier ran up. "Creole called. The Chief's vitals are stable. He's groggy. While hugging him, the woman jabbed a needle in his shoulder.

He didn't lose consciousness but said it rendered him useless in getting away. I'm going to drive over to the hospital and be there when Creole is ready to go home."

Kevin nodded, and the two men walked over to Brad.

"I'm going to go check on Lark." I rounded the building and found her sitting on a bench at the picnic table, feet up, arms around her knees.

Fab brushed her hair out of her face. "You doing okay? Need a ride to the hospital?"

"Or I can call a doctor to come check on you," I offered.

"Oh, heck no. I'm over wanting to puke." Color bloomed in Lark's cheeks. "Crazy broad blindsided me. I'm going to start carrying a piece."

"Make sure you have a carry permit," Kevin snapped. He had approached unnoticed in time to hear what she said. "If you don't already have one, good luck. They're hard to get."

Lark struggled to hold back what she wanted to unleash.

"Let me introduce you," I said to the two, who were glaring at one another. "Lark Pontana, our newest employee. And this is Deputy Kevin Cory. You'll see a lot of him, as often times he's the one who ends up responding to calls for one of our properties or another."

"I know you said you don't want to go to the hospital, but if you're still feeling queasy tomorrow, give your doctor a call," Kevin told her.

Lark shook her head vehemently. "It doesn't hurt as much as it did, so I'm not worried."

"Are you up to answering a few questions?" Kevin asked.

Lark nodded and launched into how she ended up in the middle of the drama. "My desk faces the window, so I saw the woman drive in, then heard the elevator. Figured it was a client of the Chief's." She gently rubbed her stomach. "Not long after, I heard a bunch of banging that sounded like it was coming from the elevator and went outside to check it out. As I came out the door, she was rolling the Chief out of the elevator. I thought he was dead and shrieked, then recovered and asked what happened. When I reached out to touch his cheek, she hauled off and kicked me."

"You ever see the woman before?" Kevin asked Lark.

"First time." Lark shivered. "Hopefully, the last."

"What about you two?" Kevin asked.

Fab told him about the Chief's old building going up in flames and how, when she went to check it out, the woman introduced herself as the real estate broker Robbie Lee, who owned the neighboring building. Also that we'd met the real Ms. Lee and knew this one was lying.

"I need to remind the Chief that the second

time the cops show, he's out," I said, to Kevin's amusement. "It's not in the fine print of the contract, so I'll have to hope that he's rattled enough over crazy chick's attempted kidnapping that I'll be able to get him to sign an addendum."

Kevin shook his head.

"Where did Brad go?" I asked.

"Heard the phone ringing off the hook," Lark said. "He knew I was fine, as I'd told him so several times. The guys were waiting on a call from one of our contractors."

Brad must have sensed we were talking about him because he appeared at the table. "You ready to go inside?" he asked Lark. She nodded. He held out his hand and helped her to her feet. "Come on in," he said to Kevin. "I'll give you the tour, and you can get something cold to drink."

Chapter Twenty-Six

A finger brushed down my spine. A hand swept the hair from my shoulder. Warm lips pressed against my own. I opened my eyes and stared into Creole's. "Very happy that you're not a prowler."

"That would spoil the mood."

"You got home late; the Chief okay?" I pressed my lips against his.

"The doc ran some tests and prescribed rest. The Chief wasn't staying in the hospital one minute longer than he had to. I dropped him at his house and told him to call if he needed anything."

"Is he looking forward to being a father?"

"You know what they say about sarcasm...?"

"That it's fun."

"Chief swears that if the woman—Raine Morris is her name—is really pregnant this time, he's not the father. It would be impossible, since they haven't had relations in months."

"This time?" I wrinkled my nose.

"Raine claimed to be pregnant once before. When he asked for a pregnancy test, she 'miscarried.'"

"Did you sit him down and give him the talk? You know, how the bloom of hot sex with crazy chicks fades quickly, and the reality is that they're more trouble than it's worth."

Creole laughed. "You're not far off. After their first romp, it didn't take long for Raine's 'issues' to show themselves. After some digging, he discovered that she'd received years of psychiatric therapy. He didn't give it any thought once they stopped seeing one another."

"That's because his other friend was hollering, 'she's so much fun.'"

Creole buried his face in my neck. "Please… don't… anything about his friend."

"Fun-sucker."

"Where were we? Anyway…" He gave me a stern headshake, to which I smiled. "Raine is in need of intensive mental health care, but her parents, who are stinking rich, have used their connections to get her problems swept aside. They have a history of convincing judges that they can help her at home."

"Hmm… let me guess." I tapped my cheek. "She's bailed out already. How long before she's back in the Cove?"

"Raine's psycho antics got her a stay in a psych ward until a judge decides otherwise. Long before she gets released, and hopefully it won't be anytime soon, I'll have made it clear to the Chief that she's not welcome back on the property."

It suddenly dawned on me how early it was; it was light outside, but the sun hadn't made an appearance. I realized that Creole had on sweats and a t-shirt—overdressed for sleep attire. "Isn't it a little early for you to be dressed and all perky?"

Creole rolled over, and his hand disappeared beside the bed, coming back with a box a little larger than ring-size, wrapped in ribbon and a bow.

I shook it, and it rattled ever so slightly. "It's not my birthday."

"You're stalling, babes." He kissed me again. "We've already blown through a fair amount of time, and we need to make a clean break before the other two wake up."

"Sneaking around under Fab's nose?" I shook my finger, which he nibbled on. "She'll be grouching you out. Now, if she catches you… she'll be ecstatic, and you'll never hear the end of it."

He tapped his wrist.

Ah, yes, hurry up. I slid the ribbon off the box, removed the lid… He couldn't miss my surprised look as I removed the key inside. I held it up to the light. "Clue?"

"No. Now, get up." Creole pulled me toward him and rolled the two of us to the end of the bed, setting me on the floor. "I picked out your wardrobe." He pointed to the chair. "You need to hustle."

I looped the black sweats and white t-shirt over my finger. "We're going all fancy and matchy?" Except he had on a Boardwalk tee and mine was plain. "Five minutes." I held up my fingers.

He snapped his fingers.

I was back out of the bathroom, looking halfway presentable, a full minute before time ran out. At least, my hair was smoothed down and not sticking on end.

Creole grabbed my hand and pulled me through the patio door and out past the pool.

"Now, do I get a clue?" I skidded to a stop and planted my feet.

Creole laid his finger across my lips. He crouched down and motioned for me to get on his back. No need to ask, as it was my favorite way to ride. He hustled us across the patio and down the few steps to the beach, then lowered me to the sand. I wiggled my toes. He hooked his arm around me, hugging me to his side, and we headed down the beach in the direction of our new house. The single-story on stilts towered over the semi-private beach. We took the stairs to the large wraparound deck, which had been transformed into an outdoor living space, complete with kitchen.

I'd worked up a design that would make the best use of the space. I'd showed Creole the preliminary plan, and he loved it. Seeing it finished, so did I. Furnishing it would be fun.

I leaned against the railing and surveyed the exterior, loving that he'd opened up the wall, replacing the sliding door with a bank of sliders that folded into themselves and making the deck an extension of the main living space. When the doors were open, we'd be able to hear the lapping of waves on the sand.

"Does this mean my wait is over and you're giving me a tour of our new digs? I get to ooh and ah over your upgrades?"

"This is a two-part unveiling. The interior is this morning. The front of the house got behind schedule, and my guy promised two more days." Creole reached in my pocket and pulled out the key, then took a lockpick from his pocket. "Your choice."

I laughed, reached for the key, and pushed open the door. Creole scooped me into his arms and carried me across the threshold. He set me down in the middle of the living room, the oversized space also encompassing the dining room and kitchen, all blending into one another with the kitchen on the far wall. All shared the same view of the blue waters of the Gulf. The layout was similar to Fab's house, except it was L-shaped, with one hallway that led to two guest bedrooms, an office, and the master at the far end.

"The dark hardwood flooring throughout was a good choice." I ran my feet over the smooth finish.

The house had come with a small island, which Creole had removed and replaced with one that could easily seat six, as it was our top choice of a place to sit and enjoy morning coffee.

He pulled out one of the two stools for me and picked me up, sitting me down.

"Does Fab know that you boosted a couple of her stools?"

"Didier warned me to get them back before she noticed."

Creole moved around the kitchen and paused in front of a new coffeemaker, switching it on for his favorite brew and heating water for my concoction. He'd planned well, pulling two mugs out of the overhead cupboard.

I oohed at the garden window that ran from half the length of the counter. "You remembered." I'd loved the one in my old house.

"The window needed to be replaced and brought up to code. It was a good choice, and I know you'll enjoy filling it with plants."

"I'm hoping that this surprise of yours means that we're moving soon."

"Week, tops, and it'll be ready for occupancy. I have a short punch list for the interior, and in that time, the driveway and front landscaping will be finished."

"Love the renovations and upgrades, not that I had a doubt that it would be anything but first-class. Good job, babes." I leaned forward, crooking my finger at him to meet me halfway so

I could brush my lips over his.

"This house was priority one for me, since we're going to be living here. Instead of leaving signing off on work to my foreman, I came and inspected everything myself." He cast an approving eye around. "As soon as we get furniture..."

That job had been delegated to me. Fab had lobbied hard to have input, and no one could deny that she was good at it. "The bed will arrive soon. As for the rest, we can take our time and be minimalist." I grinned at him.

"Don't go anywhere," he said when the coffeemaker dinged. He poured the coffees, putting them on a tray, then carried them outside and set them on a small table that came with the house. He came back inside, held out his arm, and I slid off the stool and hooked mine through his. Once outside, he picked me up and set me down on a double chaise that he'd covered with a beach towel.

The waves sparkled in the sunlight, which was now shining brightly. The white sandy beach beckoned. "Let's do this every morning."

He handed me a mug. "To our new house," he toasted.

"This is just what I needed to get excited about furniture choices. Don't be surprised when a truck rolls up. I emailed you the same file of ideas that I sent Fab. Haven't heard back from her." I sighed. "She probably doesn't know how to tell me my choices are too pedestrian."

Creole pulled me closer. "Fab-o is up to something," he said conspiratorially. "Contractor called, asked if she had permission to measure the rooms. I laughed and told him not to get on her bad side; she'd shoot him. He didn't think it was funny, saying, 'I got that impression.'"

"She'll be shooting you if she hears your new nickname for her."

"I shared it with Didier, and he groaned." He took my empty mug, setting it on the table. "It's sad that it sounds like you're not going to have a lot of time for running around, backing Fab up on her jobs." He faux-frowned.

"You might want to work on sounding a little more broken up." I tilted my head and grinned. "Sorry to disappoint you, but I plan to up my multi-tasking game. Not about to leave my bestie hanging. Can't let her go chasing down trouble by herself."

Creole groaned.

"This will make you happy—Fab's gotten a couple of calls from old clients, and I've heard her telling them she's out of business. I'm going to pitch setting restrictions for the cases she does accept."

"Make sure you get it in writing." His tone held disbelief that it would ever happen. "I'm a bit surprised that Didier didn't mention anything. It's his contention that the old clients only call when they have some criminal act they need committed and want to keep their hands clean."

I snuggled up to him, and we sat in silence, enjoying the quiet of the morning. An egret flew in and landed, beginning a hunt for food.

When Creole finished his coffee, I asked, "Are you going to give me a tour, so I can ooh and ah some more over all the renovations?"

Creole stood, held out his hand to help me to my feet, and ushered me inside.

Chapter Twenty-Seven

Creole snuck us back into the mansion the same way we made our getaway. We showered, and I changed into a black short-sleeve A-line dress. Creole sat on the edge of the bed and watched as I strapped on my Glock and slid into a pair of low heels, then tossed a pair of flip-flops into my tote. Before he could grill me on my day, I said, "I need to make sure my businesses are still standing. The Chief was also on my list, but I'm thinking he'll follow doctor's orders to rest and stay home." I slid a couple of files into my briefcase.

"Not much keeps him down. I don't remember him taking sick days. Vacation, yes, and he'd be off on a golfing trip now and then."

"I'll stop by the office. I don't want him saying I didn't show." My phone beeped. I picked it up and read the message, putting the phone in my pocket. "Fab texted Hurry up."

"At least, she's not kicking the door down." Creole grabbed his briefcase in one hand and my hand in the other, and we made our way to the kitchen.

"You ready?" Creole asked Didier. "We've got

an early meeting."

"You want coffee to take with you?" Didier held up a travel mug.

"Already had two cups." Creole smirked at Fab.

She squinted, glaring like Creole was a giant bug she had in her sights, and he bit back a laugh and beat it out the door, Didier mumbling something neither of us could hear.

"You two were up early." Fab settled a searching look on me.

Creole didn't say it was a secret. "The husb surprised me with coffee at our new digs. Fair warning: since we'll be moving soon, we need to go shopping."

"I found some great pieces, keeping to your guidelines—beachy and comfortable. I'll send the file over for your perusal." Fab finished her coffee and looked at the clock. "Gunz wants to meet at the office."

I thought her announcement deserved a big groan but wasn't up to it. "Gunz would be much happier if you ditched me and dealt with him on your own. In fact, he'd be ecstatic," I said as we walked out and got in the Hummer. "Drive by my house slowly so I can catch a glimpse of the work being done on the front." Another surprise from Creole. It was cheating, but only a little if the fencing was open. I couldn't be blamed for looking.

"Checked it for you. That way, if it was

something hideous, I could yell woah." Fab spoke over my laughter. "They're in the midst of construction on the driveway. Went over the plans with the guy, and you're going to love it."

"The gardener folks?"

"It's the same crew that keeps the compound looking great, and I spoke to the owner. He said Creole made choices in keeping with our little neighborhood."

"Palm trees and tropical flowers. I'm going to love it."

Fab backed out and slowed. Nothing to see, since the construction fence was closed, two trucks parked off to the side. "I offered to redo the security system, framed it as a gift—how could Creole turn that down?"

"You know that he wouldn't trust the job to anyone else."

Fab drove out of the compound, cut across the highway, and took three shortcuts to her office, where she hit the button for the security gate. After pulling in, she waited for it to close before parking. It was a rule at the compound and here, so we knew no one had snuck in behind us.

Fab parked in the garage. As usual, Gunz had beaten us to the office, his SUV in the only visitor space. We got out and hiked up the stairs.

Theodore Gunzelman, gigantic bald dude, opened the door and stood grinning at Fab. If you didn't know him, you'd be tempted to turn tail and run. He certainly wasn't a sweetheart, but at least he'd stopped shooting first and then asking questions.

"You're looking beautiful," Gunz gushed at Fab as she brushed by him. She'd also chosen a black dress and accented with her Walther strapped to her thigh.

"I'm certain you meant to include me in that gracious compliment," I said, and slid past him.

Gunz grunted.

We took our usual seats, Fab behind her desk, Gunz in front, and me in the corner to keep an eye on the other two and be the voice of reason for any craziness. The meeting had a high chance of being about one of his relatives. They were an unstable bunch and likely to be up to almost anything.

"I've got a couple of jobs for you." Gunz shifted around and settled his considerable bulk in the chair.

I'd been reprimanded in the past and told not to roll my eyes under penalty of something dire—what hadn't been specifically spelled out. So I'd try to behave until he spilled the details.

"Tomorrow, I need you to drive my cousin Ronnie up to Dade and get him checked into prison. I warned him not to be drunk or high, as more charges could be leveled. If he is, call me. I told him I'd beat the smoke out of him if he caused more problems for himself and that he'd have to clean up his messes in the future if he screwed up." Gunz never said no to his family members, and there were a considerable number of them. I'd asked him once to guess how many and gotten a cold stare.

"What was Ronnie convicted of?" I asked.

Fab shook her head as Gunz turned to me.

I shot her a tough totems, I want to know look.

"In general, drunkenness. Drunk driving more than once, in public another time, and I forget what the other two were for. Dude can't hold his liquor," Gunz said, unleashing an irritated sigh. "After the first arrest, I took his keys away, figuring he would stay out of trouble, but it didn't work out that way. He was lucky to get three years, since it was his fourth arrest. I'm hoping that he dries out and stays sober once he gets out."

"Just so we're clear, we're driving Ronnie to the hoosegow, dropping him at the front gate, and that's it?" When Gunz turned back, I glared at Fab for not asking these questions.

"That's it. And if you run into the slightest snag, give me a jingle." Gunz took a long suck on his designer water bottle. "The second job is a maybe, and I'll give you a call to firm up. But I want you ready to go on a moment's notice. I'm using my considerable mediation skills to get my cousin's numbnuts boyfriend to return her car before I report it stolen."

"Do you issue your cousins a number so you know where they come on the pecking order?" I asked, not mentioning the assorted other twice-removed relations.

Ignored.

"You want us to pick up the car and deliver it back to your cousin?" Fab asked.

"No!" I said before he could answer. "This is where I feel compelled to remind you that the last car-retrieval case we did for Gunz, we were arrested for grand theft auto. Hate to repeat myself, but no."

Fab shot me a you're not helpful stare. "What we could do once you locate the vehicle is drive your cousin over to pick up her own car."

Gunz swiveled his head in my direction. "Would that meet with your approval?"

I shot him a thumbs up.

Fab shook her head at me.

"I'll know by tomorrow if I'm going to get any cooperation from the boyfriend, Jeff Lane." Gunz scrolled thorough his phone as he talked. "I've got a call in to Jeff and will remind him that if he doesn't cooperate, he'll end up in jail."

If that was the case, then he wouldn't be needing us. I snuck my phone out of my pocket, laying it in my lap, and called Xander. When he answered, I hung up, knowing he'd call back, which he did. I stood as it rang, saying, "I need to take this," and disappeared into the alcove. I settled behind my desk, enjoying the view of the water, even though it was a bit mucky from boat traffic.

"You hung up on me, didn't you?" Xander laughed.

"Thanks for not being dim and calling back."

"I saw that big galoot arrive a little while ago and figured you needed an excuse to escape."

We laughed over a couple more things and hung up. I flipped open my laptop with the intention of hiding out and had checked a couple of emails when I heard the front door slam. I peeked my head around the corner to make sure Gunz had left before joining Fab at her desk, sliding into the chair Gunz had vacated.

"Since I've got your full attention..." I snapped my fingers at her. "I do, don't I?"

Fab settled back in her chair.

"I'm thinking that the two of us should take over the top floor of the Boardwalk offices. Big plus, we'd be close to the guys. Then you rent this space for top dollar."

"You stole Didier's idea."

"Then there's two of us with a good idea. Think about it." Didier on board; that was good. "Any more client appointments?" She shook her head. I took out my phone and texted Creole, wanting to know if the Chief had showed up for work. He texted, No show. I texted back, Going shopping. "Shopping?" I asked Fab.

She jumped up, grabbing her purse, and slowed as she headed to the door to say, "Hurry up."

I laughed and ran back to my office, grabbing

my purse.

Fab made the decision that the best place for shopping was Miami and headed north, promising an exhausting trek through all her favorite stores.

Chapter Twenty-Eight

The next morning, we hit the road at an early hour, having agreed that we'd add extra time in case something went awry. Ronnie Dowell, Gunz's cousin, had a check-in time of ten at the prison to the north of us, and he couldn't be late. Early was acceptable.

Ronnie's house turned out to be a well-kept bungalow on a quiet residential street in the middle of the Cove. None of the neighbors were hanging in the street or camped in the driveway, which left plenty of room for Fab to park. I followed her up the walkway. Fab knocked discreetly, and the door opened. A burly, disheveled forty-something in wrinkled dockers, a plaid dress shirt missing a few buttons, and tennis shoes hung his head out. Off to one side, an older white-haired woman with a pinched expression peered out. A collie bounded to the door, sticking his head out for a sniff. The dog was friendlier than the two people, neither of whom had said a word.

Ronnie, who matched the picture Gunz sent, turned and wrapped his arms around the woman and sobbed his eyes out.

I stepped closer to Fab and whispered, "You need to tell Ronnie to step on it or he's going to be late."

The woman gave Ronnie a hard shove to the chest that broke his hold. "I'm Ronnie's mother," she said in a tired voice.

Ronnie blew his nose on the tail of his shirt.

The woman slapped Ronnie's arm. He flinched, and she jerked on his shirt, pulling him down and whispering in his ear. She looped her arm in his and led—or dragged, it was hard to tell—him over to the SUV and opened the back door. She gave him a shove, and he got in. She leaned in and kissed him, then kicked the door closed.

I almost told her that if I found a shoe print, she'd be buying me a new door. Better to bill Gunz. I climbed in, only then noticing that the collie had jumped in at the last second. Fab clearly had no clue, since she didn't react. I flicked her arm and raised my eyebrows. Getting the message, she looked in the rearview mirror and turned in her seat. "You can't take a dog to prison."

"Lewis is my support animal." Ronnie sniffed and started to cry, hooking his arms around the dog's neck.

I got a package of tissues out of the glove box and handed them over the seat, lest he arrive at the jail in a snot-filled shirt. Or worse, it landed all over the interior.

"You do know that the dog won't be allowed to check in with you," Fab said in a patient tone, which was new for her. She must have been practicing.

"I need Lewis for the ride, so I won't barf."

I covered my face with my hands and did my best to swallow my laughter.

"What are we supposed to do with Lewis after we've dropped you off?" Fab snapped and squealed out of the driveway, her patience having flown out the window.

Ronnie rolled down the window and stuck his head out, waving frantically as his mother walked back into the house without a backward glance. "Return Lewis to my mom," he said, leaving the window cracked for Lewis's nose. "If she's not home, the door's never locked, so you can let him in. Don't let the other dogs out."

I turned, and looked back at the man splayed against the seat. "How many dogs?" More importantly, do they bite?

"You gotta crack the door open, shove Lewis inside, and get it closed fast before the other five get roused and make a beeline. If they get the jump on you, one or more might get out, and then they'll be on the run, which is what I wish I'd done, but I've got nowhere to go." He sighed heavily. "Rounding them up can be difficult."

"Good to know," I mumbled and shot Fab the stink eye. It was swell of Gunz to make no mention of the dog, who'd gotten bored with fresh air and was now sacked out on his owner's lap.

Ronnie leaned forward and tapped Fab's shoulder. "It's nice of you to drive me to jail." She growled. I turned my head. "Riding with Gunz would've been too much. He's… uhm… excitable at times."

That's an understatement.

Ronnie settled back, hung his head to the side, and started mumbling to Lewis, who slept through his meanderings.

"Before we get out of town, does the dog need to go to the bathroom or anything?" Fab asked.

"No worries, got it covered. Lewis can go on the floor. I brought a paper towel." He pulled one out of his pocket. "I can clean it up and throw it out the window."

Another charge for Gunz: footing the bill for detailing the interior. Ignoring the punch to my arm, I turned and stared out the window as if I found the passing scenery, which I'd seen a million times, riveting. After a mile or two, I entertained myself making faces at my reflection.

"Don't be throwing anything out the window; it's illegal, and you're in enough trouble." Fab had trotted out her Mom voice. "I'm more than happy to pull over so Lewis can do his business."

"I'm going to miss him." Ronnie started sobbing again.

I flipped down the visor. Ronnie had buried his face in the dog's neck. I'd looked it up, and it was an hour's drive, depending on traffic. I bet myself that Fab would break the record, and she did.

When Fab turned off the Interstate, Ronnie's ramblings turned to song, and he didn't stop until she pulled up to the front gate. Ronnie sat there, not getting out.

"We're here," Fab stated the obvious, since he was staring out the window.

Ronnie shifted back and forth, then emptied his pockets onto the seat and shoved everything in the seat crack. "I can't be taking any personal items. If you could save them for me, that would be great." He scooted forward and stuck his hand between the seats. "I'm going to need some money."

Fab sputtered and stared at me and finally asked, "Gunz didn't fix you up?"

Ronnie shook his head. "I've got to have some to get started. Then if you could remind him to put more in my account?"

Fab stared at his outstretched hand.

I reached into my purse and handed him enough cash to get him loaded up with enough junk food to last a week.

"You're a sweetheart." Ronnie flashed me a tobacco-stained smile. "You'll take care of Lewis if my mom won't take him back?"

I noticed he directed the question to me. "I'll make sure Lewis gets home."

He gave Lewis a long hug and several sloppy

kisses and got out. He stood by the passenger door and motioned for me to roll down the window. "I'm billing you for all these extras," I said to Fab before sticking my head out the window.

"You're a sweetheart. So you know, I'm going to be on my best behavior so I can get an early release." Ronnie waved and turned without waiting for an answer.

We both watched as he presented himself to the guard and disappeared through the gate.

"I'm thinking Ronnie thinks I'm going to step up and be a dog mom while he's in the pokey." I scratched the head of the dog, who'd shoved it between the seats. "If he'd known that it was going to be you, he'd have called you sweetheart."

Chapter Twenty-Nine

"Before you hit the Interstate, you might want to let your dog out to do his business on a tree trunk or wherever and not in the back of my Hummer." Fab ignored me, as was her usual when she thought I'd lost my mind. I almost laughed at the thought of her jumping out of the car to walk the dog. "If he does, either you or your client will be buying me a new ride."

"Lewis might run off," Fab whined.

"Try not to shoot him." Teasing Fab never got old. "You're a renowned investigator, you'll think of something."

If looks could kill…

Fab pulled over and got out. She went around, popped up the lift gate, and dug through the bag of tricks she kept back there, producing a piece of rope. She whistled, and Lewis cleared the seat. She tied the rope to his collar while he sat patiently waiting on her, then pointed to the weeds, and he took a flying leap.

I rolled down the window. "Good job." I shot her a thumbs up.

She let Lewis set the pace.

I whipped out my phone, snapping pics, since

no one would believe me without proof.

Fab let the dog romp around and sniff to his heart's content. It didn't take long before she and her new bestie were back and we were headed down the road. Lewis hung his head between the seats and stared out the windshield.

She beelined it to Ronnie's house to drop off Lewis.

"I've got him. Least I can do." I jumped out and opened the back door. Lewis barked and jumped out. I expected him to make a dash for the door, but instead, he sat by my side. I grasped his collar, and the two of us walked down the walkway. I knocked, and the only response was barking dogs. I'd forgotten about opening the door first. I tried again, coaxing Lewis in front of me and twisting the knob. Locked. I straightened, and this time gave it my best cop knock. The dogs inside went into a barking frenzy. I stepped back and surveyed the front. The drapes were pulled across the front window, and the rest of the property was wrapped with a fence.

Fab jumped out, stomped up to the door, and almost kicked it in, which sparked another round of barking. She whipped out her lockpick.

I cleared my throat.

Fab turned. "I'm not here to rob the place. We're bringing Lewis home." She got the door open, and from inside, we heard the sound of a shotgun being racked. Fab slammed the door and grabbed my arm. "Get in the Hummer."

We both ran back and jumped in. I'd almost forgotten Lewis, who'd wandered off to sniff around the yard. He came running back when the car doors slammed and looked up expectantly.

"I get shot, you shoot back." I got out and opened the back door for him. "Did you think we were going to leave you cooling your paws?" Lewis barked and jumped in.

Fab pulled out of the driveway and parked down the street. She got hot on the phone, and from the gist of the one-sided conversation, she was grouching out Gunz.

Good.

She hung up and tossed her phone in the cup holder. "Gunz is out of town and can't take the dog."

"I bet if we dropped by his homestead, you'd find him kicked back with his big feet in the air." Fab laughed, which surprised me.

"He's supposed to call right back."

"Premonition coming on." I rubbed the middle of my forehead. "This is going to end with you dog-sitting. Mommy dearest racking her shotgun was her idea of a friendly way to tell us 'not taking the dog back.' Right now, you're not a believer, but you'll come around." You'd think, being family and all, she wouldn't cross Gunz. Then again, we weren't him, so maybe she saw that as a loophole.

Fab's phone rang. "Yes," she grumbled, then screeched so loud that if Gunz had his ear to the phone, he'd probably gone deaf. "Hold on." She attempted to pass her phone off to me. "You're the one with animal rapport."

"Forget it, baldy," I yelled and added, "No way, Gunz-o."

Fab covered her mouth so he wouldn't hear her laugh, and after a one-sided conversation on Gunz's part, she finished up the call, saying, "I'll board the dog until you get back to town and then you need to figure something out."

"You don't just call the first dog boarding joint you find listed on your phone." I scratched Lewis's head. "You have to check the place out, make sure it's not a flea hole. If you plan on making calls for the rest of this hellish day, let's at least go home."

"Stop being mean." Fab pounded on the steering wheel. "Come up with one of those plans of yours."

"Since you whined so nicely…" I got out my phone and scrolled through the contacts. "This is Madison Westin. Would you by chance be able to board a collie for a day or two? Our client would compensate you generously." I was surprised that Fab hadn't thought of Blanche herself.

"No problem at all," Blanche assured me.

I told her about the morning jaunt up north and lied, saying that when we tried to return Lewis, no one was home.

"We've got plenty of room," Blanche said.

I hung up and told Fab, "You need to make a run past the teller machine and withdraw cash. This is going to cost Gunz's big-ass behind. Then you need to hoochie on down to Blanche's house."

Fab huffed as she shot away from the side of the road. After a stop at the bank, she tore down the highway, took the exit to Blanche's, and pulled into the driveway.

I jumped out and let Lewis out. "There's other dogs here, dude." I scratched his neck, giving him a reassuring pat. "So be on your best behavior until you make a friend or two."

Blanche opened the door before I could get there. I introduced Lewis to the woman, and he responded by wagging his tail. He knew a kindred spirit when he saw one. "I so appreciate this."

"No problem at all. I'm used to last-minute boarders. We'll take good care of him."

Three dogs and a horse chasing one another around a corral caught my attention. "I hope no one gets hurt."

"Those four are inseparable. They play like that every day," Blanche assured me. "If you ask me, the horse thinks he's a dog."

Fab, who'd followed me, grabbed Blanche's hand and wrapped her fingers around a wad of cash.

Blanche eyed the money. "This is too much."

She attempted to hand it back.

Fab pushed her hand away. "It's my client's money. He can afford it. It's my opinion that he should pay triple."

Blanche laughed and opened the door.

Without waiting for an invitation, Lewis ran inside and straight over to Timothy. The two checked each other out. Then the little boy dropped to the floor, and Lewis laid his head in his lap. The four other dogs asleep on the floor opened their eyes, checked out the new arrival, and went back to sleep.

"Tessa's going to be disappointed that she missed you; she's gone to the store with my husband." Blanche left the door cracked and motioned for us to sit on the porch. "I don't want Timothy to hear anything." She cast another glance inside before sitting down. "I can't thank you enough for everything you've done for my grandchildren. The court gave me temporary custody, since Karla is in jail and can't make bail, which I think is a good thing. Mr. Tank has been very helpful."

"How are the kids doing?" Fab asked.

"The social worker thinks that they both need to see a therapist, and I'm willing to do whatever I need to to keep them here on the farm." Blanche smiled. "Tessa's the resilient one. It's going to be a longer adjustment for Timothy; he's fearful and doesn't want to leave our side." She glanced over her shoulder. "I'm surprised he's so taken with

Lewis. Before I forget, that Crum fellow showed up."

"I was just going to ask if you'd heard from him," I said.

"He's an odd one. I was uncertain about letting him in the house, but that only lasted a second. The kids love him. It was the first time Timothy really came out of his shell. Crum was brusque with the kids, which made me want to clock him a good one, but when they laughed, I calmed down." Blanche laughed.

I laughed with her. "That's Crum. Kids love him. They don't notice that he's short on manners and niceties. He does have them but doesn't like to trot them out unless he's compelled to."

The door opened, and Timothy and Lewis ran out, barely giving us a glance as they bounded into the yard. Blanche got teary-eyed watching.

"I want you to know that we're both appreciative that you're willing to take Lewis," Fab said. "Neither of us knows anything about dogs."

"Animals are my specialty. I'm happy you called. For Lewis's sake, I hope whatever the misunderstanding is, it will get cleared up and he can go home soon."

"Grandma, Grandma, come play," Timothy yelled.

"I'll be in touch," I said as the three of us stood. Fab and I said our goodbyes and walked back to the Hummer.

"Misunderstanding." An eyeroll was evident in Fab's tone as she slipped behind the wheel. "Ronnie's Mom was adamant about not taking Lewis back. You need to pull a plan out of your… well, somewhere."

I groaned at that sneaky smile of hers. "Three years. No one's going to take Lewis for that long and give him back, even if was a dick of a dog, and we already know that's not the case." I was tempted to lean close and growl. "My plan is this: you convince Gunz what a dog lover he is. In the meantime, in addition to boarding fees, he ponies up a huge donation."

Chapter Thirty

I had big plans for the day—sitting out by the pool, catching up on paperwork, and enjoying the sunshine. Creole and I had gotten up early and gone for a walk on the beach. Before he left, I promised to stay out of trouble. He laughed.

My phone rang, and Doodad's face popped up. I groaned inwardly and answered.

"Good news, bad news," Doodad said in a cheery tone. "I've heard from our favorite bartender that that's the best way to break the news."

Kelpie turned every situation into a positive, and if there wasn't a scintilla of positive news to be told, then she made something up. Her backup plan when she couldn't come up with anything was to not tell me at all and foist it off on someone else.

"Can't wait to hear."

"There was a slight mix-up last night," Doodad said.

"That's nice and vague." I wanted to roll my eyes but had to keep my forehead wrinkles to a minimum. "Wait while I use my powers of deduction." He chuckled. "What you're really saying is that a fight broke out."

"You can't suck all the excitement out of the retelling," he said, amused with himself.

"That's me, excitement-sucker," I mumbled.

"A guy called and wanted to book a couple of tables. Told him we're a bar, not the Waffle House."

They don't take reservations either.

"Always thinking, I suggested the deck, but he was adamant about wanting to be inside."

I motioned with my hand for him to speed it up, which he couldn't see.

"In walks the soon-to-be bride and groom, which we didn't find out until later, and ten or so of their closest chums, hogging all the available tables. Rounds of drinks ensued. Here's some good news: they ran up a big bar bill and paid, so no issue there."

They probably knew Kelpie would shoot them before they got to the door.

"An hour or so into their boozing, the groom decided it was a good time to get up on the table. Bouff told him to sit his butt down, which he ignored, then shouted for silence and said, 'I've got an announcement.' He holds out his hand, has the bride climb up on the table and stand next to him, and says, 'You're the last woman I would ever marry.' He got mostly gasps, a few chuckles, and a couple of attaboys."

I shook my head. This is going to be bad.

"The bride was rendered speechless. Groom dude turned to a paunchy fellow—you know, gut hanging over his belt buckle—who turned out to be the best man. Dickface—in the spirit of the festivities, I think that's appropriate for the groom—told his friend, 'You're welcome to her. I know you've already sampled the goods... and in my bed.' He held up his phone, flashing it to his friends. Heard afterwards that he was showing nudie pics but didn't get to see for myself." Doodad sounded disappointed.

"And then they filed peacefully out the door?"

"Oh, hell no." Doodad chuckled. "The bride attempted to leap on Dickface, who jumped onto the best man and wrestled him to the floor. They fought like a couple of girls—one or two punches hit their mark; the others were more like flailing around. I know you want to know what happened to the bride. She landed in a heap on the floor. She appeared disoriented but got to her feet, jumped on Dickface's back, and pony-rode him."

"The regulars must've loved every minute." I sighed. "Anyone die?"

"Nooo... Hooting and hollering and yelling for more went on until the cops showed. One of the turncoats enjoying the show called them. As per usual, a few of our patrons with outstanding warrants beat it out the back, and that included Dickface and the best man, who apparently decided to let bygones... well, you know. Neither lent a hand to the bride, who was crouched on all fours, threatening to barf."

"Please tell me—"

"No worries. Her girlfriends dragged her ass out to the deck and held her head over the railing."

"Make sure it didn't stick to anything going down."

"Gotcha. The cops, party-killers that they are, told everyone to hit the road. Warned the drunks to get rides, and if they attempted to get behind the wheel, they'd be arrested."

Thank goodness. "Is that the good news?" I asked.

"Nopers. The good news was that it was almost closing time. Not real close, but close enough. Nice to have an early evening for a change."

Probably seeing me on the phone, Fab made an appearance and pulled up a chair next to me, not disguising the fact that she wanted to eavesdrop.

"Here's something you'll like—the bar is getting a good cleaning. Last night's mess will require a good brooming and a bit of spit. Shouldn't take more than a couple of hours, even if I have to do it by myself. Since we're opening late, we'll miss the breakfast drinkers, but we'll make up the sales since I'm sure stories have run rampant."

I let out a long sigh. "I'll be in in a little while.

Take pictures in case I need to report it to insurance."

"No worries. I'll get one of Cook's kin out here pronto to fix the hole in the wall." He hung up, chuckling.

"It would've been a lot easier to hear if you'd hit the speaker. Now, you have to repeat everything," Fab snarked.

I unleashed an aggrieved sigh, putting extra drama into it. I knew before asking that Fab would come up with some hokey excuse for not going to Jake's with me. "Two guys got into a fight last night at Jake's. Shots were exchanged. No one died. But I need you to come along and assess the damage, since you're better at it than me."

"I'll get changed." Fab stood and went into the house.

I gave myself a figurative pat on the back; I'd be using that trick again.

* * *

Fab and I jumped into the Hummer and made the short trip to Jake's. Pulling into the driveway, she checked out her lighthouse and Junker's. All was quiet. She pulled around the back, and we entered through the kitchen.

"Hey, Bossaroo." Kelpie waved frantically, hands over her head. "When I got in this morning, I told the guys that they should've called you last night." She shook her finger at Doodad.

Broom in hand, Doodad rolled his eyes. "Suck-up."

Wielding a push broom, Bouff, another of our bartenders, dragged an empty trash can over to one of Cook's kin, who'd been recruited for clean-up. Another can full of bottles, cans, glass, and debris sat by the front door next to a stack of broken furniture.

Hands on her hips, Fab stood at the end of the bar and scanned the walls and ceiling, her phone out to record the damage and give a boost to the retelling of events at the next family dinner, inviting more recommendations that I should sell. Not happening.

All eyes, except mine, went up and stared at the ceiling.

"I lied," I announced, struggling to hide my smirk.

All eyes were now on me.

"You know how you pick and choose where you'll accompany me and I don't get the same courtesy?" I said to Fab. "For off-the-cuff, I thought it was a good story. Don't you think?" She glared. Guess not. "Sometimes… the expedient way is the best, because here you are."

"You so owe me. I'll be collecting." Fab flounced over to a barstool, slid onto it, and slapped her hand down. "I'll have my usual. She can pay."

I didn't remind her that as a friend of the owner, she never paid. "Anyone get hauled off to the hospital?" I threw out to anyone who wanted to answer.

Doodad shook his head. "None that were reported." He waved to Bouff. "He wants to toss in his two cents."

Fab grumbled under her breath.

"Interesting thing," Bouff said, coming over and leaning against a barstool. He had a prosthetic leg from his time as a bomb specialist in Afghanistan, but was in better shape than anyone else who worked here. I'd overheard hot, hot, hot… from more than a couple of women. "In the middle of the melee—spitting, hair-pulling, etc—it somehow registered that sirens were approaching. I found it interesting that, in addition to the usuals that scurry for the exit, so did Dickface and the rest of his friends. And it appeared that he and the best man had decided that sexing it up with the same woman wasn't a relationship-killer. I, for one, was impressed with their disappearing act."

He laughed at the face I made.

"Didn't spend much time being impressed, since the ones still in here were getting out of hand. I cocked the rifle, which garnered a few wide-eyed stares, but I didn't shoot anyone." Bouff frowned, then laughed. "Decided the cops could handle the laggers. They trooped through the door in bad-ass mode and shut everyone up."

I was afraid to ask which deputies got the call.

"They had their ten dozen questions, which I answered, and I was about to direct them out to the deck to chat with the bride when she stumbled through the door, clutching her midsection. You could tell neither cop wanted to question her, but one stepped up and asked for her name and the names of everyone involved. She hemmed, hawed, looked everywhere but at him, and burst into tears. If she'd toned down the sound effects, it might've been more believable."

"Then she hurled, and the cop hauled her off to jail," I said.

"Not taking any chances, he pointed to the door and told her to get a ride home. There's one of those happy endings I hear you like." Bouff grinned.

"I don't know why the good stuff happens after I've split for the night," Kelpie complained.

"Please… you already make more tips than anyone else here," Bouff teased. "It's about time one of us raked it in."

Kelpie shook her enormous chest, the bells around her neck ringing. "How many times have I told you? Show a little skin and cha-ching, cha-ching."

"You never gave me that advice," Doodad grumbled.

"Before I forget, why would the bride protect the groom and not give up his name?" I asked.

Doodad shrugged. "Maybe it was her way of

saying sorry for having relations with his best friend."

Fab spun on her stool and snorted. All eyes turned to her. "This is so interesting, don't let me interrupt."

I made a show of taking a head count. "Since the full-time staff is here, we could have a meeting. Won't that be fun?" No one said a word. "One or all of you can update the part-timers."

"That's if it's any of their business," Kelpie said, finishing up her manic chopping of the garnishes that she'd need for the day.

"In the spirit of being kind to your coworkers, please don't frame it like that," I said.

"Gotcha." Kelpie pounded the bar top with a spoon. "Call this meeting to order," she belted out.

I slid onto a stool and reached out to stab several cherries, signaling I'd need a soda to put them in.

"We need some catchy ideas to bring in the customers," said Doodad, who'd moved closer and now stood next to Bouff at the end of the bar. "Fight night news will spread but will only be good for a couple of days of increased traffic, and then we need to pull a new trick out of the bag."

"Research weird theme nights and see what you get," Fab threw out.

"That's so helpful," I said.

A spray of bullets hit the front of the bar.

Thank goodness for brick walls and the thick entry door. It was hard to gauge—it probably lasted less than a minute but seemed like a never-ending assault.

We all pulled guns and hit the floor. I rolled next to Fab, and we crouched under the bar.

When the shooting stopped, Bouff roared, "Everyone stay down until we figure out what's going on."

"Don't anyone do anything heroic," I yelled as I sat up and leaned against the base of the bar. "What now?" I directed the question to anyone who wanted to answer.

"We're sitting ducks here," Fab grumbled, moving to sit next to me.

"We stay down until the cops show and give the all-clear," Bouff ordered.

"I'm calling 911," Doodad yelled from the other side of the bar.

I heard him tell the operator what went down and that he wasn't sure if the shooter or shooters were still hanging around. I tugged on Fab's arm. "For once, let's sit out the excitement."

Kelpie crawled around from the back of the bar and sat next to Fab and me.

It didn't take long before we heard sirens wailing into the driveway.

Bouff got up and went to the front door. "It was unlocked. We're lucky whoever sprayed the place with bullets didn't want inside because it would've been easy enough." He inched the door open, stuck his head out, and then went outside.

Doodad came over and sat with us. "We might as well all sit together and stay out of the way. Makes us easier to find and question."

The first cop in the door was Kevin, and I waved. He squinted at me. I couldn't see who was behind him. I moved closer to Fab. "Let's hope he's in a decent mood," I whispered in her ear. He hung back and talked to Bouff, who'd followed him inside, and the two men went back out.

"Don't worry about Kevin," Kelpie said. "He starts to go off and I'll shake my girls at him. Never fails to distract a man." She demonstrated.

The other cop, who I didn't recognize, walked over and questioned each of us. It didn't take long, since none of us knew anything.

"How long are we going to be sitting here?" Fab grumbled.

"It varies, as you well know. Sneak out the back if you'd like. If Kevin asks, I'll say, 'Fab who?'"

Kelpie laughed. "Good one."

Fab glared at her.

Kevin rounded the end of the bar and handed me a large piece of cardboard, which Kelpie attempted to intercept. Kevin jerked it back and thrust it at me. "You might want to update your sign."

I flipped it over, seeing "Closed for Brawl Clean-up. Give us a couple of hours" in black marker. I tried not to laugh. "Thanks. We'll take care of it." I shoved it at Kelpie, who yanked it out of my hand.

"Dark-blue older model pickup truck, man behind the wheel, ring a bell?" Kevin asked.

Fab and I shook our heads.

"You'd think one of you would know who'd want to shoot up the joint," Kevin said.

"I'm hoping for a fast arrest and you'll tell us," I said.

Chapter Thirty-One

While we waited for the cops to let us go, Fab's phone had rung—Gunz demanding a meeting regarding his next job. Once Kevin dismissed us, we slipped out the back and took a shortcut over to her office.

Walking up the stairs, I said, "Seriously, Gunz-o needs to stop wasting your time and mine with these in-person meetings. It's old already."

Fab paused on the step and turned. "Be nice," she said, punctuating that with her best behave stare.

Gunz was already seated at Fab's desk, making himself comfortable as though it was his office.

Once we were seated, he said, "As you know, this job is a straight retrieval. You'll pick up my cousin Sia, drive her to where the car's parked, and wait until she's safely on the road before you leave." He texted the address to Fab and added, "Maybe follow Sia for a few miles to make sure that stupid ex of hers isn't following her."

Why couldn't the boyfriend just drop off the car? Afraid of Gunz? I knew Fab didn't want me asking "none of my business" questions, so I kept my lips zipped.

"Why can't Sia get one of her friends to take her?" Fab asked, like me, suspicious that there was more to this 'simple retrieval job.'

"They all washed their hands of her when Sia hooked up with Mr. Bad News and turned a blind eye to his illegal activities. Until the day he cleaned out her bank account, that is. Fed up, she threatened to burn his clothing if he didn't move out of the apartment, which she paid the rent on. He left immediately and said he'd be back to pick up his belongings. Two days later, while she was at work, he stole her car, then went back and cleaned the apartment out. He missed a few things but didn't leave much behind."

"What was Bad News's name again?" I asked.

"I texted all the information to Fab."

Okay then.

"Why not call the cops when she realized her car was gone?" Fab asked. "She couldn't have known at that point that Jeff had made off with it."

"Actually, she knew from the start. He called just as she was getting ready to leave work and boasted about what he'd done. Said if she called the cops, he'd kill her. That's when she called me."

"Since you know who this guy is, why not force a sit-down?"

"My reputation precedes me. He refused to

meet in person. He's keeping a low profile." Gunz gave Fab a toothy grin that promised mayhem. "Despite my warnings, Sia still has a soft spot for the weasel and made me promise I wouldn't kill him. I didn't tell her that I'd find breaking all his bones an equally effective message. He wouldn't even think about looking at her again." He cracked his knuckles. "I did my best to talk her into reporting him to the cops and letting them book him for grand theft auto, but it fell on deaf ears."

"What'll stop the ex from stealing it again?" I asked.

Gunz spun halfway around in his chair. "If he knows what's good for him, he'll keep his end of the deal. He parks the car in a public place and walks, never to be seen again. I had to guarantee no retribution, but I made it contingent on never hearing his name again."

"Is the car already at this address and ready for pickup?" Fab pointed to her phone screen. Gunz nodded. "Then we'll take care of this today."

"I'll text Sia a heads up." Gunz had his phone in hand.

"Have her bring an extra set of keys, in case he didn't leave them," Fab said.

My phone rang, and I pulled it out of my pocket. Blanche Bijou. I flinched, knowing this could be more trouble. I got up and crossed to the sliding door that opened to the deck, standing in the doorway with my back to the room.

"We may have a problem," Blanche said, her tone an odd mix of worry and excitement. "My grandson and Lewis have become instant best friends, and Timothy would be devastated to be separated from him. He's bloomed and actually said a complete sentence."

"That's great news. I promise they won't be separated," I assured her recklessly.

"Oh, thank you! It warmed my old heart to see them bond." Her relieved tone turned concerned again. "I do worry about what will happen when the man in prison gets out and wants Lewis back."

Me too. But surely I could con Ronnie with a lookalike dog. He might not notice after being separated for years. Or better yet—make it Gunz's problem. That had me smiling. "Don't you worry. Once Ronnie hears that Lewis is helping a kid, I'm sure he'll be happy." Talk about jumping into a no-win situation. Another job for Gunz. He could convince Ronnie.

"You're the best. You snap your fingers and make things happen. One of the few people I know that keeps their word."

I laughed. "If I had that superpower, I'd wear my fingers out. I think Tessa and Timothy deserve a better life, and it makes me happy to do anything I can. If it weren't for you, their options wouldn't be great."

"There's one more thing," Blanche said tentatively. "If you could stop by in the next couple of days, Tessa would like to talk to you. She's remembered a few things about that man. We don't mention his name around here," she whispered.

"I'll stop by later. Is everything else going okay?" Blanche reassured me that everything was going better than she could hope and they were all adjusting really well.

After hanging up, I slipped my phone in my pocket and stepped back inside, sliding the door closed. When I turned, Fab frowned at me, looking annoyed that I hadn't put the call on speaker. I'd remind her later that she'd been busy with a client.

"That was good news," I said, returning to my chair. "Lewis has been offered a forever home."

"What are you talking about?" Gunz was clearly irked about being interrupted.

"Cousin who went to the pokey—the one that left his dog to poop in my Hummer? Ring a bell?"

Fab struggled to bite back a laugh.

The skin on Gunz's forehead got all bunched up. His skin wouldn't fold like that if he hadn't waxed off his eyebrows. "I already told you—Ronnie's mom doesn't want the dog back. Turns out he brought it home a week ago, and his mom has been after him ever since to get rid of it."

I sucked back a sarcastic retort, knowing Fab

wouldn't want me to share. "Here's the deal. Lewis has bonded with a young boy, and he's worked wonders to bring him out of his shell. Would you please work it out with Ronnie and convince him to let the dog go to a new home?"

"How am I supposed to do that?" Gunz snapped.

"You'll think of something." I gave him a phony smile.

"Add it to the list. Ronnie's mom doesn't want him back either." Gunz sighed. "At least, until he's worked out his issues and is sober. I'm thinking of moving him into one of my units with a set of expectations that he'll need to fulfill in order to stay. And I have a strict no pets policy."

"There's one more thing." I didn't flinch from his glare but didn't back down either. "I'd like you to make a generous donation to Sanctuary Woods. It's an animal rescue, and the money would help them take in and rehome more animals."

"I already paid through the damn nose on the charges for that dog Hilton."

"Money well spent." My lips were feeling strained from the fake smile I'd sported throughout this conversation.

"It was difficult to find a place to board Lewis at the last minute," Fab said to placate him. "We were lucky that they had room and were willing to take him."

"If you have other friends that would like to donate to a great cause, I'll get some business cards for you to pass around." I fully expected him to turn away and ignore me, but he didn't.

"The ones that could afford to send over a bag of cash don't meet your legal-only standards."

"I guess I can skip the selling point that it's a tax deduction."

Gunz's phone rang, and he glanced at the screen. "Appreciate you jumping on this car job. If you need anything, call me." He stood and headed to the door, slamming it behind him. His booted feet could be heard clumping down the stairs.

"You should be a little nicer when you're hitting someone up for money." Fab got her purse out of the drawer and grabbed her briefcase.

"The big man hasn't heard the last from me on the donation issue."

"I'm sure." Fab smirked.

I stood. "Let's get this job over with. And so you know, I'm going to need caffeine."

Chapter Thirty-Two

The cousin turned out to be a perky blonde, not long out of high school. She flashed us a smile. "Thank you for picking me up." She was clicking away on her phone the whole time as she hopped into the back and never once looked up.

Fab and I were always happy not to have to resort to small talk. You wouldn't hear us complain about being ignored.

We drove Sia to the pickup spot in Florida City, a short jaunt north.

Fab pulled off the highway and flicked down the visor. "Be on the lookout for your car," she told Sia and turned to make a loop around the perimeter of the outlet mall.

Sia rolled down the window and stuck her head out as Fab cruised slowly by the aisles. She pulled her head back in, scooting forward and pointing. "It's the black Wrangler parked next to the road, off to the side of the large welcome sign."

Gunz had sent a picture, and we both recognized the Jeep.

Fab turned into the parking lot and cruised over several aisles and had barely come to a stop before Sia jumped out. "Thank you," she yelled and ran to her ride.

"Do you offer a refund when the job is easy?" I asked.

"I'm sort of annoyed there isn't a good reason to bill double." Fab coasted into a parking space.

We both laughed and waited until Sia backed out and headed to the exit. Fab hung back, and when Sia turned onto the road, she sped up and followed at a discreet distance.

A short distance from the mall, we were about to turn onto Highway One when Fab had to pull to the side of the road, out of the way of the cop cars approaching, lights flashing. They flew past us and surrounded the Wrangler.

"What the heck?" I leaned forward and stared out the windshield. "Don't park here; find a location where you're not going to stick out to do your spying on what's about to go down."

Fab inched her way to the corner as the cops got out of their cars, guns drawn, and surrounded the Jeep. Fab U-turned and went back in an attempt to find an out-of-the-way parking spot, which was impossible thanks to road signs that read "No stopping." She pulled over anyway and idled, along with several other lookie-loos.

Sia was out of the Jeep and being led over to the side of the road. She turned, putting her hands behind her back, and was cuffed and questioned by one of the cops.

Two other cops were searching her vehicle.

Another cruiser pulled up. The cop got out and opened the back door for the K-9 to jump out.

"That could've been one of us." Fab grimaced.

"They're looking for drugs." My neck hair was telling me this wouldn't end well.

Fab fished her phone out of the cup holder. I knew from the description she gave of the unfolding events that she had Gunz on the other end. Whatever he said had her jerking the phone away from her ear. "I'll do my best. Call you later." She hung up.

"I take it Gunz was furious."

"Oh yeah. He's going to hit up a couple of his cop friends and see if they can find out what's going on. In the meantime, he wants me to watch and see how this plays out. He's afraid Sia's ex set her up somehow."

"If any of those cops are paying attention to the traffic backed up on this side of the road, they'll be on their way over here. I hope not giving out tickets."

"They'll just give us a warning to get moving."

"That makes four." I pointed as another cop car pulled up. "It's not looking good for Sia."

It took another five minutes for the cops to finish searching the Jeep. One led the dog over, and he circled the exterior for a sniff before jumping inside. The cops conferred; then one approached Sia, walked her over to one of the cruisers, placed her in the back, and drove off.

"No matter the circumstances, this is the last recovery job for me." I sighed a breath of relief that it wasn't Fab or me rolling down the road in the back of the cop car, but I felt sorry for Sia. "If that were us, Creole would have killed Gunz."

"What do you suppose is going on?"

"I could throw out a couple of creative guesses. I wonder how long it will take for Gunz to find out."

"If the ex set up Sia, he's lost his mind and better have moved to another state. The only way Gunz will let this go is if it's Sia's fault."

I shuddered at the thought of Gunz hunting me down.

Chapter Thirty-Three

Good thing I'd told Fab that Tessa had information for us and we needed to stop by. I'd forgotten about that and stared out the window as we cruised home, lost in thought, feeling bad for Sia. I knew she wouldn't be enjoying her trek to jail and hoped that Gunz would be able to bail her out pronto.

Fab blew past the Cove and turned off the highway on the outskirts of town, towards Blanche's house.

"This is proof that you pay attention to what I say. Once in a while." I smiled at her. "I'd forgotten that I promised to stop by. Now, I won't have to bug you to drive out here."

"I'm curious what Tessa's remembered about Colton. Hoping it's something that can help us locate him." Noticing my frown, she said, "Not you and me but the cops. I promised Didier to not get any more involved."

"Creole warned me that if we back the man into a corner when he's looking at a lengthy prison term, he'll do whatever it takes to make sure he isn't arrested. He didn't need to get into grisly details to press his point home about leaving it to the cops."

It was so peaceful out here, the homes on acreage, well separated from each other. Large oak trees dotted Blanche's property, their massive limbs shading the house. Fab pulled into the circular driveway and parked. Instead of running around the pasture, several dogs were sacked out next to the fence, the horse nowhere in sight. Two more dogs were fast asleep on the porch. Our arrival had them lifting their heads, and after a quick glance in our direction, they went back to sleep. Tessa and her grandmother were rocking on the porch swing. They waved and called hello as we got out of the car.

"It's beautiful out here," I said.

"We'd miss the beach and the sound of the waves." We walked up the steps of the porch, and Blanche stood and directed us to wicker rockers with oversized pillows.

"Iced tea?" She reached for a tropical flowered pitcher. We both nodded, and she filled glasses with ice from a matching bucket and handed them to us.

Anton called from inside the house.

"I'll be back. You go ahead and talk." The screen door slammed behind her.

Tessa sat across from us in jeans, a crop t-shirt, and bare feet, a pair of flip-flops not far away.

"You look great," I told the young girl, who'd blossomed in her new environment, her face not marked with fear as it had been in the past.

"Just thinking the same thing." Fab smiled at her and leaned forward, lowering her voice, "Everything going okay? You know if you ever need anything, you have our numbers."

"So many nights, I wished I could see my grandmother again, and here we are." Tessa sniffed and looked away, taking a deep breath. "My little brother's even coming out of his shell. Says he's not a baby anymore and we need to call him Tim." She smiled. "You wouldn't believe the changes, for both of us, and it's all good. Right now—" She looked over at the pasture. "—he and Lewis are out with a few of the other dogs on a long walk. It's good, because it tires out the dogs and my brother."

"Any word from your mom?" I asked.

Tessa grimaced. "Nooo. I hope it stays that way. Tank tells me I have nothing to worry about, and I believe him. All my life, adults have gone back on their word, but since I met you two, not a liar in the bunch."

"That's because they're afraid that Fab'll beat the smack out of them," I said in a conspiratorial tone.

Tessa laughed, which was good to hear.

Fab made a face, but I knew she loved the description.

Blanche shoved the screen door open with her foot and came out, setting down a tray of cookies on the table in front of us. "Refills?" she asked, hand on the pitcher. We shook our heads. She grabbed a glass and sat back down next to Tessa.

"Did you tell them?" Blanche nudged Tessa.

Tessa shook her head. "It's about Colton," she said in a low tone, glancing around. It would take her a while to stop looking over her shoulder. "I remembered some things I'd overheard and told Grandmother. She thought you two were the best to tell." She scooted closer to the woman, who clasped her hand.

"You can tell us anything," Fab said. "We'll do whatever we can to help."

"As you know, we have lots of friends, and I'm not the least bit bashful about asking for favors." I smiled at the two.

"That's the truth."

Hey, Pot. I wanted to laugh at Fab.

"I've thought a lot about the other girl locked in the bedroom, and someone needs to help her." Tessa shuddered at the memory. "When Colton was drunk or high, he'd pass out on the couch and snore the roof off. Other times, he'd go into the locked bedroom, and every time, I heard the lock turn once he banged the door closed. I feel guilty, knowing that he kept someone prisoner and I couldn't do anything."

"Now, none of that," Blanche soothed her granddaughter.

"Good news, although I can't tell you very much. The other girl managed to get away and was rescued," I told her, not wanting to give too many details about Kathryn.

"Colton won't be able to find her?" Tessa asked in a hopeful tone.

"No worries there; she's with family," Fab said.

"I hope he can be stopped before he snatches up another girl." Tessa stared down at her fidgeting fingers.

"I don't know how he's managed to escape the notice of the cops so far, but he won't be able to hide forever," I assured her.

"It's surprising that, with all the cars you two stole, you weren't already on the cops' radar," Fab mused.

"That's because Colton's favorite hunting ground was the Miami area and the cars were immediately delivered to a couple of different drop-off locations."

"Could you find them again?" Fab asked.

"I'm not sure. In a stolen car, no driver's license, I didn't give a single thought to my surroundings, only to following Colton and getting there in one piece." Tessa frowned at the memories and finished her tea.

This was a long shot… or maybe not. "You told us Colton drove a sedan and a pickup. Can you tell us anything about either of them?"

"Just a regular car, the truck's a Ford, dark-blue, with a few dents but not bad."

Fab and I exchanged a look, thinking the same thing—was Colton the shooter in the blue truck at Jake's? Neither of us was a believer in coincidence.

"There's more," Blanche reminded Tessa with a raised eyebrow.

Tessa took a deep breath. "I wanted to tell you about Club X. Colton claimed to be one of the owners. Bragged you had to be a member to get on the top floor. I thought he was full of it, because when we went there, we didn't stay long."

"What's Club X?" I asked.

"Nightclub," Fab said. "I've seen their advertising; they cater to the young and hip—a place to be seen, party, and drink."

"Owner of a nightclub, that would be easy enough to check," I said, but like Tessa, I wondered. Xander had run a thorough search on the man and hadn't turned up that interesting tidbit.

"Be good to know one way or the other," Fab said. "I doubt the owner story. He wouldn't be living out in the boonies if he was, and why would he need a side gig stealing cars?"

"Some nights, his phone would ring late, and I'd pretend to be asleep and listen to him talking. He mostly grunted his answers. I always knew that the next day, we'd be stealing a car." Tessa took an ice cube out of her glass, running it across her cheeks. "Several nights a week, he'd leave but never let it slip where he was going. The first few times, he woke me and threatened that if I moved, he'd know. Then turned a camera on me."

"You need a break?" I asked.

Tessa shook her head. "Fear kept me from leaving. Also, how would I get around in the pitch dark and back to town... and then what? On the nights I knew I'd be alone for a few hours, I'd obsess over getting away, then laugh at myself."

I reached over and squeezed her hand.

"Another conversation I overheard..." Tessa said. "He needed to find three women for an upcoming auction. Big spenders were coming to town, and they couldn't disappoint or it would be his ass. He laughed, but the sound made my skin crawl."

"Auctioning women? Is that big business in Miami?" I asked Fab.

"Back in the old days, I used to hear about all sorts of criminal activity, but nothing linked to any place in particular," Fab said. "You know how it is—when one person finds out, it's no longer a secret. I'd be surprised if that kind of enterprise could be kept quiet and not attract the attention of the cops."

"Another night, Colton yelled at someone on the phone that he didn't care what the women wanted and told the person to just do their job."

Thinking about how many women Colton may have kidnapped made me sick. He needed to be found and stopped.

"I wondered what would happen to me a lot. Would I ever have a normal life? Whatever that is. I thought a couple of times about taking off in one of the stolen cars, but fear kept me from acting."

"I'm happy that I caught you trying to boost my SUV," I told her with a smile.

"That was a good day. Gunshot and all. Meeting you two changed my life." Tessa looked embarrassed. "What I didn't tell you or him was that I recognized your ride right off. I felt bad for trying to steal your car because you were always so generous to me and Tim."

"We know Colton targeted my Hummer because he caught a picture of it outside his property, but it would be interesting to know how he tracked it to me. I don't have any memory of ever meeting the man." I'd studied his picture in case I ran into him. "I did know a couple of people that lived out where Colton did, but they've since moved."

"Colton joked a few times that he knew the secrets of the mangroves better than anyone," Tessa said.

"If that's true, then it explains why the cops haven't found him yet," Fab mused.

"The folks that live out there are known to keep to themselves," Blanche said.

I tried not to shudder, thinking of the few times we'd been out there. Nothing good had happened.

"Can you stand a couple more questions?" Fab asked Tessa, who nodded. "You remember anything in particular about the club?"

"It wasn't far from the Causeway. Once Colton exited, the streets were mostly one-way. No houses, but the street the club was on had other similar buildings. Colton said it was a party street. Whenever we got close to any place where we'd be stopping, he ordered me to lie down on the back seat and not get up if I knew what was good for me."

"All the threats must've gotten old," I said.

"One thing about being with my mom—I learned how to survive and avoid sporting a pair of black eyes."

"You're safe now," I promised.

"Both you and Tim are safe." Blanche kissed the top of Tessa's head. "Even when your mom gets out of jail, she has no way of getting down here."

"What if the court says that Tim and I have to go live with her again?"

"Once a judge hears everything she put you through, I can't imagine her ever getting custody," I said. "Plus, you'll be eighteen in a few years, and it's moot at that point."

"What about Tim? He can't go back and live with her again. He won't survive."

"I'm making you a promise that Fab and I will always be around, and nothing's going to happen. Tim will be safe." It was a promise I intended to keep. "I want you to know that I'll be sharing all the information you've confided to us with a retired cop friend. He'll know exactly what to do with it. He's got kids of his own, so he'll be motivated to get Colton locked up." Another promise I felt good making. Casio would hunt him out of any hole he crawled into.

"I hope I was helpful and not a waste of your time," Tessa said, a hopeful note in her voice that she'd done the right thing.

"You're great." I smiled reassuringly. "This is the best lead so far."

Fab's phone beeped. She pulled it out of her pocket, read the screen, and smiled. "If you remember anything else, no matter how inconsequential, call, and we'll pass it along." She stood. "We need to be going."

I stood and hugged Tessa. "Call anytime."

Fab enveloped Tessa in a hug and whispered a few words that made her laugh. It was a sweet sound. Blanche and I smiled at one another.

"That was Didier, reminding me that we have plans for later," Fab said as we walked back to the car. "Tessa's snippets of memory make me believe that the nightclub is a cover for rich men buying women that may or may not be willing."

"You'd think rich guys could get a woman without having to avail themselves of a criminal service." I rolled down the window and waved going out of the driveway. "I'm telling you now that you need to leave Club X to the cops. If you ignore my good advice, you'll be going by yourself."

Chapter Thirty-Four

The next morning, Mother called and had organized a family breakfast at the Bakery Café. "Everyone's coming," she said, and hung up to, I was certain, call the next one on her list and run the same con. She didn't trot it out every time, so it tended to work.

I tugged on Creole's hand and motioned to the door. I wanted him to myself, even if it was only for the short ride across town.

"Wait up," Fab called. "We can all ride together."

"Then the guys won't have a ride."

Didier laughed and wrapped his arms around Fab.

Creole and I scooted out the door and into the Hummer.

My phone rang as the compound gate closed behind us.

"You got an update on the Beckett case?" Casio grouched.

"I'm fine and you?" I put it on speaker and nudged Creole, crossing my lips with my finger. Manners and all, I should ask if it was okay. Maybe next time.

"Swell. Beckett's blowing up my phone. I get it, since I have my own daughter and would want to find this cretin and kill him, making damn sure that nothing floats back up."

Creole grinned.

"That kind of talk is unbecoming of law enforcement."

"Ex. Checking your impulses when it's your family is difficult." Casio unleashed a grumbly sigh. "Back to the reason for my call…"

"I was going to call you later."

"More favors for me? Good, because I'm running low."

Creole turned away, laughing. I punched him on the shoulder. He continued to laugh.

"You're going to owe me. Huge. At some point, you're never going to be able to pay them all back." I laughed, thoroughly amused with myself. "You in the area? I can meet you after breakfast. I'd spill over the phone, but Fab would kill me, and then probably you, and think of the mess."

"Breakfast? I'll be right over."

"Family hoopla at the Bakery Café; maybe next time."

"I'm meeting the Chief today, so how about we meet at the office?"

"I'll text you." That must have sounded like good-bye to him, since he hung up. I placed my hand in Creole's. "I'm sorry. Our few minutes alone didn't go as planned."

Creole found a space in front of the Bakery Café and parked. "We're the first to arrive. I know a great way to spend our time." He pulled me into his arms and kissed me.

It wasn't nearly long enough before the locks went up and the door opened. "Hey, not in my car," Fab roared and slammed the door.

"I'm getting the locks changed. She can follow me on these jobs of hers."

Creole and I laughed.

We both got out, he draped his arm around my shoulders, and we walked into the covered patio where Fab had claimed a table. Mother and Spoon entered from the back, Brad hustling to catch up to them.

"I don't know why we can't sit out on the sidewalk," I said to Mother with an air of innocence, knowing she hated it out there. Our usual table was empty, but there wasn't enough room for all of us to crowd around it, since the neighboring table was taken.

"How many times have you been shot at, sitting out there?" Mother asked in exasperation.

"Fab would know that." Surprisingly, I didn't wilt under her hate stare.

Brad winked at me and hijacked the conversation with stories about Mila's latest escapades. I'd thank him later.

The server came over and took our orders.

Casio barged up, added to the order, and sat next to Mother. "You said my favorite word, food, and here I am."

So much for meeting later. I rolled my eyes and shook my head. "This is a family get-together, not a business meeting."

"Madison," Mother admonished. "No better time than now to hear what the two of you are up to. It saves you from having to call."

Brad bit back a laugh.

I kicked him under the table but not hard, conveying, Help.

He shrugged. You're on your own.

"Oh look, coffee's here," I said, as though grasping a lifeline. "When we're on our third or fourth cup, Fab can take center stage."

Coffee must have been the magic word, as the server was back and serving the concoctions we'd ordered. I licked my lips at the extra whipped cream on mine.

Fab launched into a retelling of the conversation with Tessa. There were several shocked looks, Mother's most of all.

"There's been rumblings about illegal activities over on that street of clubs," Casio said. "They've been under investigation several times, but nothing came of it. It's hard to believe that there wasn't any confirmed criminal activity, considering the area and knowing it's packed with drugs."

"It was my thought that you'd be the one to know what to do with the information," I said to

Casio, hoping to convey that we weren't getting involved.

Creole covered my hand with his and squeezed.

The food arrived, and conversation slowed until we finished eating.

"Speaking of drugs, wanted you to know that I tossed yours." Spoon tipped his coffee mug toward me.

"I don't do drugs." I shot him a flinty stare. "Just caffeine. When they start home delivery of IV bags, I'll be the first to sign up."

Spoon laughed, enjoying putting me on the spot.

Payback, I mouthed.

"How often do you sit in the back seat?" he asked.

"Only when we have Investigator Madeline in the front." Mother grinned, which made me laugh.

"As you know, after a service, we detail inside and out, and my guy came to me with the paraphernalia he found stuck in the crack of the rear seat."

I growled at Fab, and all eyes shot to her. Didier was the first to laugh.

Fab elbowed him. "It wasn't my stash either."

"Then you don't mind that I dumped the weed, papers, and pipe?" Spoon smirked.

"It was Prisoner Ronnie," I said, louder than I intended, and heads at the next table turned my way. "Her client." I pointed at Fab. "I saw him leave something in the back seat but forgot to check."

"Here we go," Fab said, sounding annoyed but clearly amused. She took center stage again and sauced up the details of that job, not leaving Lewis and the shotgun-toting mom out of the story.

"If any of you have extra dough under the mattress, Sanctuary Woods is needing an influx of cash," I said. "And if you could shake some coin out of your richy friends' pockets, that would be amazingly cool."

"Honey, we should organize another fundraiser," Mother said to Spoon. "The last one was successful, and everyone had a great time."

"Doing it around an adoption event would bring out the folks," Spoon suggested.

"Under no circumstances do any of you mention a d-o-g in front of my daughter," Brad admonished the table.

"It's dog, dude," I teased.

"Mila wants something furry and four-legged; she vacillates between a dog and a cat. You're lucky she hasn't pocketed one of your cats and taken it home with her." Brad squinted at me.

"Good luck to that, stuffing twenty pounds in her pocket. They're spoiled and smart enough to know that they've got it good right where they are. Even more so at Casa Fab."

"Speaking of..." Mother said. "I'm looking

forward to today."

I glanced first at Mother and then Fab, not having a clue what she was talking about.

"Madison doesn't know," Fab said.

"Know what?" Creole grouched.

Didier hooked his arm around Fab. "I've got your back, babes."

"Surprise furniture delivery," Fab said. "A couple of pieces, anyway. Don't ruin it by snooping around before the unveiling."

"The bed's the only thing I've ordered. And why call you and not me?" I asked.

"Because it really is a surprise." Mother clapped her hands together. "We might've changed the order a bit, but better," she assured me.

I loved it when Mother and Fab planned a surprise… except when I had no clue what it was, and now I'd have to practice my smiley I love it face.

"I went through the same drama when I bought my condo. I'm proof that you'll live through it," Brad boasted.

I turned to Creole, who shrugged. He didn't care about furniture unless it was uncomfortable.

"Big announcement," Casio said. "I finally negotiated a lease, and me and the kids are moving down here, where the kiddos can run wild on the beach." He turned to Mother. "I'll hire you to boss the furniture movers around and tell them where to put things."

Fab's phone rang. She ignored it, and seconds later, it rang again. "Sorry." She took her phone out, glanced at the screen, and grimaced. "I have to take this. Good news maybe?" She answered. Judging by her tight-lip expression, I guessed it was Gunz. She shook her head in an "I don't want to" gesture but inserted the occasional, "Okay," before hanging up. "Sia's getting out on bail and is being processed now. Gunz wants us to pick her up." She launched into a retelling of that job.

I wasn't sure, but it could have been the first that our husbands were hearing about how that job had gone down, hence their irritated expressions.

"Gunz called a friend in law enforcement, and once he heard that cocaine had been found in her Jeep with an estimated thirty-thousand-dollar street value, he got hot on the phone to Cruz."

"I thought hotshot Miami lawyer Mr. Campion only took murder cases," I said.

"I thought the same. Gunz volunteered that they're old friends, and he has Cruz's private number on speed dial. You know, when you need the best..."

Fab and I knew that to be truth—he'd gotten the two of us out of trouble more than once.

"Gunz let it slip that Cruz owed him, for what he didn't say. He talks more when he's irritated out of his mind."

"There was a time when I had Cruz's private

number. Then Granny blew into town and got her hoochie on with every beach boy she could find. Next person that wants to book their relatives into The Cottages, I'm going to make them sign a disclaimer that they understand I'm not the morality police."

"Really, Madison," Mother admonished.

"You know Granny's a handful and a half."

Laughter went around the table.

"Gunz's cousin is in a boatload of trouble," Casio said when everyone quieted. "She's looking at prison time, even if it's her first time. She won't walk."

"My money's on the boyfriend setting her up to take a fall," Fab said.

The guys all nodded.

"Thirty grand?" I said in disbelief. "That's a lot of money just to get revenge, when supposedly the guy couldn't even kick in on the rent."

"Wouldn't be surprised if the bust wasn't meant to go down like it did," Casio said. Creole nodded. "It could've been that he was the one set up, and the girlfriend got caught in the middle. He needs to be investigated, but unless he fesses up, which I find unlikely, she's taking the fall."

"The dude better have blown town," Fab said. "He's going to regret it if this case doesn't get dismissed… and might anyway. Gunz isn't going to let it slide that someone set up his cousin to spend years in prison—intentional or not."

"Makes more sense that he was the one set up, since he was the one driving the car around," Casio said. "And if so, he angered someone big if they were able to take that kind of write-off. If that's the case, whoever it is isn't going to be happy he skated."

Creole nodded. "I feel sorry for this Sia person, but I'm happy it's not either of you in jail."

"No more car retrievals," Didier said. "Unless they come with legitimate paperwork that shows it's just a pickup job and absolves you of any criminal wrongdoing, if there is such a thing."

I vote for just turning any future jobs down.

"While you two are picking up Gunz's cousin, I'll go to the house and wait for the furniture delivery," Mother offered.

"Do you have your phone?" Fab asked. Mother nodded. "I'll text you the codes."

"I'll be going with Madeline. Make sure she doesn't take any guff, and the job gets done like she wants it." Spoon kissed the top of her head, and Mother beamed up at him.

"No doing anything naughty on the furniture," I said with a smirk. "Creole and I get first dibs."

Groans went around the table.

Didier shook his finger at me. I laughed.

"You might want to tell Mr. Beckett to let law enforcement deal with Colton," I said to Casio.

"Remind him that he's got a family that needs him."

"Beckett's not the kind of man you give advice to unless he asks, and trust me, he won't be asking."

From what little I knew of the man, I imagined that he was used to snapping his fingers and putting an end to any situation not to his liking. "Text me your new address," I told him. "Once you and the kids are settled, we'll have a big beach party to welcome you to the Cove."

All of us stood and exchanged hugs and goodbyes.

Chapter Thirty-Five

Fab and I walked into the lobby area of the jail as Sia was being released. She headed for the door to freedom, turned in on herself and stared at her feet as she scurried to the exit. Fab and I hurried to catch up. When Fab called her name, she yelped and turned, fear on her face, calming once she recognized us. We each took a side and walked with her back to the car. Fab helped her into the back seat, and she settled back, closing her eyes. Fab and I exchanged what now looks.

Before either of us could say anything, Sia burst into loud, wracking sobs. I reached into the glove box and handed her a package of tissues, then fished a bottle of water out of my bag, putting it in the cup holder.

"I can't go back there," she choked out between sobs. "You have to believe me; they weren't my drugs."

I turned in my seat. "You've got Gunz on your side, and he's already gotten you a top-notch attorney."

Sia nodded, blowing her nose. The tears continued to roll down her cheeks.

The ride south was silent except for her

wracking sobs.

For once, I wanted Fab to step on it and push the speed limit. She wouldn't get a word of complaint out of me this time.

Fab kept her eyes glued to the road. She finally turned off the highway into a residential area of well-kept houses and pulled up in front of a large bungalow-style house with a wraparound porch. It wasn't the same address where we'd picked Sia up yesterday.

I raised my eyebrows, and Fab nodded toward the house.

An older woman who'd been sitting in a rocker jumped up and ran down the walkway, stopping at the passenger door. Fab popped the locks, and the woman jerked the door open.

"Mama," Sia cried, and the woman enveloped her in a hug.

"Thank you for bringing my baby home," she said as she helped Sia out of the back and shut the door.

"I need a drink. Make it a double," I said as Fab pulled away from the curb.

"Jail's not a fun place, but Sia was only there one night. She'll never survive a lengthy sentence, which is what she'll get if Gunz isn't able to conjure up a miracle."

"I tried to come up with something comforting to say and had nothing." I glanced out the window and realized we were close to home. "I need you to stop at the strip mall so I can hit the bank and grocery store."

While I ran into the bank, Fab looked in the windows of a couple of nearby stores. We both went to the grocery store, each adding more drink-related items to the cart than food.

Fab went through the checkout line ahead of me and was waiting nearby, the barely legal bagger flirting with her and getting nowhere.

When I handed the cashier a hundred-dollar bill for my purchases, she ran it through the reader a couple of times. Then, shooting me a nervous smile, she pressed a button on the side of the register.

"Is there a problem?"

She stared at me blankly.

"What's wrong?" Fab asked, moving to stand next to me.

A middle-aged man walked over and examined the bill the cashier held out to him. Then he closed the register and routed the waiting customers to another line. He ran the bill through the reader again and held it up to the light. "This is counterfeit," he said emphatically. He turned away and said something to the cashier, then turned back to me. "You'll need to come to the office."

"That won't be necessary," I said, opening my purse. "I can pay with a credit card. I want the bill back so I can take it back to the bank." I held out my hand.

"We don't return counterfeit money," he said,

as though I should know that. "We hand it over to the police. They've been called and are on their way."

"You called the cops?"

"It's a crime to pass phony money."

"I suppose it is if I'm printing it in my basement and attempting to spend it around town," I said, matching his snotty tone. I felt a nudge in my side and calmed slightly. "I got that bill at the bank a few doors down. The teller will remember me." That was one of the perks of frequenting the same location the majority of the time.

"You can hardly blame us for following the rules." He motioned for me to follow him, stepping closer to me than I found comfortable. I wondered if he'd give chase if I made a run for it.

"You can easily verify her story by contacting the bank." Fab shot him a hair-raising glare.

I enjoyed the manager's discomfort at facing down Fab.

He stepped away and sniffed. "Once you leave the bank, there's nothing that can be done. We're required to file a police report against you. You should have realized the mistake and handed it back."

"What a scam," Fab said in disgust.

I agreed with Fab. "What's going to happen now? I'm supposed to take your word that it's counterfeit, you keep it, and I'm out the cash?" I wanted to beat the smug look off his face.

He unlocked the office door and pointed to a chair. "That's up to the police." He turned to Fab. "You'll need to wait outside."

"Not happening." Fab cut in front of me, taking a seat with a try and make me move look on her face. "No offense, but I don't trust you." It was clear she didn't care whether he was offended or not. "Your customer service skills are non-existent, treating a regular customer this way."

"If you're innocent, it'll get sorted out."

The three of us sat in silence. The manager moved paperwork around on his desk with barely a glance at us. There was a knock on the door, and the manager jumped up to open it. Kevin Cory walked in and briefly eyed Fab, his smirk settling on me.

"Hey, Officer Kevo." I waved.

Fab bit back a smile. That made two of us that enjoyed my greeting of our local deputy.

The manager introduced himself as Harry Close and handed Kevin the phony bill, relating the sordid tale of how I attempted to defraud the store.

Kevin held the bill up to the light and waved it around. The manager handed him a special light, and he re-examined the bill.

I whipped out my phone and scrolled through the screen.

"What's your story?" Kevin turned and asked me.

"It pretty much happened the way Mr. Personality related." Who cared if he was offended, judging by his shocked face? I didn't plan to ever step foot in this store again. "I don't have the time to print dough in my spare time." I told him about the stop at the bank and stuck my phone out to show him an email. "You're looking at a receipt for the cash I withdrew. The rest of the cash is in an envelope in my purse if you'd like to count it and check those bills."

"Since there hasn't been so much as a whisper of you passing phony money, I'm not arresting you. The bad news is that you're out the cash, unless you'd like me to accompany you back to the bank, and you can make your case there. The banks have machines that catch the fakes, but I suppose a few get through."

"What you're telling me is that I should get one of those special pens, and the next time I need cash, stand at the counter and mark up each one?"

"Chances are low that you'll get another one," Kevin said. "So far, we haven't had any calls suggesting that it's becoming a problem." He picked up the light, which he'd set on the manager's desk. "Do you mind if I look at the rest of the bills from the same transaction?"

I fished the envelope out of my purse and handed it to him.

He took the light and ran it over each of the bills, then handed them back. "These are real…

or you did a better job."

"You're in a good mood today," I said in a suspicious tone.

"It happens every once in a while." Kevin grinned. "You're free to go."

I gave the manager a dead-on stare. "I'll never be back." I followed Fab out the door, Kevin behind me. We didn't say anything until we were outside.

"What are you going to do with the bill?" Fab asked Kevin.

"I'm taking it into custody."

"Did the manager have to call the police? Is that protocol?" she asked.

"I'd say he was protecting his own backside. Calling the cops could have gone either way… unless you threatened to shoot him." His tone was laced with amusement.

"If you have time," I said, "we could go to the bank now. I'd like to speak to the bank manager so it doesn't happen again."

"I've got time. No other felons to go chasing after. For the moment."

The three of us walked back to the bank. The door was locked. Glancing at the sign, I saw it was closed for the day.

Kevin turned to me. "I'm going to investigate this, and I'll get back to you on what I find out. I wouldn't hold out hope that the bank will make it good. They'd probably say you could've switched bills."

I nodded, figuring that would be the case. "You missed your opportunity to arrest me."

"Next time." Kevin grinned and cut across the parking lot.

"You forgot your groceries, and I didn't pay for mine," I said. "We're going to need to stop somewhere else."

Fab handed me the keys. "I handed the cashier my card while you were talking to Mr. Personality, and they better still have our purchases." She stormed back to the store.

Chapter Thirty-Six

The next morning, Fab wanted to cruise over to The Boardwalk offices and refused to give a hint as to why. We left the house, and she slowed going through the compound. When I asked, "What the heck?" at seeing Mother's car, she said "surprise" with an annoying amount of exuberance.

Another one? I ignored her, still annoyed at seeing Mother's car parked in front of my house and having no clue what was going on. I loathed surprises, and this was a big one. Who gets their house decorated with no input? People on television. But who knows if that's real?

Fab pulled into the parking lot of The Boardwalk offices, and slowed. "When is the security fence going in?" She cruised around the back and parked. A quick car count told us that, in addition to our husbands, a few more people were inside. She grabbed my arm before I could get the door open. "Do you trust me?"

"I suppose."

Fab smirked, knowing that I wasn't in the mood to admit that I did. "All this secrecy has to do with Didier's and my housewarming gift. You can't ruin the surprise with surliness."

Oh, okay.

"I promise I was restrained. Mostly. You'll be happy to know that I didn't ignore Creole's veiled threat to 'keep the receipts.' I was worried that with your foot-dragging, the only thing you'd have to sit on was a cardboard box, and that's only if the liquor store is still putting them out curbside."

"You're going overboard, I just know it." I sighed. "Whatever you've got going on with Mother, she's thrilled, so there's that."

"Promise—" Fab smiled big. "—you're going to love everything, and if not, we'll change it."

I smiled lamely, then got out and scoped out the property. "The gate goes in tomorrow. I asked for a rush job, and they didn't give me a bunch of excuses. It's an overpriced 'No Trespassing' sign, but as long as it works."

"If not, we can get it electrified."

"Zzzz... That would be hard on the hair." I tugged on my slightly tamed mop.

Fab opened the lift gate, motioned me over, and handed me a pink bakery box, then took one herself. We'd made a quick stop at the Bakery Café, everyone's favorite. There'd been coffee, but we'd both sucked ours down already.

"Are the pastries a bribe or out of the goodness of your heart?" I asked as we crossed the parking lot.

Lark stood under the rollup door and waved,

her arm ringed with bracelets halfway up to her elbow that jingled up and down. I hadn't talked to her about dress code, but her multi-colored A-line dress and sandal slides were a great choice. Arlo barreled past her, skidded to a stop for a quick sniff of the two of us, and took off again.

"There's one more surprise," Fab whispered as we crossed the threshold.

Before I could demand, "What now?" Lark took the bakery box from me. "I'll put this in the kitchen and anyone can help themselves?"

"Great idea." I took notice of the addition of potted plants and the ginormous tree that had initially annoyed Creole, and I hadn't heard another word about. Lark had moved her desk to center stage, just inside the doors; no one would be sneaking past her. A divider had been rolled out, offering privacy to the guys. I waved to Didier and Brad, who were sitting at the conference table with Creole, who was on the phone.

Creole hung up and crooked his finger. I didn't hesitate, crossing the room and leaning down to kiss him.

"Just the woman I wanted to talk to," came the Chief's voice from behind me.

I straightened, pasted on a smile, and turned. The Chief stood in the middle of the room. "Before I forget," I said, loud enough for everyone to hear, "we're having new security measures installed tomorrow, and I'll need the names and license plate numbers of anyone working for you." His brows went up. "That way, the night guard will know there isn't a prowler on the loose."

"Who?" Creole whispered.

I gave him the stink eye.

"Oh yeah, him." He bit back a laugh.

I winked at Fab, who smirked back. She was sitting on Didier's lap on the other side of the table.

Brad knew I was full of it and had a goofy grin on his face.

"Once again, sorry about the Raine Morris fiasco," the Chief said, exasperated. "Turns out she was more obsessed with me than I knew. Not sure what she hoped to accomplish with her criminal activities. She's still being held for a psych evaluation. Should she be released, I'll be contacted, and I'll let everyone know."

"Raine shows back up here, we'll just shoot her." Fab made guns with her fingers and accentuated with poofs. "End of problem."

The Chief was not amused. I grinned behind his back, but I'd wiped it off before he turned to face me. "Since you haven't found a tenant for the third floor, I'd like to move my offices up there."

"Sorry, Chief." Fab stood. "The new tenant is moving in as we speak." She waved to a moving van that had just pulled in and parked. Two men bounced out of the cab, and one lowered the loading ramp.

The guys all said, "Who?" at the same time.

I recovered quickly from the shock and wasn't in the mood to cover for whatever Fab was up to, lest I be held responsible. "You need to pony up the details, and pronto, before the movers start unloading that truck," I said in a tone so low, only she could hear. I started toward the door, and Fab stepped in front of me.

"Remember, I said I had another surprise?" she whispered. "I feel compelled to remind you that this was your idea."

Get to the good part.

Fab hooked her arm in mine and turned us to face the room. "Madison and I are the new tenants," she announced.

The only one not surprised was Didier, who winked at me.

"You?" the Chief sputtered.

"Madison and I talked and decided it would be a good idea if we were all in one building. It was Madison's idea that I rent out my warehouse. Since I'm sure she'd give you a recommendation and you can probably afford the rent, you're welcome to look at that space."

I took his snort as a no and noticed Fab didn't ask for clarification. I wanted to turn and look at Creole but didn't, lest the two of us start laughing. "My desk and the rest of my office better have been packed and loaded on the back of that truck."

Fab whipped out her phone. "Here's the furniture layout."

I had a view of the water—okay, the canal below; however murky, it was perfect. Plenty of room for that mammoth desk she'd had custom-made from shiplap. "Love it." I smiled at her.

Casio breezed through the door and bowed to Lark, setting a bottled four-pack of Dad's Root Beer on her desk. He whispered something that left her blushing, then waved to the room at large and nodded to the Chief. "What did I miss?" He took a seat and rolled the chair across the floor.

Fab shared her news.

"You'll be easy to find." He grinned at her.

"Beckett still burning up your phone?" I asked Casio.

"I told him what Tessa shared, not mentioning names, and he's determined to bring someone to justice."

Him or the legal system? "Maybe the club will burn down and that will be the end of it," I said. Another problem solved.

"They'll just move to another location. The lot of them need to be behind bars," Casio said. "Anything new, keep me updated."

"Will do." I stopped short of saluting. Now that Tessa and Kathryn were back with their families, fear would motivate me to keep my nose out of the club's business.

The Chief turned to Brad. "Another condo come up for sale in that building of yours?"

My brother owned both top-floor condos in a building the family had renovated. When the one next door to him had come up for sale, he'd scooped it up, wanting to control who lived next to him.

"I just heard that a unit below mine is going on the market, although it hasn't been listed yet. I can put you in touch with the owner, and you can work out a deal." Brad scribbled on a notepad, tore the page off, and pushed it across his desk.

Fab tipped her head toward the parking lot and walked out. Three movers were ready to get to work.

"Since you didn't sign the first lease I sent over," I said to the Chief, "you still have an out if you want one. No hard feelings." I wanted to do month-to-month leases, but the guys weren't having it. I warned them that we'd better hope we didn't have to evict anyone. We could be forced to have a court decide the matter.

"It's all good," the Chief assured me.

I reached in my briefcase and pulled out a folder and pen. "If I can get your signature on the last page, Fab and I will get out of here, and you guys can get back to work." I handed it to the Chief, who took it and settled back in his chair.

He ran his finger down the paperwork. "The concessions I wanted aren't here."

I sat down across from him. "That's because it's an as-is contract. My husband was already more than generous with the changes we'll be making to the space. The rest are on you."

Creole grinned at me.

"I won't require a cashier's check, since I know where to find you and it would be unpleasant if your check bounces. Just sayin'," I added at his raised brows.

"You're a piece of work." The Chief scribbled his name on the bottom of the contract and handed it to me.

"We're very happy to have you as a tenant." I smiled at him. "Any issues not of your own making, give Lark a call and she'll get it handled."

The Chief shook his head. "Are you available to negotiate a sales price on the condo? I have every confidence that you'll squeeze every last nickel out of the deal."

"That would be fun," I said and meant it. "You'll also need a lawyer to orchestrate the legalities, and I've got just the legal eagle to handle the deal."

"That doesn't surprise me."

I put the paperwork back in my briefcase and moved to Creole's side.

"The Chief planned to worm every last upgrade out of me, but for you, he signs," Creole grouched in a whisper.

"If you'd only been a dick to him…"

"Old boss and all, he knew I wouldn't."

"The good news is that our buildings are all

rented, and that means we're free to buy up the rest of the block." I'd already reminded him a couple of times to be on the lookout for opportunities.

"I may have a tenant for your building," Creole said to Fab. "It's a non-profit. I'll forward the details if you're interested."

Fab looked at Didier, who nodded. "I like that idea. I'll give them a call."

Chapter Thirty-Seven

Fab and I hung out at the warehouse for a couple of hours, making sure the movers put the furniture where we wanted it. I hadn't been up to the third floor since updating the place. One look around, and I knew Fab had been busy. The grey walls had been painted white, and the entire space had been cleaned. I had an update of my own in mind: new windows.

The guys left for a lunch meeting, and we finished up shortly afterwards. Fab offered to run through Roscoe's for hamburgers, a red flag that I ignored. She claimed to hate the food but always ate every bite. We got out and ate on the patio, where you had to know the owner to get a seat.

Once back in the car, I expected we'd head home. I was wrong. Fab turned north and blasted up the highway, but I didn't get suspicious until she made the turn for Highway One.

"Where the devil are we going?" I entertained the idea of wrestling the wheel from her and driving my own vehicle but discarded it, knowing it had a zero chance of success.

"Oh, did I forget to tell you? I have a quick

errand to run and knew you wouldn't want me to go by myself."

"The innocent act you've got going on right now fools no one that knows you. Now fess up before I report my Hummer stolen."

Fab snatched my phone from the cup holder before I could get it. "It'll be fun."

I crossed my arms, giving her a militant stare. "Spit it out, whatever it is."

"I'm checking out a building, then turning back and heading home. Promise." Fab hit the gas and squealed down the road.

"My next set of tires is on you."

"I've thought a lot about what Tessa told us." She ignored my groan. "I did some research, and it confirmed everything I remembered."

"I don't hate to be the party pooper in this case, but if they're selling sex, wouldn't that be a nighttime activity?" I knew that she'd never get out of the house at night to make a clandestine run by herself, and if Didier had a heads up on this investigation, she'd be cuffed to his wrist. "What are we likely to see in the middle of the afternoon at a club that doesn't open for hours?"

"Promise, just a drive-by and we're out of there. I have no intention of breaking and entering."

"Do you have a good reason for wanting to do this?" No answer. I sucked in a breath, not certain I believed her and knowing that if she found what she felt was a compelling reason to whip out her lockpick, she would. "You have to know that if anyone catches us, we'll be dead or sold off to the highest bidder, which is worse than dead. The little we already know suggests that they cater to men with money to burn, and the owners aren't going to want their side business outed. They'd do whatever it takes to make sure word doesn't spread. To the wrong people anyway."

"I find it odd that the cops wouldn't have undercover officers inside. Busting sex trafficking would be big headlines."

"Or they do, and Casio wouldn't endanger the investigation by telling us," I said.

"Another promise: I'm not going to do anything to draw attention to either of us."

I knew her better than to believe she'd be able to help herself.

At that point, Fab changed the subject and distracted me by talking about furniture. It didn't take long to get to Miami. Fab exited the Interstate, made a couple of turns, then another one onto a one-way street with two wide lanes, and slowed in front of a ginormous black building taking up one side of the block, Club X painted in red across the top. In the front was a massive rollup door, in addition to a pair of solid doors on each side. Not a single window, at least not across the front.

Fab eased off the gas. It wasn't a heavily trafficked street, as only one car sped by. She cruised past a black van and two spendy cars, which were parked at one of the fire exits on each end of the building, one of which had been left cracked open. A parking lot fenced with barbed wire backed up to the far side of the building, a half-dozen cars in sight. It could only be accessed from the street behind it, where a man was posted, his head visible through the glass of a small guard house.

I knew Fab wasn't going to be satisfied with one spin down the block, and I wasn't wrong.

It took several turns, negotiating one-way streets, to get back to the club. This time, Fab focused her attention on the other side of the street. The neighboring businesses were all nightclubs, none as big as Club X. She coasted slowly by the club directly opposite it, the exterior white and brick and not as intimidating as its neighbor. This one appeared to be locked up, but unless we cruised through the alley, we couldn't know for certain.

I was nervous and jittery and ready to jump out of my skin, and the third trek around the block did nothing to calm my nerves.

Instead of making another trip down the block, Fab pulled over and parked. She opened the door, one leg hanging out. "You're going to cut across to the other lane and park just past the parking lot. Before you start…" She waved her hand. "I'm going to walk past the club, snap a couple of pics of the cars, and not break stride.

Then get an eyeful of the parking lot and take a couple more pictures." She got out and closed the door, leaving me talking to myself.

I climbed into the driver's seat. I moaned on and off about wanting to drive, but if I'd had a choice, I'd have passed this time. Superstitious or something, I waited until I cleared the black building to switch lanes, doing what Fab directed while keeping one eye on the side mirror.

As retribution, I planned to drive home and give her a taste of my slow-pokey driving skills, which irked her no end. Really, though, what I should do was attempt to replicate her racing skills. My nervous laugh was a welcome break in the silence.

I flipped down the visor and kept my eyes peeled, not letting her out of my sight for a second, flicking my attention between all the mirrors.

As Fab passed the main door, a big lug came out of one of the side doors, his bald head swiveling. He whistled at Fab, and it wasn't a "you're cute" one. He yelled something that I couldn't hear. She didn't break stride, but turned slightly, giving him a quick wave, and sped up.

Lug broke into a run, reaching out and jerking Fab around, confrontation on his mind, judging by his glare. Fab's leg swung, and Lug doubled over, hugging his knees. At the same time, another massively built man exited the building and ran over to Lug.

Fab broke into a sprint, ran to the passenger side, hopped in, and yelled, "Step on it," before slamming the door.

"What the heck happened?" I squealed along with the tires. The light turned red at the end of the block. I slowed and, not seeing cross traffic, blew through.

"Not sure why, but the guy was spitting mad. I heard his lumbering footsteps and knew he was getting close; then he jerked my arm, but I was ready for him. I kicked him in the jewels as hard as I could. His loud groan told me he wouldn't be in hot pursuit, at least for a few minutes and… here I am."

Once I cleared the signal, I slowed slightly. I nodded toward the mirror. "We're being followed, and there's no time to change seats."

"Listen to me; you can do this. I'm going to tell you exactly what to do." Fab pulled her weapon. "The next corner, you're going to slow way down as you make a right turn."

My fingers gripped the steering wheel. As the dark sedan pulled up on the bumper, I gave the gas one last punch before slowing into the turn. Although the area was quiet for a weekday afternoon, there were a handful of pedestrians to watch out for, which the sedan behind us appeared to ignore, though they swerved around one that stepped off the curb and almost in front of their car.

Fab powered down the window, hung out as

we went into the turn, and took a shot that punctured one of the front tires on the sedan. It swerved across to the far side of the street and came to a stop under a freeway overpass. Back on the gas, I shot onto the on-ramp for the Interstate and avoided looking at the speedometer as I sped down the highway.

Fab flipped down the visor. "No one's following us now."

My heart hadn't stopped pounding at an alarming rate. I took the next exit and pulled into a gas station. The two of us jumped out and ran around, changing seats.

"Good job." Fab clapped my shoulder with a big grin. "Proof you pay attention when I'm driving like a crazy woman."

"I'm just happy that I didn't wrap us around a pole."

Fab exited the gas station and kept the SUV under the speed limit until we merged back onto the Interstate. "I honestly didn't think I'd attract attention. I wasn't doing anything other than walking past. I was snapping pics of the license plates on the cars parked in front, but he couldn't have seen my phone, as I had it down by my side and kept my body turned—I thought I was snapping them on the sly."

"Nothing happens on that block during the day. You're probably the first pedestrian out for a stroll in forever and not another in sight until we cleared the signal. Driving by twice probably didn't help. The whole time we were loitering, only one car flew by, ignoring the speed sign. Though I did spot two delivery trucks in the alley on one side."

"You're probably right. I was thinking I wouldn't attract attention, but I stuck out."

"Chances are good that they have someone running our plates as we speak. You maimed one of their men, not to mention their tire, and maybe did body damage to the car." A nervous laugh escaped me. "Trust me, friend, they're not going to let it go; in fact, they will want to know everything about you. Except it's my information that will pop up. They'll probably deduce they've ID'd the getaway driver, and that will make you more of a mystery."

"We're going to have to lie low. Keep an eye out for any unwanted attention."

I eyed the side mirror, expecting a car to roll up on us out of nowhere. "Lug's reaction was over the top when all you were doing was walking by."

"Lug?" Fab laughed.

"Name fits him. I hate to think what he would've done if you weren't so kick-ass." I shuddered. "I was afraid he'd get the better of you and I'd have to call in the cops."

"If I ran the operation, I'd dial back anything illegal for a day or two to see if the cops showed. Or move the auction."

"Wonder how Colton Roberts fits into this operation?"

"If his job is to procure unwilling women off the street to be sold for sex, he's the bottom of the food chain. He gets picked up by the cops, bet he doesn't live long, depending on what he knows."

"We have another problem," I said with a smirk. "Need a hint?"

What? Fab's brows went up.

"Creole and Didier. More hints: this trip wasn't sanctioned, and neither of us has reached for our phone to relive the almost-ass-kicking details."

"Since nothing happened, I don't think we need to say anything unless asked."

"If I get wrinkles from all this eye rolling..." Okay, I didn't have a good threat. "Something did happen. Although the Hummer isn't registered to the compound, we can't just hope Lug will stop trying to find us and go away."

"We can't be held responsible when situations out of our control go awry."

"I'd love to see a video of you telling Didier that with a straight face."

"I suppose you'll race in the door and announce what went down?"

"You're looking for a way to weasel out of telling your husband. You should rework that plan; it's not going to work for you. Listen up, I'm about to impart some advice." I could hear her eyeroll. "Sex him up and then roll me under the bus; it's what I'm going to do, except my bus will be rolling over you."

"You give me a headache."

"Cure for that is a drink. I'll take a double."

Chapter Thirty-Eight

Fab and I agreed that we'd tell our husbands what had happened privately and not make it a big reveal during dinner. I warned her that they had a right to know, since odds were high that trouble would be showing up on the doorstep.

"You worry too much."

Whatever.

The next morning, I snuck out of bed early and tiptoed around the kitchen, filling two thermoses with our preferred blends of coffee. Back in the bedroom, I grabbed a blanket and shoved it all in a bag.

"What are you up to?" Creole, now wide awake, had rolled onto his side and was watching my every move.

"A little surprise."

He groaned. "I should've known. You were a little too quiet last night."

I tossed his sweats and a t-shirt at him. "It's been too long since we enjoyed morning coffee on the beach."

"Must be a doozy." His feet hit the floor. Two seconds to dress, or so it seemed; then he grabbed the bag, and we headed barefoot down to the sand.

We sat and faced the shore, and he looped his arm around me.

I waited until he'd sucked down a healthy sip of coffee. "About yesterday."

"Hold on." He downed more coffee. "Maybe we should wait on the details until I've finished every last drop."

I leaned my head against his chest. By the time I finished explaining the events of the previous day, I'd wiped every trace of amusement off his face.

"I'm going to kill Fab," he growled.

I wound my arm through his so he wouldn't jump up and hunt her down. "I could've—"

"Jumped out of a moving vehicle?"

I grimaced at that visual.

"Tell me again what happened."

I did, and he was even more unhappy than the first time.

"We're going to have to support Didier in his time of grief." He blew out an irritated sigh.

"I should've known—Fab's insatiable curiosity. It seemed innocent enough…" I wasn't going to add to his irritation by telling him I had reservations from the start.

"Three possibilities: either no one ever walks past there in the daytime, Lug spotted her furtive picture-taking, or they're so deep in illegal activities and anything out of the ordinary sends them into high alert." He turned and enveloped me in a hard hug. "If Lug had caught her…" He hugged me harder.

I made a choking noise.

He peered into my face and grinned. "You think this is bad? I'm not letting you out of my sight."

"That kind of threat only inspires me to misbehave more often."

He stood and pulled me to my feet. We walked along the shore, kicking the water at one another, laughing and letting the tension roll off, silently agreeing that we'd worry about the situation later.

As usual when Fab and Didier had a personal problem, they beat it out of town, leaving a note: "Don't forget to feed the cats." Most likely, Didier feared for his wife's safety, knowing Creole would be livid. Fab might as well save her breath than attempt to blame me; Didier would see through that ruse in half a second.

It turned out to be "take your wife to work day" for the next couple of days. Instead of floating up to the third floor, I took over Didier's desk and used the time to catch up on paperwork.

Two days later, Fab and Didier were back, Fab contrite and apologetic. I pinched Creole hard on the backside as a reminder not to strangle her.

One reason for their return: a Gunz job.

Creole ground his teeth so hard, I thought they'd snap off. "What now? Are you sure he doesn't go out and recruit people to claim a relationship with so he can use them as an excuse to slobber over you?"

"Eww," Fab said in huff.

Eww is right. I struggled not to laugh and noticed Didier doing the same.

"Finished?" Fab snapped, then dialed it back, managing a smile, but just barely. "Not a relative job this time. Sort of. He bought a property with his sisters. Now that the deal has closed, he wants me to do a check."

There's a couple of freak-jobs! I didn't enlighten the husbands. Any description I could give of the sisters wouldn't capture their eccentricities.

Creole put his hands on my shoulders, turning me to face him. "I'm asking you—" To heck with Fab implied. "—not to put yourself in any danger."

I nodded, knowing that it would be an impossible promise to keep if Fab was in trouble. "I'll use my best powers of persuasion to ensure that we don't go looking for trouble."

It didn't quite satisfy Creole, but he let it go.

"How about a promise out of you?" Didier asked Fab.

"I know it doesn't seem like it, but I'm getting better."

Good thing she missed Creole's grunt of annoyance. Didier saw and bit back a smirk.

"Don't forget your Glock." Creole pulled me

into his arms, laying a big kiss on me despite the audience. "Call me—before, after, and in between," he whispered in my ear.

The guys left for the office, and we were right behind them.

"Maybe we should trade my baby in for my beater truck." I leaned forward and patted the dashboard.

"Vigilance has to be our new mantra, and not just because of recent events."

"How about some specifics on this job of yours?" I asked as Fab turned south on the Overseas, not bothering to say it can't be as simple as you made it out to be.

"The threesome bought a house from an online auction, sight unseen. Now that Gunz is one-third owner, he'd like me to make sure it's squatter-free."

"Hmm…" I sighed dramatically, intending to irk her; she turned away, cheating me out of her response. "That's an interesting tidbit that you left out when selling the job to the guys."

"It's hard to remember everything." That line would be a hard sell to the guys—with the exception of names, Fab remembered everything.

"And if—"

"Then I'll report back to Gunz, and he'll get eviction proceedings started," she snapped in a happy now? tone.

Not really. "You need to tell Gunz that buying something he hasn't checked out is stupid. And bad business, if you ask me."

"I said something similar, only nicer." Fab smiled. I shook my head. "He went in as a silent partner with his whack-job sisters; it wasn't until after the fact that he found out they hadn't seen it first. He was livid, but you know he excuses their antics. The duo are out of town, and he wants to get started on renovations."

When I heard that this job had to do with a Gunz property, I'd known it would be local, but hoped for a longer drive south to enjoy glimpses of the Gulf.

Eventually, Fab turned off the highway onto a narrow residential street. A row of two-story homes on stilts ran down one side, with sandy driveways and overgrown trees. The other side was a virtual jungle of overgrowth, typical of the area. She found the property by process of elimination, thanks to the addresses on neighboring mailboxes. Unlike the rest of the houses, there was barely a glimpse of this one from the street. It was nestled on the oblong lot amidst trees and wild, untamed growth. She parked on a gravel patch in front of the property.

"You're sure there's a house back in there?" I glanced down at my bare legs and winced. Florida plus humidity equals bugs and plenty of them.

"Let's get this over with." Fab motioned me out.

I took a step back and surveyed the

overgrowth as Fab snapped pictures, walking from one end of the property to the other. I ventured off to one side. "There's a path of sorts over here." I pointed. "Sand, gravel, weeds, and goes straight back. I'll wait in the car."

"You will not," Fab shrieked.

I lifted my skirt and drew my Glock. "I'll carry it at my side, in case I'm tempted to blow someone's head off."

Fab and I ventured down the so-called path, which led to a broken-down rotted double-wide that had been transported right out of a horror film and dumped in the foot-high weeds. An enormous mud nest was attached to the right of the screen door, which hung precariously by one hinge, hornets buzzing in the air.

"My suggestion is that you snap a few pics of this thriving jungle, don't forget the wasp nest, and we get the heck out of here," I said.

Fab stood at the bottom of the crumbling steps and yelled, "Anyone home?"

The eerie silence that had followed us since we turned on the street was only briefly disturbed by her voice.

Never one to call it a day, Fab ventured farther down the path and disappeared into a clump of trees. I was about to yell for her when she reappeared. "This is the only entrance."

She hadn't been gone long enough to completely circle the double-wide to verify that, but I wasn't about to suggest that one could probably be found on the other side of the trailer. I wasn't volunteering to tromp through the weeds and trim the overgrowth to find it. A pair of clippers hadn't made it into the Hummer as a potentially useful item.

"Come in with me." Fab motioned for me to follow.

"You've lost your mind. You go in, you're on your own. Keep in mind that if you disturb the homestead hanging on the wall, the war is on, and you'll be on the run. I'll be driving you to the hospital to pick stingers out of your skin." I took a step back—being allergic, I knew I'd be puffed up before we reached the end of the block.

"Don't go far," Fab whined.

"Bad idea," I warned and took another step back. That would never stop the woman.

Fab reached out and gently pushed the swinging door back. It made a cracking noise, and the only hinge gave way. She jumped out of the way as it hit the rotted step, splintering.

To my shock, the hornets weren't bothered. Yet. I took two more steps back.

Lockpick in hand, Fab managed to lunge up to the door, but tried the knob first, and it opened. She stuck her head inside and instantly jumped back. She caught herself, managing to stay upright, and leaped to the ground. "Let's go."

Already in flight mode, I took off running back to the Hummer and jumped in.

Fab climbed in seconds after me and slammed

the door. "It's hard to believe that anyone is living there, as the stench of death is overwhelming." She shook her head, rubbing her nose to get the smell out of her nostrils. "I'm thinking human as opposed to rats."

I hit the door locks. "Just in case. You might've let the spirits out to roam, and I don't want to give them a ride to the house."

Fab groaned.

"You need to get hot on the phone and ring up Gunzy. He's got friends on the force; it's an unfortunate part of their job that they get to ferret out the source of the odor."

"Gunz is going to want a walk-through."

"Party killer that I am… It might be a crime scene, and cops take a dim view of disturbing the evidence, no matter how smelly." If she thought I was going to volunteer… ha! "My answer to him would be 'tough totems,' and to you too, if you suggest I do it."

"You need to be nicer to him and me."

"Ba-loney. Wading through death stench is not in the friend contract."

Fab laughed, and it was clear she wasn't going to make the trek. She pulled out her phone and called Gunz, letting him know that he'd need to bulldoze the property but not before the police conducted a dead-body search. "Talk later." The conversation had been short, and she tossed her phone back in the cup holder. "Gunz didn't even hint that I go back inside, which made me happy.

He said I didn't have to wait around either, that he'd take care of it." She backed out, headed to the corner, and didn't so much as glance back.

Chapter Thirty-Nine

We'd just turned onto the Overseas, headed home, when my phone rang, Tessa's face popping up.

"You said I could call if I needed help, and I do," she said, her fear radiating through the line.

"Take a breath and tell me what you need." I hit the speaker button.

"Mom found me, and I need a ride home. I'm at that billboard for the Crab Shack next to the Goodwill store. I wiggled between the trunks of several palm trees and crouched down. I don't think anyone saw me or that I can be seen."

"Don't hang up." My phone beeped in my ear, and I ignored the incoming call. "You don't need to worry; we're on our way. The way Fab drives, we'll be there in a few minutes," I said in an attempt to calm her down. "What happened?"

"Grandpa and I stopped at the grocery store, but he left the list in the car and I ran out to get it. Mom appeared out of nowhere and forced me into a car. Don't know where she got it and wasn't stupid enough to ask. When she slowed at a light, I jumped out and ran." Tessa started to cry.

"I'll call the cops."

"Can you come get me first?" Tessa hiccupped. "I don't want to face them, and maybe my mom, by myself. It might take her awhile to get here, since this is a one-way strip, but she'll be back. I know it."

"Stay down and out of sight; I'll stay on the line until we get there."

Fab's phone rang. I kept one ear on the conversation and knew she was talking to Blanche. She told the woman we had Tessa on the other line and were en route to pick her up and not to worry.

I reassured Tessa.

"Mom can get pretty worked up about almost anything, but today, she took it to a new level, ranting and yelling that everything was my fault and I had to fix it." Tessa paused and gulped in a few breaths. "No clue what she was talking about. I never ask her about anything; it only makes her madder."

"It was brave of you to jump," I said, thinking I wouldn't have suggested it.

"I had to get away from her. It took a few minutes to work up the nerve; then I didn't think about it, just did it. Knew if I didn't, whatever she had planned would be far worse."

"Did she mention Colton?" Fab asked.

"No. I wondered if they'd hooked up and he was the reason she grabbed me."

"I can see the billboard now," I told Tessa. "If

there's room, we're going to pull up in front of the trees. Don't come out until you see my SUV."

"I'll make room," Fab reassured me and drove up onto a dirt path for pedestrians.

I threw the door open and jumped out as Tessa bolted out of the trees. I yanked the back door open and helped her inside, then got a bottle of water out of the cooler and put it in the cup holder. "You need to call your grandmother."

She held out her phone. "It died. I forgot to charge it."

I handed her my phone and got back in the front. "Call Tank," I told Fab. "There needs to be a record of this incident to use against Karla, and he'll know what to do."

Fab pulled back into traffic and made the call, which she put on speaker.

After we relayed the events, Tank said, "Take Tessa home. I'm on my way, and I'll call the cops."

Tessa hung up from talking to her grandmother and dried her eyes. "Grandmother got ahold of Grandfather, and he's on his way home. I can't believe how badly my mom scared the two of them. They thought I was gone, and they'd never see me again."

Familiar with every shortcut, Fab was able to zip around traffic and head back south of town. When she turned off the highway and pulled into the driveway of Sanctuary Woods, Tank and two cop cars were right behind her.

The front door flew open, and Blanche and Anton darted across the yard to the SUV. Tessa bounded out and into their arms. It was hard not to get choked up as the threesome wrapped their arms around each other.

Tank got out of his car and headed straight over to us.

I had hoped to sit in the car until we were needed, but guess not.

"Thank you for calling me," Tank said. "You can bet that I'm going to protect Tessa and Tim from this latest stunt of Karla's and make sure it doesn't happen again."

"Isn't this a 'she said, she said' situation?" Fab asked.

"There's a cop at the grocery store right now, reviewing the security footage. They got right on it as soon as Anton reported Tessa missing."

I sighed with relief.

"I'd appreciate it if you two didn't disappear into the wind until after the cops have had a chance to talk to you."

"Sure thing." Fab shot Tank a cagey grin.

One of the cops called for Tank and waved him over.

"I'm not interrupting the family reunion." I nodded to the porch, where everyone had gathered around Tessa, then walked over to the pasture fence, where a cow grazed. No sign of the horse.

Fab walked up beside me. "You know anything about wild animals?"

I laughed at her. "A thing or two about the two-footed variety."

"How long do you think we're going to be here?"

"Not long, I hope. I'm ready to go home and see what my husband is up to," I said. "He'll be happy to know that dead spirits didn't suck us into that hovel of a house that Gunz now proudly owns."

Fab made a face. "When I talked to him, I didn't let on what a pile it was; let the pics speak for themselves."

We both laughed and hung out at the fence, waiting to be called on. It didn't take long.

"Hey, you two," barked a voice from behind us.

We turned to watch Kevin approach, a smirk on his face.

"I used to think you drew the short straw when it came to cases involving us; now I think you volunteer. I mean, what are the odds?" I said.

"One of these days, you're going to call the cops first on one of these situations you get yourselves into. You should've called immediately after Tessa called you," he reprimanded us.

"Unsure what to do, I called Tank and followed his instructions," Fab told him. "And look, you all turned out."

Kevin questioned us. Our stories were the same, since we were together. "Before you run off," he said to me. "Your bank manager, who had glowing things to say about you, I was tempted to show him your pic, verify we were talking about the same person." He smirked. "He believed your story and credited the money to your account."

"I appreciate the update." And surprised, not expecting to hear anything back.

"You two are free to go. Next time, and we both know there'll be one, make the cops your first call."

I nodded, thinking maybe. "See you soon."

As Kevin walked away, Fab hooked her arm around mine and steered me toward the SUV.

"I'll send Tessa a text that we're on call 24/7," I said, sliding into the passenger side.

"Stress to call, even if she thinks it's nothing. We'll make the decision," Fab said as she drove out and back to the highway.

I took out my phone. "Are we picking up dinner or having it delivered?"

"Delivered."

I texted Creole and shoved my phone back in my pocket.

Chapter Forty

We were almost back to the Cove and coming up on a red light when a sedan cut us off, pulling in front of us and slamming on the brakes, forcing Fab to skid to the side of the road.

An elongated black SUV with dark-tinted windows cruised up on the driver's side, leaving just enough space to get the door open. A man got out of the passenger side, wearing dark glasses, and a baseball cap pulled low. He stood at the driver's window and smirked at Fab.

Cars were honking, but being hemmed in, we weren't going anywhere.

"Be prepared to shoot," Fab ordered, pulling her Walther and moving the seat back. She snapped up her phone, tossing it in her lap.

I drew my Glock and hoped I wouldn't need to use it.

The thug reached for the door. Finding it locked, he drew his weapon.

"Get down," Fab yelled.

I was already copying her and slumping back.

He took one shot and then another. The glass shattered but stayed intact, and he hit it with the butt of his gun.

Fab cracked open her door and shot him, her bullet taking out a chunk of his cheek. He screamed, dropped his weapon, and stumbled back.

Another man hopped out of the back passenger seat and wrestled the injured man to his feet, then shoved him into the car. He turned and drew his weapon, and Fab shot him in the upper chest. He fell to the ground. Someone else jumped out of the SUV and muscled the body inside, barely getting the door closed before the SUV squealed off.

Two lookalike thugs hopped out of the sedan, sunglasses and baseball caps covering their faces, and headed for the back end. They lifted the trunk lid, which had been smashed in at some point, reached in together, and came out holding either end of a body, which they threw at the Hummer. The thud as it hit the hood and slid off onto the ground was sickening.

The driver ran back and got in the car. The other man stood at the grill and laughed. He made double fingers and shot up in the air, then saluted and pulled a real gun, shooting out the Hummer's front tires before jumping back in. They sped off.

Cars were still honking, slowing as they passed with their windows down, cameras out. They'd soon figure out it wasn't just another fender bender.

"What the…" Fab burst out.

"You okay?" I took out my phone and texted myself the first three numbers on the Florida plate of the sedan before I forgot them.

Fab pushed the door open.

I grabbed her arm. "Maybe we should wait."

"I'm going to check out the body on the off chance whoever it is isn't dead. You call 911."

"Thumbs up or down for whether an ambulance is needed." I couldn't remember when my hands started to shake.

Fab got out and waved traffic around the Hummer. She rounded the front bumper, came to a sudden stop and stepped back, then shot me a thumbs down. Phone in hand, she snapped a few pics.

The operator answered, and I said, "There's been a shooting, and someone threw a body out of a car and drove off." I gave her the cross streets. The cops would know right where they were needed as soon as they saw the traffic backed up.

Fab came around to the passenger side. I rolled down the window and said, "Standing on the shoulder makes you a target."

"The cops are going to want to question us and will probably haul the Hummer away. Maybe us off to jail. Depends on whether they believe that we didn't murder the guy lying under the front bumper."

Squeamish about asking, I did anyway. "Anyone we know?"

Fab shuddered. "Dude was worked over pretty good. Identification will probably require DNA testing."

"Put your gun away," I said, looking in the side mirror.

Two cops rolled up, lights flashing. They parked behind the Hummer and got out, Kevin in the lead.

Fab holstered her gun, put away her phone, and went to meet them.

Kevin circled the Hummer, surveying the damage, and stopped short at the discovery of the body. After a moment, he moved closer, and I heard him say, "You're not dead; what about your friend?"

Fab answered his questions, then spoke to the other officer. After a brief conversation, he made his way over to me and motioned me out of the SUV.

"What happened?" he asked as I joined him on the side of the road.

I told him succinctly. "I never got out of the car. I didn't look at the body or anything else. My friend warned me off; I don't have the stomach for it."

"Do you think you can pick any of the men out in a lineup if we're able to locate any suspects?" the cop asked.

I shook my head. "They did a good job of covering their faces. Honestly, from the moment the body landed on the hood, I freaked out and still am."

"You're going to need to arrange for a ride. You're welcome to sit in your vehicle while you wait."

Fab joined me a couple steps ahead of Kevin. "Friends of yours?" he asked her.

"No clue who they were," Fab said. "There were at least four in the SUV, two in the sedan. They were all dressed the same—dark clothing, kept their faces covered. Two should be showing up at a hospital somewhere, unless they have a doctor who'll ignore the law and not report it." She ID'd the SUV as a Yukon with the brand plate removed.

"We'll also check the morgue," Kevin said grimly, then turned to me. "What's your version?"

"They pulled up alongside us and opened fire," I snapped.

"I'm not suggesting that any of this is your fault," he said.

"Here." I reached in my pocket and pulled out my phone, showing him the text I'd sent myself—the numbers on the plate of the car. "That was on the sedan. And I'm thinking there can't be that many extra-long SUVs on the road with a shattered back window."

"This will help." Kevin nodded and headed back to his patrol car.

"Can I call for a tow truck?" I yelled.

He turned and shook his head. "It's going to Impound; you can pick it up after Forensics has been over it."

I turned to Fab and laid my head on her shoulder. "You're amazing."

"My only thought was getting us out alive. Sort of surprised that there wasn't more gunfire before they roared off."

"Do you want to venture a wager on what this is about? I've got a fiver on Lug and his friends."

"Not taking that bet. If it turns out to be them, I'm really sorry for not minding my own business and getting you involved." Fab shook her head. "Wish I could've ID'd the dead guy." The other cop had covered him with a sheet.

"Stop already. I'd have killed you if you'd gone by yourself." I nudged her shoulder. "Any clue how the guy died?"

"Lucky for us, it's clear he wasn't run over. His death was gruesome." Fab winced. "It's clear that he pissed someone off. I hope he died of the gunshot in the middle of his forehead and the mutilation came after, not the other way around."

"Tossing John Doe on the hood of the Hummer was deliberate. Wonder what message it was meant to convey, since they didn't kill us but wanted to? Be interesting to know who John Doe is."

"One of us needs to call for a ride. I'd rather walk than get in the back of a cop car, even if

Kev-o offered." Fab wrinkled her nose, staring down the highway.

"Doing it now." I pulled out my phone and called Creole. "Hey, babes," I said when he answered. "We're on the Overseas with a flat tire." I told him where we were located.

"On our way," he said and hung up.

"You left out… a lot." Fab made a face.

"I didn't want them to break the speed limit getting here. If one of us were on the way to the hospital, it would be different."

"Could there be a worse day?" Fab asked.

"Yes, and you can bet that whoever wants us dead will be back."

"How are we going to stop them?"

I rubbed my temples. "No clue."

I collected our purses from the car while Fab walked around, snapping pictures inside and out. Then we stood as far off the road as we could. Cars slowed, some folks waved, and others whistled and cat-called.

It wasn't long before the guys rolled up in Creole's truck, parking in front of the ambulance that had just arrived.

They got out and trekked toward us, and we met them halfway.

Creole's lips brushed my cheek as he stormed past me. He paused, staring down at the sheeted body, then sought out Kevin.

Fab got a way better kiss before Didier hustled to catch up to Creole.

After a brief conversation, Creole stomped back. "You left out a lot of details," he grouched and pulled me into a hug.

"That's because I didn't want you breaking the speed limit to get here, and you did anyway."

Didier had his arms around Fab. "Were either of you hurt?"

We both shook our heads.

"Neither of us was hurt, and I didn't want you to worry on the ride here," I said.

"Good news." Didier smiled at us. "Kevin says you're both free to go."

In that moment, one thing Creole and Didier had in common was that they were angry at what had gone down and biting back all the questions they'd like answered.

Creole helped me into the truck, and Fab and Didier got in the back.

"Other than recent events, is there any reason someone would want you two dead?" Didier asked.

"Madison and I talked about this, and the answer is no," Fab said.

I leaned my head back against the seat and closed my eyes.

It didn't take long to get back to the compound. When Creole parked, I didn't get out, taking out my phone. He opened the door and leaned in. "I didn't order dinner, and we need to eat… although I'd rather drink my dinner."

"Hold off on that for a second." Creole pulled

out his phone. "Where are you?" He mouthed Casio. "Need a meeting. Now." He gave him the short version of events. "Meet at the house. Free food." He hung up and turned to me. "Order extra, since I forgot to ask who Casio's with and if he's bringing anyone."

I called Jake's and placed an order on steroids; anyone who wanted to could take home a to-go bag. I asked for delivery, knowing that wouldn't be a problem, as we were notoriously good tippers.

"One more call." I held up my finger. "I got the first three numbers off the plate of the sedan and want to see what Xander can do with them."

"Invite him. We can have him run down any ideas we come up with."

I called and offered food and, of course, billing me for his time, which he readily accepted. I found out that Toady was in earshot and invited him, too. I wouldn't tell anyone and let that be a surprise.

Chapter Forty-One

"While I'm setting the table for all the guests, would someone make me a pitcher of margaritas?" I winked at Didier, who had his hand in the liquor cabinet. "You do have plates for twenty?" I asked Fab.

Fab did a double-take. "Let me guess, the bus is about to roll up and our guests will be jumping down?"

I pointed at Creole, who was filling an enamelware bucket with ice. "He extended the invites. I only ordered the food." I turned to see if the black clouds that had suddenly appeared in the sky had rolled on by, and they hadn't. I'd have preferred to sit out on the patio but didn't want to chance that it might rain. "It'll have to be buffet-style, and I'll set everything up here on the island. We're going to need more chairs." Other than Casio, I wasn't sure who Creole'd invited and had added two to my guesstimate.

"Do you have an exact head count?" Fab asked Creole, who pointed to me and grinned.

"Twenty or so, probably not thirty, and likely less," I said.

Creole and Didier laughed.

"'I don't know' would've been faster than whatever that was," Fab said.

"You could be helpful and order me about. I wouldn't want to forget anything and make you look bad." At her raised eyebrow, I added, "It is your house."

Fab and I worked efficiently and got dishes and silverware set out on the countertop, leaving the island open for when the food arrived.

Didier set a martini in front of Fab and a margarita in front of me. I licked my lips and cautioned myself not to down it.

The front door opened, and Mila stood there grinning, holding up a lockpick, Brad behind her.

"You're ridiculous, dude," I told him with a smile. "You won't be so amused with yourself when your daughter figures out how to work that pick and you have to go fetch her from j-a-i-l."

Brad snorted a that's never going to happen. "When I got wind of a big to-do at the mansion, I knew I was invited, even though my invite never actually arrived. I had plans with Mother and Spoon, and here we are." He stepped into the entry and held the door open for the other two. "If I'm mistaken and we're not invited, you can be the one to tell Mother," he said to Creole, loud enough that everyone heard.

Mother quirked her head at Creole, a look of amusement on her face. Spoon's look matched his wife's.

"Dude, you are a dick," Creole told Brad. He crossed to Mother and kissed her cheek, leading her over to the island. "The door is always open to Madeline."

I laughed and shook my finger at Brad.

Mila ran into Fab's open arms, and she took her into the living room, where the two sat on the floor, opened a cabinet door, and proceeded to pull out toys and books.

Spoon took Brad's post at the door, sticking his head out and holding it open. Everyone looked more than a little surprised when Toady and Xander walked through the door.

"Howdy, folks." Toady waved.

Creole turned to me.

"What's one more?" I shrugged.

Good thing there was a large refrigerator in the garage packed with the favorite beverage of the evening—beer. Foreign, local, craft, you name it—if it was a good brand, there was probably a cold one inside.

Fab, Mother, and I went for the harder stuff—vodka, Jack Daniels, and tequila. Didier filled a glass with ice, topped it with Jack, and handed it to Mother.

I pulled Xander back into the entry. "Were you able to find out anything on the license numbers I texted?"

"I don't have the ability to run the numbers, so I contacted my friend, who can get anything done for a price." Xander checked his phone again. "Nothing yet."

"I don't want you doing anything that will put you in legal hot water. Don't forget to include his fee on your invoice."

The door opened again. Casio stuck his head inside and yelled, "Anyone home?"

I chuckled and waved, since I was standing less than a foot away.

Fab crossed the room, Didier behind her. "You ever heard of knocking?" she asked Casio.

"Yeah," Didier said, and laughed.

Casio pushed the door wide, stepped in, and turned. "They welcomed us in, told us to make ourselves at home."

The Chief breezed by the man, knowing he was full of it.

"Big gun is here," I announced.

Before Casio could get the door closed, it was shoved open again, and Caspian walked in. "Good thing I was in town or I'd have missed out on..." It was clear he wasn't sure what but was happy to be included, most likely by the Chief or Spoon, since they were friends.

The gate buzzed, which was a first that day. "It's the food," Fab said, looking at the monitor and buzzing the driver in. She opened the door and ushered in one of the cooks from Jake's, directing him where to set the several shopping bags he had in his hands.

Didier made sure everyone had drinks while Fab and I set out the food. It was clear I'd gotten carried away when I ordered several of Cook's sampler platters. Creole told everyone to grab a plate and take a seat at the dining table—all serious talk would be tabled until we finished eating.

I wasn't hungry and fluttered around, pushing back the sliders to the patio and welcoming in the fresh air. The downpour had so far only threatened. I decided on a taco, ignoring Creole's raised eyebrows conveying, 'that's not enough food.'

The conversation around the table was amiable, oftentimes funny, as everyone updated everyone else on the latest in their lives. Fab and I abstained, but no one seemed to notice.

I'd called it on the food order, as it entirely disappeared. The guys cleared off the table and refilled everyone's drink of choice.

Fab settled Mila in an oversized chair and handed her a tablet with a movie to watch. The cats jumped up and snuggled against her side.

"All of you know about Tessa…" Creole started and looked around the table. Everyone nodded. "She was able to remember a couple of Colton's conversations that she'd overheard." He went on to give details to those that didn't know them. "A few days ago, Madison and Fab drove to Miami and checked out Club X and the surrounding area." Not much of a reaction except from Mother, who gasped.

Fab raised her hand. "I admit it wasn't one of

my better ideas. In hindsight, I wouldn't do it again."

Creole told them about the chase that had ensued, and all eyes shot to me and Fab.

He went on to share today's events. "My guess is, today is related to the Club X adventure. Since Madison has a fairly distinctive ride, they may have just gotten lucky, seen you on the highway, and followed you."

"No, it was planned, since it's unlikely they'd drive around with a dead body," Casio said. "Got a bit of news for you on that front. The body has been tentatively ID'd as Colton Roberts by the driver's license in his pocket. It won't be official until the DNA results come back."

Good riddance.

"It's clear his killers wanted us to know he's no longer among the living," Fab said.

"Takes a large amount of hubris to orchestrate a body dump in broad daylight," Spoon said.

I was on a two-drink maximum so I could be lucid enough to answer questions. To heck with that. I poured another. "You convey the news to your buddy, Beckett?"

"I called, even though it's not official; I couldn't take him slamming my phone constantly. He took the update with icy reserve. Needless to say, the conversation was short." Casio huffed out his annoyance.

"That club needs to be closed." Toady grunted. "I know a couple of cops that, with this kind of information, would show up there tomorrow with a search warrant."

The Chief nodded. "I've kept in touch with a few of my sources at Miami PD, as Casio's kept me in the loop. It's rumored that the owners have connections within the department, which they're attempting to ferret out now."

"I'm not the professional here," Brad said. "But with one man possibly dead and another nicked, won't they be back to shut you up?"

"You two should keep a low profile," Mother suggested.

"I second the low profile." Didier smiled at Fab and hauled her to his side.

"Spooner?" He shook his head at me. "My coach will be sprung from auto lockup in a day or two. When you replace the Hummer's windows, how about bulletproof glass?"

"You already have it." Spoon smirked. "A little gift from me the last time I replaced them. Forgot to tell you. That's why the glass didn't blow out."

I should've known, since he always looked out for us.

"Like it did on their SUV," Fab said. She and I exchanged a smile.

"You know who could bring down the wrath on that club? Henry Beckett," Casio said. "And I wouldn't be surprised if he's already working on it. He's got more connections, legal and otherwise, than any of us. He's definitely frustrated that law enforcement hasn't already surrounded the place and put them out of business."

We sat around and threw out ideas, most of which involved giving law enforcement agencies time to do an investigation and not second-guess what was happening behind the scenes.

Brad was the one to stand and break up the party. He needed to get his daughter, who'd already fallen asleep, home.

All discussion was tabled. Anyone with a good idea was encouraged to call Creole or Didier.

Chapter Forty-Two

Everything had been quiet for a couple of days. Moving day was rapidly approaching, and this would be one of the last mornings the four of us would share coffee as housemates, though I had no doubt that we'd be in and out of each other's houses all the time.

Creole's phone rang, cutting off conversation. He answered, stood, and strode into the living room, opening the drawer for the remote and turning on the television. He flipped through the channels, motioning us into the room. "Thanks." He stuffed his phone in his pocket.

A young news reporter stood off to one side of a charred building. The camera pulled out and showed that the street, both sides, had suffered the same damage—burned to rubble.

The banner running across the bottom said: "Explosion in Miami!"

Fab and I exchanged wide-eyed stares, both recognizing what was left of Club X… and the entire street it sat on.

Creole flicked through the channels and found wall-to-wall coverage on all the local stations.

One channel had scored a coup, getting video

of flames leaping in the air. "The fire, rumored to have started due to a gas leak, leveled Club X and leaped down the block. It's a sad demise to this trendy street of nightclubs," the blonde lamented.

The explosion had happened in the wee hours of the morning, long after closing. The club was the first to go up in flames, which then took out all the buildings on both sides of the street. No fatalities had been reported.

I went back to the island, grabbing coffees for Didier and Creole, then went back for Fab and I. The four of settled on the couch and watched the coverage.

Fab broke the silence. "Show of hands: who believes this was a coincidence?" No takers.

"It sounds like everyone got out, which is good," I said.

"It will be months before they can rebuild," Didier said. "Trust me, they'll have a lot of hoops to hop through, getting all the permits from the county building department."

"They might not find it worth the trouble, depending on how lucrative the legal side of the business was. We know the illegal side was raking in money," Creole said. "If the fire was deliberate—and it's hard to believe it wasn't—then the owners know that they have a big enemy. It wouldn't make sense to open in the same location."

"Xander did some digging for me. The club is

owned under a corporate name. After more research, he found the names of the three partners," I told them. "Xander said that they had gone to great lengths to remain anonymous."

Creole's phone rang again.

"More good news?" I asked.

Creole took note of my sarcasm and shook his finger at me. He took his phone out, glanced at the screen, and answered. "We've got it on." After a pause, he said, "Mind if I put you on speaker? Wouldn't want Fab to shoot me." He laughed and motioned us back over to the island. "Casio," he told us as he pushed the speaker button.

"Hey everyone," Casio said. "Breaking news. Surprised it hasn't hit one of the local stations, but it'll become public once next of kin has been notified. One of the owners of Club X, Kent Cook, was found dead in his driveway. Bullet to the forehead. Fancy-ass neighborhood. The neighbors didn't hear or see anything, which wouldn't be uncommon at that early hour. The sun hadn't made an appearance yet."

"Oh, yeesh. Gruesome." Fab expressed what we were all thinking.

"An old colleague called right after they discovered the body. He knew I'd want to know, since I blew up his line with more than a few questions about the club. He questioned me about what I knew. Nothing! Here's something interesting, though—Kent Cook lived behind security gates, and when the cops went to inform him about the explosion, they were standing wide open."

Hit job? No one was asking, or maybe it was understood.

"What about the other two partners?" Creole asked.

"My friend mentioned them, and once a check is made on them, he'll call," Casio said. "If those men are still alive, they better watch their backs; they annoyed someone big."

"It's hard to believe that the gas leak was a fluke. Now murder?" Fab questioned.

"Brilliant in my book," Casio said.

Creole nodded.

"Thought you'd also want to know that the body pitched at your car, positively ID'd as Colton Roberts," Casio informed us all. "One more thing, there haven't been any sightings of Karla. Ran the plates on the car she was driving when she kidnapped her daughter—stolen and nowhere to be found. Yet, anyway. APBs have been issued for both her and the car." He had another call and hung up.

No one disagreed with Didier's suggestion that the four of us work from home. We spread out on the dining room table, the television on mute in the background in case of breaking news.

Two hours later, Creole's phone rang, and it

was Casio again.

I tried not to hold my breath, wondering what the news would be.

They talked for a few minutes, and Creole hung up. "All three owners are dead. Same MO—bullet to the head. One in the entry of his house, no sign of forced entry. The other behind the wheel of his Mercedes, still in the driveway."

Chapter Forty-Three

Housewarming Day!

I'd finally been allowed into my house, and Fab made great choices based on the file I sent her. She'd found an overstuffed, down-filled sofa in white, with footrests that could double as tables. Pushed together, it was perfect for sprawling out or curling up. There were glass tables on each end. She'd contacted the man who made my desk and had a dining room table and long bench made from reclaimed wood. A large area rug made for a cozy feel. She'd also found cute padded-back barstools for the island. I was happy to see that she'd stuck to my edict to keep it simple.

With a few minutes left to myself before my family arrived, I hung over the railing, staring off in the distance at Creole and Didier coming back from their run. Didier hollered from the beach as he passed, and Creole came running up the steps. "You staying out of trouble?" Creole brushed my cheek with his lips as he swept by.

"I'm saving up for later," I said to his retreating back and heard him laugh.

There were a few wispy clouds over the calm

water, disappearing into the horizon, but otherwise, a clear and gorgeous view. "Wow," I said at the sound of the water crashing against the deserted beach below on sand that looked—at least, from here—soft and perfect.

Waving like a lunatic, Fab caught my attention. She strode across the white sand in an off-the-shoulder black dress, her sandals hooked over her finger, and ran up the steps to the deck, stopping to look at the changes I'd made. I'd been busy moving the chaises and chairs around and had unloaded a big bag of colorful pillows. "I'm here early to tell you what to do." She gave my fuchsia linen tier dress a flinty stare. "You went shopping without me." She pouted.

"It was a quick trip, and I came home with this one dress—" I twirled around. "—and not half the store."

"Pretty. Now that you have a tricked-out closet to fill, we're going to have to go on a shopping bender."

"Creole told me he called the closet designer you recommended. I got the feeling you strong-armed him." I laughed. He'd liked the job the man did, so didn't complain about the full-court press she ran on him.

"Didier's exact words were, 'you can't hold a gun to the man's head.' I promised not to be so bossy in the future. He laughed." Fab threw her arms around me. "I had so much fun decorating your house… what little you'd let me do." She was back to pouting.

"Have you thought about hanging out a shingle?"

"I'd miss the adrenaline rush."

The doorbell rang.

I winced.

Fab grabbed my arm. "What? I didn't gun up for today's festivities. Should I have?"

Creole walked in, decked out in shorts and a tropical shirt, just in time to hear Fab. He laughed. "Madison doesn't want anyone parking on the new driveway… or walking on it either."

"I don't want tire marks on the crushed shells," I said.

Creole had a truckload of clam shells brought in and poured over a thin layer of cement. He'd bargained with the clam dealer, who he swore had a mountain of them next to his fish shack, the amount needed for the driveway barely making a dent.

"You're the best husband." I made a kissy face.

Fab did her best to hork up a furball as Creole headed through the house to the front door, laughing.

After a moment, Kelpie's laughter joined his. She'd eavesdropped on me hiring one of Cook's kin to deliver the food and work the party, and insisted we needed a bartender and she was the chick for the job. We didn't really—there wouldn't be enough people to keep her busy—

but she'd brushed aside my objections, saying, "Piffle."

"I had a talk with her and told her to tone down the sexiness, that there'd be kids here," Fab said.

"Mila loves her. I went out on the deck at Jake's one day, and the two were singing off-key like drunken sailors. It was a little hard on the ears."

"Where do you want me?" Kelpie jiggled her way outside in a low-cut tankini top and flirty skirt, lights and bells around her neck.

"We're doing everything outside, since it's a beautiful day. I stole Fab's bar cart and umbrella and started to stock it but got sidetracked." I'd requested that Creole and Didier move it over before they went on their run.

Someone was playing on the doorbell. It surprised me that when the door opened, it was Mother who stood grinning in the doorway, Spoon behind her. Both waved. In Spoon's arms was a large tropical bouquet in a glass vase: anthuriums, bird of paradise, and ginger lilies. I waved him to the dining room table.

"So beautiful." I hugged Mother and then Spoon.

"I'm so used to bringing food, I was at a loss. This was Spoon's idea—he thought you'd like them more, and we got them locally."

"When isn't your husband right?" I asked.

Mother giggled.

Spoon hauled her to his side. "She's right, you know."

The door opened, and Didier ushered in Caspian and the Chief in hot discussion.

"Party's on." I let out a nervous huff. It had been a long time since I'd done any entertaining, and I was looking forward to jumping back in.

Creole sidled up to me, standing at my side with his arm around my shoulders.

Fab took her phone out and checked the screen with a sneaky smile. "Listen up, everyone." Still in sneaky-smile mode.

I stepped closer to Creole.

"I have a surprise. Madison is a big believer in 'the more the merrier,' and so…" She swept her hand toward the door, then walked over and flung it open.

From my vantage point, I could see that two SUVs had pulled into the driveway, the windows tinted on both, so it was hard to see who was behind the wheel.

I wasn't sure how I got to the door, but I stood next to Fab and watched as the passenger doors opened.

"This will make more sense a little later on," Fab said. "Hope you ordered enough food."

"Embarrass my mother by running out of food?" I gave her the crazy look. "Not happening."

Brad got out of the second car and caught Mila as she jumped from the seat into his arms. My gasp caught in my throat. It was clear that they'd done that trick a time or two.

He stopped at the first SUV, holding out his hand, and Lili Famosa hopped out, followed by her brother Alex, his cocky smirk a carbon copy of his dad's. "Casio, get out here," Brad bellowed. Cisco and Diego, the twins, jumped down and reunited with Alex and Lili, and they ran screaming around the driveway.

Casio, who'd been on his phone, shoved it in his pocket and got out. The biggest surprise was Crum. I assumed that Fab had invited the kid wrangler, who was thankfully fully covered in casual beach attire.

I turned on Fab. "What are you up to?"

"You invite people to my house."

That wasn't an answer. "It's your job to make sure that nothing goes wrong. After all, trouble wouldn't be festive."

"I bet Kelpie has drinks ready for us." Fab tugged on my arm.

Everyone had gathered out on the deck, drink of choice in hand. I corralled Crum before he could disappear with his charges and had a secretive conversation. He agreed to my request, and I handed him my phone. He then led the kids down to the beach, laughing and yelling.

"One more surprise," Fab yelled to get everyone's attention. "Do you want to tell them or should I?" she asked Casio.

He stepped forward, a big grin on his face.

"Fab and Didier have rented their empty house to me and the kids. We're going to be neighbors."

Most clapped.

"That might not be so bad," I hedged. "Love your kids."

"Hey, what about me?"

"Yeah, you too."

That got everyone laughing.

"It's a good time to tell you all," Casio added, "that you'll be seeing Crum hanging around. I hired him to help me get my kids situated. So don't shoot him. I need his help."

"And you insisted on a dress code?" My brows went up—mostly attired would make me happy.

Casio made a face. "I'll get on that."

Creole tugged me to his side. "Madison and I have an announcement. We hired someone, who has to remain anonymous, to track the money that my brother stole out of our bank accounts." Several of our guests clapped. "Most of the money was found, and we now have it back and in an account that he can't get his hands on should he get out of jail anytime soon."

No one mentioned the illegalities of how that went down.

Crum's shrill whistle floated back across the sand. He made eye contact with me and jabbed his finger toward the road. Then he and the kids ran down to the access stairs.

"Got a surprise of my own. Got to keep up

with Fab," I said.

"I know about this; you're going to like it." Creole shot Didier a thumbs up.

Two good-sized men came down the stairs carrying water bikes, four in total. Yelling, the kids followed them down to the water.

"No way the kids aren't going to want to go for a ride. This is going to take another adult." Brad took off down to the sand at a run.

Fab and I hung over the railing and stared down at the beach and the shimmering blue water, which sparkled in the afternoon sunshine.

"We're going to have the best parties." Fab toasted.

"Yes, we are."

~*~

PARADISE SERIES NOVELS

Crazy in Paradise
Deception in Paradise
Trouble in Paradise
Murder in Paradise
Greed in Paradise
Revenge in Paradise
Kidnapped in Paradise
Swindled in Paradise
Executed in Paradise
Hurricane in Paradise
Lottery in Paradise
Ambushed in Paradise
Christmas in Paradise
Blownup in Paradise
Psycho in Paradise
Overdose in Paradise
Initiation in Paradise
Jealous in Paradise
Wronged in Paradise
Vanished in Paradise
Fraud in Paradise
Naive in Paradise

Deborah's books are available on Amazon
amazon.com/Deborah-Brown/e/B0059MAIKQ

About the Author

Deborah Brown is an Amazon bestselling author of the Paradise series. She lives on the Gulf of Mexico, with her ungrateful animals, where Mother Nature takes out her bad attitude in the form of hurricanes.

For a free short story, sign up for my newsletter. It will also keep you up-to-date with new releases and special promotions: www.deborahbrownbooks.com

Follow on FaceBook: facebook.com/DeborahBrownAuthor

You can contact her at Wildcurls@hotmail.com

Deborah's books are available on Amazon

amazon.com/Deborah-Brown/e/B0059MAIKQ

Made in the USA
Las Vegas, NV
28 September 2024

95918223R10223